THAT WAY MADNESS LIES

Don D'Ammassa

Managansett Press

"Complexity" first appeared in *Shock Totem*, 2009
"Context" first appeared in *Souls in Pawn*, 1992
"Dealing with Stress" first appeared in *The Quiet Ward*, 2003
"Echoes" first appeared in *Shivers VII*, 2013
"Forever in My Thought" first appeared in *Hottest Blood*, 1993
"Friday Nights at Home" first appeared in *Sinistre*, 1993
"Inspiration" first appeared in *Shock Rock 2*, 1994
"Leave Me Alone" first appeared in *Night Terrors 6*, 1998
"Misadventures in the Skin Trade" first appeared in *Borderlands 4*, 1994
All other stories appear for the first time in this volume.

Cover art inspired by *The Scream* by Edvard Munch

Managansett Press First Edition 2015

DEDICATION

For Algernon and Sarah

Some of my best for two of the best

CONTENTS

FRIDAY NIGHTS AT HOME

Friday, October 2

Louise Tyler's transformation began after she arrived home from work at precisely 5:12 on a Friday evening, although it had been gestating for some time before that. She parked her subcompact car on the right side of the driveway, snug up against the rear wall of the carport, and carefully locked the doors.

She opened the kitchen door with practiced ease, emptied the mailbox mounted on the wall, and stepped inside. Still wearing her coat and gloves, Louise sorted the mail into three piles, trash, Tom, and her own, which today consisted of a magazine she'd never have time to read, bills from the electric company and Sears.

After hanging her coat in the hall closet, she slowly climbed to the second floor, turned right, knocked on the first door she encountered and stepped inside without waiting for an answer.

"I'm home, Terry."

The twelve year old looked up from where she'd been lying on the rug staring at television. The room was in its usual state of chaotic disorder, and Louise carefully avoided looking at it in any detail. The lack of organization was almost physically painful. "Oh, hi Mom. Didn't hear you come in."

"That's because the television is so loud. How did school go today?"

"Umm, all right, I guess." Louise nodded, even though it was the same answer, syllable for syllable, which Terry always provided.

"Have you done your homework yet?" Her automatic riposte.

"Mom! It's the weekend. I've got plenty of time to do it."

"Oh, right."

Downstairs again, Louise removed an eye of the round from the microwave where she'd left it to defrost all day. Friday night was always beef night, the roast providing leftovers for at least one weekend meal. She added her customary garnishes and some scrubbed potatoes, started the oven, and removed a package of green beans from the freezer.

With dinner underway, she set the table, places for three, then stepped out through the sliding glass door onto the deck, where as usual the paperboy had managed to find a new and awkward place into which to throw the newspaper. Frowning, Louise reached under the chaise lounge and pulled it out, glancing at the front page on her way back inside.

In the lower right corner was a brief story about the latest round of layoffs at Eblis Manufacturing. Louise bit her lip and determinedly shifted her eyes to the headlines. She had worked at Eblis all her adult life and while her salary as a quality control inspector wasn't spectacular, she had little confidence she could get as much or better elsewhere.

Tom arrived at exactly 6:30, grumpy as usual following the hour and a half commute. "I never should have taken this job," he told her in greeting. "And next week they're closing down two lanes on the Braga Bridge for repairs and it's going to be even worse."

"Something better will come along eventually," she reassured him, but it was mechanical, a learned response. "And it pays better than the temporary jobs you were doing before."

"Well, it's not as if we needed the money. We were getting along just fine on your salary."

Louise shook her head. "We managed to pay minimums on all the bills is all, and most of our savings are gone." She didn't want to have this conversation again. Tom was a great programmer but he had no conception of how to manage money. He would not understand that she had been compelled to cash in both their IRA's, absorb the penalty, and use the funds to keep creditors at bay. And their credit cards were all pushing their limits.

Terry came down for supper after three calls up the stairs, Louise brought the food to the table, began to slice the roast. Her hands were trembling so violently that she had trouble with the first cut.

"Hey, want me to do that?" Tom made no move to rise.

"No, of course not. I always carve the meat. I'm just tired is all." Tom always ended up with slices of different thicknesses and ragged edges, where Louise produced a uniform series with relentless precision. He'd insist the meat tasted the same regardless of its shape, and was always impatient when she tried to explain that there was a right and wrong way to do things.

After supper, Louise cleaned up with some grudging and generally useless assistance from Terry while Tom went to the living room and turned on the television. Terry disappeared upstairs a few minutes later and with a last look around to make certain everything was in place, Louise followed, turning left this time and walking to her own room. She had converted the guest bedroom a year earlier, after Tom had complained that her restlessness kept him awake at night. They hadn't had sex together for over two years.

Louise changed into a housecoat, then sat on the edge of her bed, drained emotionally if not physically. One button was loose and she retrieved a needle and thread from the night table drawer in order to make the necessary repairs. She winced once as the point of the needle nicked the flesh of her leg.

"At least I can still feel pain," she said softly. "So I know I'm still alive."

Friday, October 16

Louise Tyler pulled into the right hand corner of the carport at precisely 5:12, sat quietly for a few seconds to calm the fluttering in her stomach. It had been a bitch of a day. The whole week had been crisis piled upon emotional scene upon foreboding of doom.

After locking the car, she crossed to the kitchen door, calmly unlocked it, retrieved the mail, and stepped inside. Without taking off her coat, Louise sorted through the envelopes and magazines, set aside the bills for gas, telephone, and the bank loan payment. At the bottom of the stack was an envelope with her name on it, the return address Terry's school.

She removed her gloves, left them on the kitchen table while opening the letter. It was brief and clear; Terry had consistently failed to turn in her homework assignments for the past few weeks and the school thought a conference was advisable. Which meant she'd have to take time off work.

Louise tried to remain calm while hanging her coat in the hall closet, but it didn't work. This time she didn't knock before entering her daughter's room.

"What? Oh, hi mom." Terry sketched a smile and turned back to the television screen.

Louise stormed past, stabbed at the on/off switch, then crouched and pulled the cord out of its socket for emphasis.

"Hey! What's going on?"

"You know perfectly well what's going on, young lady!" The

words tried to come out too quickly, stumbled one over the other, but Louise was past caring. "I've just had a letter from your teacher about your homework!"

Terry's head dropped forward, but she seemed more annoyed than contrite. And was that the shadow of a smirk at the corners of her mouth? "Yeah, I guess I forgot a couple of times."

"Judging from Mrs. Thompson's letter, it's been more than a couple of times."

"Yeah, well Mrs. Thompson doesn't like me so she exaggerates things. She's always trying to make me look bad. Ask any of the other kids."

"I don't care what the other kids say. Now you get to your homework right now. As far as I'm concerned, you're grounded until this is all straightened out, and that includes no television. Your father will have more to say to you about this when he gets home."

Back downstairs, she removed the roast from the microwave and set it in a pan, along with a half dozen unpeeled potatoes, one of which she forgot to scrub. She also removed a package of squash from the freezer, stared at it for a full minute before realizing her error, swapped it for green beans.

After setting the table, she walked out onto the porch and found the paper caught in the branches of her prize fern. Eblis Manufacturing had made the front page again, this time a short piece about the efforts of several terminated office workers to sue for severance pay.

Tom arrived at 6:40, so enraged by the length of the day's commute that it was several minutes before she could break in to tell him about the letter from school. When she was finished, he shrugged and picked up the newspaper.

"Well, aren't you going to go upstairs and talk to her about it?"

Tom didn't even glance up from the paper. "What would be the point? You already punished her. Besides, it's just some overdue homework. No big deal."

"No big deal? I suppose it doesn't matter to you if she has to repeat sixth grade?"

He shrugged, clearly not paying attention. "It won't come to that. She's a smart girl."

Louise's hands trembled so much that evening that she took

twice as long as usual to carve the roast and the slices were not up to her usual standard. No one seemed to notice. Afterward, Tom headed for the living room and Terry went immediately to her room without offering to help clear away the dishes.

Upstairs, Louise changed into her housecoat and blinked away tears. Rage or sorrow? She wasn't sure. Everything seemed so distant, softened in texture and muted in tone, as though she were wrapped in a coat of insulation. The needle and thread still lay on the night table and she deliberately picked it up and jabbed herself just above the knee, driving the first quarter inch of the pin into her flesh. The world seemed to sharpen just the slightest bit around her and she repeated the action a half dozen more times until she felt close to normal.

"Acupuncture in reverse," she whispered, laughing slightly. "The pain makes me better, not worse."

Friday, October 23

Louise Tyler arrived home at precisely 5:12, parked the car on the right hand side of the driveway, half in and half out of the carport. She slid out and closed the door without locking it, then emptied the mailbox, sorting through the envelopes with gloved hands while standing in front of the kitchen door. Late notices for the mortgage and the car payment, along with the usual round of bills, she realized.

She dropped the mail on the kitchen counter on her way to the closet, hung up her coat, then walked upstairs and rapped on the door to her daughter's room without opening it.

"Terry? Are you in there?"

"Yeah. I'm here."

"How's the homework coming?"

"I'm doing it!"

Louise thought about responding to the tone of insolent anger but contented herself with an inadequate rejoinder. "You'd better be. I'll call you when supper's ready."

With the roast cooking, she located the newspaper, lying on the chaise lounge for a pleasant change, and scanned the front page while walking back to the kitchen. As she had expected, the announcement of a twenty percent reduction in operating hours at Eblis had caused quite a stir.

Tom arrived at 5:42.

"You must have really flown today. What happened?"

He was smiling broadly, even presented her with a rare kiss, though barely more than a peck on the cheek. "I quit."

The world began to blur around her. "You quit? Sure you did. What really happened? Another power failure?"

"No, I quit. Really. It just wasn't worth it for the salary they were willing to pay."

Louise raised one hand and rubbed at her temple, but she couldn't feel her own fingers. "Tom, we really needed that money. You were making a lot more when we bought this house and the mortgage payments are three times as much as our rent was in Providence. And we still have two years to go to pay off the loan for your operation, and six months on Terry's braces. My salary won't stretch that far. If you quit, you can't even collect unemployment."

"It'll all work out. Trust me. You'll find some way to magic the numbers like you always do. And I'll find something in a few weeks, maybe even sooner." And he turned away, clearly no longer interested in the subject.

After supper, Louise moved the dirty dishes to the sink but decided they could be scraped and put in the dishwasher later, or maybe in the morning. She climbed the stairs slowly, placing her feet as cautiously as possible, unable to feel the carpet even when she removed her shoes and proceeded barefoot.

She sat on her bed, heating the point of the needle in the flame of her cigarette lighter until it glowed brightly, then pressed the tip against the inside of her thigh. The pain was so much purer this way, it brought the world back more quickly, and reduced the chance of infection as well.

Before she went to bed, she had used up all the fluid remaining in the lighter and the inside of her left thigh resembled that of a drug addict.

Friday, November 13

Louise Tyler arrived home at precisely 4:12. She still felt disoriented, even though she'd been working shorter hours for two full weeks. She parked on the lefthand side, behind Tom's car, and slipped out quickly. There was a lot of mail today, but she carried it into the house without even glancing through the pile, dropped it on the kitchen table to be attended to later. Much later.

Tom glanced up from the television when she passed and waved abstractedly without saying anything. Louise draped her coat over the back of a chair in the hall and walked upstairs, knocked lightly on Terry's door.

"Terry, I'm home."

"Okay." As Louise turned to go, she thought she heard two more syllables spoken in a low voice, not really meant for her ears. "Big deal." Or perhaps she had been meant to hear them. Terry had been sullen and uncooperative ever since their confrontation over her missing homework.

It was going to have to be meatloaf tonight, not a roast but beef at least. She emptied the last four potatoes out of their bag and placed them in the pan unscrubbed. They were out of green beans; her food budget had been prohibitively tight this week and she'd had to forego all but the essentials. An elderly package of lima beans would have to suffice.

According to the evening paper, the owners of Eblis Manufacturing were meeting on Monday with a consortium of local banks in an effort to entice them into floating a loan to stave off a move by creditors to force the company into bankruptcy. Louise read the story calmly, no longer feeling emotionally involved with her employer's fate.

Supper was a quiet affair for the most part. Louise had been annoyed to discover that Tom hadn't run the load of towels through the washer as she'd requested.

"If you're going to be home all day, you could at least find time to help out a little."

Tom sighed. "Louise, I spent the entire day looking for work. I've been calling around to all the people I know, trying to get a lead on something that pays a decent wage. You're the one who keeps telling me how short we are on cash. If you want me to keep house instead, that's fine, but make up your mind one way or the other."

She left the dirty dishes on the table afterward and went to her room. Shedding all her clothing, she stood in front of the full length mirror mounted on the closet door. Tiny trails of scabs and red scars covered large portions of her body, everywhere she could reach that would not show when she was dressed. Even the undersides of her breasts were covered. Fortunately, she and Tom were never naked in each other's presence any more, and even if he noticed the few marks that weren't always completely concealed, he wasn't likely to ask about them. Tom had always been hesitant to discuss their bodies.

After a brief examination of the marks on the inside of her thighs, she decided the scars had healed enough to allow a second assault. She carefully folded a clean washcloth until it was small enough to clench between her teeth. With cigarette lighter and a fresh supply of pins, Louise set about bringing the world back into focus, her cries of enlightenment muffled by the makeshift gag.

Friday, November 20

Louise Tyler arrived home at precisely 3:37 and parked her car diagonally across the driveway. She failed to close the door behind her despite the buzz from under the dashboard and walked slowly to the house. Without looking at the individual pieces of mail, she removed them from the mailbox and dropped the entire lot into an open garbage can.

Tom was watching television, didn't even glance up as she walked through to the hall, where she dropped coat and gloves on the floor. Upstairs she knocked on Terry's door, but there was no answer; her daughter had been sulking ever since Louise told her they could not afford to repair her suddenly broken television set. Her thoughts elsewhere, she descended to the kitchen and started preparing supper. There were no vegetables to go along with the meat tonight, and instead of a roast she had thawed an ancient slab of swordfish she had discovered at the rear of the freezer.

The bankruptcy of Eblis Manufacturing was one of the lead stories in the newspaper. She let her eyes scan the headline casually, but didn't bother to read the text that followed. Mr. Kelleher had explained more than she cared to know as he was handing out their final checks earlier in the day.

Louise had planned to wash the last two days' worth of dirty dishes while dinner was cooking, but it no longer seemed worth the effort. Instead she climbed wearily upstairs and went to her own room, closing the door behind her. It was safe here; the pain and terror the outside world inflicted upon her daily retreated before the greater agony she visited on herself. The night table was covered with her tools, pins, razor blades, a cigarette lighter, some clamps she had stolen from Tom's tool chest along with a pair of needle nosed pliers and some sandpaper.

It had grown steadily more difficult to drive away the demons crowding around her, but Louise had an inventive mind and had always managed to find a way. There was an untouched patch of sensitive skin behind her right knee that she'd been saving for a real emergency, and she had almost finished when she glanced up and saw Terry standing in the doorway, her eyes wide with astonishment.

Louise set the pliers aside and spoke in a voice husky with joyful pain. "Yes? What is it?"

Terry made three attempts before she could force the words to come. "Dad said to tell you, he wants real meat tonight, no more tunafish or pasta. He said to tell you."

"But I've already put dinner in to cook," she answered mildly.

Terry cleared her throat nervously, averting her eyes so that she could no longer see the marks that ran up her mother's thigh. "I can't help that. He said to tell you."

Louise sighed and stood up, smoothing her dress down over the marks of her liberation. "All right. I'll see what else I can find."

"Supper will be ready in five minutes, Tom. Would you call Terry on your way?"

He glanced up from the television in time to see Louise's head draw back into the kitchen. "That was quick."

She was already out of sight but she must have heard him, because she answered right away. "You said you wanted it rare, didn't you?"

He wondered if that was meant to be sarcastic, but decided to be magnanimous and ignore whatever subtext might lie there. Besides, he was involved with the scandalous story the tabloid program was covering, and in fact waited almost ten minutes for it to end before calling perfunctorily up the staircase to announce dinner.

When Terry arrived, her father was still standing motionless in the archway to the kitchen, seeing but not understanding what lay before him. Louise Tyler sat on the floor with her back propped against the refrigerator door, her head slumped forward on her chest. The floor beneath her legs was dark and sticky.

The table had been set meticulously, with small bowls of salad, a loaf of reasonably fresh bread, and a pitcher of lemonade. And while there were neither potatoes nor other vegetables, Tom's and Terry's plates were both heaped with thin slices of red meat, all cut with relentless precision and loving care.

DEALING WITH STRESS

A small figure, almost certainly a child, moved furtively in the shadows. Teresa Gallo was standing on the catwalk above the main production floor when she caught the flicker of motion out of the corner of one eye, someone ducking out of sight behind one of the idle ten ton hydraulic presses.

"Something wrong, Terry?"

Evan Berridge's voice startled her. He had a habit of sneaking up on people. Officially he was a consultant brought in to suggest productivity improvements throughout Eblis Manufacturing, but it was an open secret that he was a professional hatchetman, hired to identify people to be dropped from the payroll.

"And you can bet he's not going to look too hard at the people in the front office. They fuck up and we pay the price." Everyone in the supervisor's cafeteria had nodded agreement when Maria Chaves put their suspicions into words the day Berridge appeared on the scene.

Terry fought to keep her voice under control. "No, everything's fine, sir. I was just looking for Bob Maxwell."

"Wouldn't it be easier to page him?" He nodded toward the intercom on the first landing.

"Sure would, but it's hard to hear down in the press room."

"I imagine it is." Berridge appeared to have lost interest in the conversation and moved away, but Terry was convinced that the incident had been recorded and filed away for further consideration.

When she recovered enough composure to investigate, there was no sign of an intruder, and she convinced herself that it had been a trick of the light. Or at least, she thought that's what she'd done.

Timmy's bicycle was leaning in its usual place against one side of the front porch, so he'd obviously gotten home from school all right. But she was dismayed to find the front door unlocked, a violation of one of her primary rules, and she slammed it angrily behind her.

It had already been a hell of a day. How dare he test her like this?

"Timmy! Come down here right now, young man!"

Tony thought she heard a quick, furtive sound from upstairs but there was no answer, no sign of the child. Just like his father, Terry told herself, breathing metaphorically on the smoldering embers of a long standing emotional fire. Before he'd deserted her, Jack had habitually backed away from their problems, refusing to discuss them. And if she tried to press the issue, he'd invariably abandon the field of battle for one of his interminable evening walks. If he'd been willing to find an accommodation, maybe they'd have been able to make it the marriage work. But eventually he'd abdicated his responsibilities completely, and Tony hadn't heard a word from him in nearly a year.

"Did you hear me!" She tried to shout, but her voice cracked, brittle with work related anxiety. Deprived of Jack's income, Terry was barely able to cover the lavalike flow of bills. If she lost her job at Eblis, had to survive on unemployment, she didn't know how she'd manage.

Continued silence from upstairs. A tiny finger of flame burst from the embers and Terry stormed up to the second floor, turned right, shouldered her way through the half opened door to Timmy's room.

He was sitting on his bed, facing the window, chin resting on his chest. Thoughtful? Contrite? Or just inattentive?

"Didn't you hear me calling you?" Her voice was hoarse with tension, the muscles around her lower ribcage tense and tingly. "How many times have I told you about leaving the doors unlocked? I worry enough knowing you'll be here by yourself every day without having to wonder if you've been attacked by a burglar or a dope addict or something."

Timmy didn't answer, not even when she sat down on the bed beside him, just lowered his head another fraction of an inch, staring into his lap. Terry became furious when he remained stubbornly silent, struck without thinking, slapping him across the right cheek.

Timmy's head broke loose and rolled off the side of the bed onto the carpet.

Sighing with frustration, Terry bent to retrieve it. Nothing was going right today.

Terry retrieved her sewing kit and made the necessary repairs. Although Timmy still refused to answer, she decided he'd already been punished sufficiently and besides, the last time she'd resorted to her usual practice of pressing glowing cigarette tips into the flesh of his thighs, he'd caught fire briefly, which had been frightening as well as messy.

Still too upset to eat, Terry changed into an old pair of jeans and walked outside to work in the garden. She was inordinately proud of the orderly rows of marigolds, pansies, daffodils, and chrysanthemums, all surrounded on three sides by rose arbor. Working with the soil was soothing, helped restore her equilibrium in times of stress.

Margie Campbell walked across from her own property. "Hiya, Terry. How're they hanging?"

Terry pressed her lips firmly together and took a deep breath. Margie meant well, probably, but her rough good cheer and casual obscenities grated. "Hi, Margie. Same as always, I guess."

"Still no word from the prick, huh?"

Terry sighed, sat back on her heels. "No, none at all. I'm not expecting any, Marge. I'm not even sure I want to. Just because Jack and I didn't have noisy fights every night doesn't mean we were getting along, you know. I'm happier with him gone."

"Sure, but you must miss Timmy. I mean, he was your only child! A good boy, too, always quiet and respectful."

Somehow Margie had convinced herself that Timmy had run off with his father. That was wrong, of course; the boy was upstairs in his room. Terry humored the woman's delusion; Margie was stubborn and once she got an idea into her head, it required a major effort to dislodge it.

"He was always his father's son, Margie. I'm sure he's just fine."

Margie was obvious dissatisfied with her answer. "Yeah, well, it just doesn't seem right."

Terry turned away and began pulling weeds with such obvious intensity that her neighbor could not mistake the snub, sniffed and retreated to her own property.

That evening she relented and allowed Timmy to watch television with her, holding his hand in her own to indicate he was forgiven.

The following day, she spotted the child again, this time in the warehouse. Terry was doing cycle counts, comparing physical counts of selected items to the running balance in the perpetual records. If the discrepancy varied beyond a certain amount, she made a note of it and would later try to track down the mistake by auditing the transfer slips. She was in one of the three rear storage bays when the sound of childish laughter filtered through the background noise of rumbling conveyors and electric forklift trucks.

"Is someone there?" Terry walked to the end of the aisle, trying to determine from where the laughter had originated.

Someone giggled briefly, off to the right. Terry made her way around the looped conveyor, moved quickly to the adjacent row.

At the far end, a small boy stood facing her. He waved once, then turned and ran off behind a row of corrugated cartons. Terry made no attempt to follow. She was rigid with shock. It was Timmy, her son. It wasn't like him to skip school, not like him at all. And to follow her to work, to taunt her like this...she couldn't find the words to describe her outrage.

"You just wait until I get home tonight, young man."

When she got home, Terry found a dog in her garden. He'd been there long enough to dig quite a large hole. Although he backed off a few meters when she approached, the dirt colored mongrel refused to leave until she started throwing stones. Even then, she had to hit her target twice before the dog turned and ran off.

It took several minutes to completely cover the elbow and forearm visible at the bottom in the shallow pit. Jack's watch was still running; he'd always been proud of its durability. Once the ground was reasonably level, she moved several pieces of flagstone to cover the freshly turned earth.

Terry spanked her son that evening. Timmy took it well, no screaming, no tears, no backtalk. When she was done, she felt mildly guilty. It was a first offense, after all, and she was afraid she was taking out her own frustrations on the boy, allowing tension from work to spill over into her family life.

"I hate punishing you, Timmy, but you have to learn to do what you're told." She took his hand in hers, trying to impress him with the seriousness of the situation. "It's for your own good. If you don't learn to behave properly, you'll end up just like your father."

Timmy ignored her, wouldn't even look in her direction. Terry hated it when he sulked so she sent him to bed without supper.

There was an unnerving memo on her desk the following morning. Evan Berridge "requested" her presence in the small conference room at 2:00 PM. She had almost six hours to regain her composure, or lose it completely. The interval was intentional, she realized, to crank up the stress level. It was some kind of a test.

"Never let 'em see you sweat," she whispered.

But she did. It went badly from the start. Berridge had rearranged the chairs so that she was forced to sit in one with uneven legs that rocked back and forth from one configuration of three to another. She was certain this was intentional, designed to undermine her confidence.

Berridge leaned across the narrow conference table and she hastily retreated from this infringement on her personal space, then realized she was projecting a weak image and tried to recover. But when she shifted her weight forward, the chair's orientation changed and she jumped when the odd leg banged down on the floor. Berridge pretended not to notice.

"You've been with us now for what, eight years, Terry?" He was staring at a yellow lined pad filled with his own illegible scrawl.

"Almost nine," she said softly.

"What's that?" He glanced up; his glasses had slid halfway down his nose.

"I said it'll be nine years in another six weeks."

"Your performance reports are all quite favorable; I notice you've received the maximum pay increase for your labor grade every year."

"I try to do a good job, sir."

"Yes, I'm sure you do. Of course, performance reports are only as good as the people who write them, and if I believed everything I read, I'd have to assume that Eblis only hires the absolute best people." He set his pad down and leaned back. "So where do you see yourself five years from now, Terry?"

She wet her lips before answering in a voice that crackled with tension. "Well, I'd like to be senior inventory clerk someday, or maybe get into expediting."

"Do you think of yourself as a team player?" Tiny beads of

sweat were visible on his upper lip; Terry found herself staring at them, forced herself to look away.

"I...I think so. I mean, I get along with people okay."

"Expediters need to be able to interact with a wide variety of personalities, you know. Sometimes you have to scream and shout, sometimes just nudge. To be effective, expediters need to be at ease with people, and able to put them at ease as well, but without letting themselves be bullied."

She nodded, not trusting herself to speak. What was he getting at?

Berridge leaned further forward, skewering her with his stare. "For example, do you feel awkward talking to me right now?"

Terry shook her head, then nodded. "A little, I guess. I mean, I'm not really sure what this is about, and with all the changes..." Her voice trailed off.

"Only dead organisms stop changing, Terry. Eblis needs to adapt to the times. One aspect of that process is to evaluate the future potential of an employee rather than just rely on past history. The most valuable employee is one who knows when to be assertive as well as when to be compliant. Do you think you'd be able to stand your ground on controversial issues?"

"I think so." Her mind was working at lightspeed, trying to interpret every nuance of word and action. This was clearly an important test, she realized. But what was the right response? What was he after?

"Flexibility is important, Terry, knowing when to be hard and when to be soft. Do you understand what I'm saying?" The beads of sweat seemed larger now, and Terry suddenly thought she understood the undertext. Berridge had read her personnel file, knew that for all practical purposes she was no longer married. Was he suggesting a sexual liaison?

"I...I think so. I can stand up for myself," she hesitated, "when I know I'm right about something." Her voice trailed off.

Berridge scribbled something on his pad without answering, then tapped the point of his pencil against the paper for a few seconds.

"That's all for now, Terry. Thank you for coming by. We'll talk again."

She spent the rest of the day replaying the interview in her mind, trying to decide if she'd missed some hidden cue, or made some horrible mistake that would result in her termination. She felt a great rush of relief when it was finally time to go home.

Two blocks from the house, she saw a dog trotting along the side of the road, recognized it as the same one she'd chased out of her garden. Without consciously deciding to act, she swerved the car, was rewarded by a solid double thump. The dog didn't even have a chance to yelp.

Terry pulled over to the curb, opened the door, and looked around quickly. No witnesses and no other traffic. There was still movement, disconnected nerves discharging their last messages, but the animal was clearly dead.

Terry wrapped the small corpse in a blanket and loaded it into her trunk. Timmy had always wanted a pet.

That night, while lying in bed waiting for sleep to overtake her, Terry fought to control the feeling that things were rushing past too quickly. If only Jack was there to comfort her, to make everything better like he'd promised.

It was all his fault of course, everything that happened on their last night together. Jack kept insisting that she talk to a doctor, refused even to listen to her reasons for not doing so. Perhaps she'd over reacted when she hit him with the frying pan, but it was really his fault for having been so stubborn and unreasonable, and when he'd threatened to take her son away, he'd gone too far. And then Timmy had made such a scene, crying and carrying on until she'd finally managed to quiet him.

Was she missing Jack now? Was that the explanation for the empty sensation, the pulsing ache below her heart and above her thighs? Terry rolled to one side, opened the night table drawer. She'd kept the best part of Jack at least, the part that had given her Timmy, stretched over a styrofoam cone. There were signs of wear, sooner than she had expected. But Jack had always done things sooner than she expected. Even Timmy had been premature, born almost a month ahead of schedule.

She fell asleep with Jack's memory cradled against her right breast.

The following day, quite by accident, Terry heard a

disturbing fragment of conversation. There was a significant discrepancy for subcomponent P414, so large that Terry suspected an entire skid of product had been logged into the warehouse without ever having actually left the production floor. She was crouched behind a row of skids, checking the lot tags, when she heard two men talking.

"Don't you think that's pretty quick, coming right after the last layoff?" It was Kimball, the plant manager. She recognized his Texas drawl.

"Best to get it over with. There are too many rumors going around right now." Berridge, a note of impatience in his voice. "You'll just worsen morale by letting things simmer."

"I suppose you're right. But it seems a shame to loosen up on our controls after spending so much time putting them in place."

"That degree of accuracy is expensive. It won't hurt to back off a little bit. Just by limiting cycle counts to high cost items, we'll save two salaries. And we can reduce some overtime in data processing and..."

They moved further on, beyond earshot, but Terry had heard enough. After she'd failed to respond to Berridge's sexual advances, he was retaliating by eliminating her job.

She didn't accomplish much else before quitting time.

That evening, she ate a plate of leftovers she hadn't bothered to re-heat first. Timmy stayed in his room, but Terry decided he could fend for himself for one meal. He was old enough to assume a little responsibility. When she discovered she couldn't concentrate on the television either, she went to bed early, but at midnight she was still awake, shivering even though it was quite warm.

"Jack," she whispered. "Why aren't you ever around when I need you?" Loneliness, uncertainty about the future, and darker, less specific anxieties pushed her to the brink of panic, and the safe harbor of sleep continued to elude her.

At half past twelve, moving as quietly as possible, working without lights, Terry went out to the garden and dug for a while, quite a while. When she was through, she struggled to bring Jack inside, finally managed to move him upstairs to their bedroom.

She slept much better within the circle of his arms.

Timmy bunked school again the next day. Terry wasn't absolutely certain at first, but early in the morning she thought she saw him duck behind a partition at the far end of the polishing department. He managed to evade her when she looked for him, and it wasn't until after lunch that she realized he was still in the factory.

Just before the mid-afternoon break, she spotted him a second time, just as he disappeared up the rampway to the lacquer department. That area had been silent for several months, ever since Custom Gifts International went out of business and stopped ordering lacquered brass figurines. Berridge had proposed relocating one of the small assembly operations to this area, and in fact she'd seen him come this way just a few minutes earlier. If Berridge saw Timmy, she'd be in even greater jeopardy.

Terry glanced around to make certain she was unobserved, then followed.

She couldn't risk calling Timmy's name and alerting Berridge, but it would only take a few minutes to search the area, despite the clutter of equipment and supplies. Unfortunately, she ran into Berridge before she found her son.

He was lying forward over the guardrail surrounding the degreasing unit. Terry couldn't figure out what he was looking at, but she was thankful for his inattention. With luck, she could back away silently and be gone before he noticed she was there.

She'd actually taken her first step backward before she noticed something odd about Berridge's posture.

"Mr. Berridge? Are you all right?"

He remained silent, motionless, absorbed in whatever had attracted his attention. Or that's what she thought before she noticed the handle of the screwdriver sticking out of the back of his head.

They let her lie down in the small first aid room adjacent to personnel while the police were called. The company nurse was sympathetic and gave her something to settle her stomach. The personnel secretary was right next door and if Terry needed anything, all she had to do was knock on the adjoining wall.

Terry was upset all right, but not because she had been the one unlucky enough to find the body. After all, people died. There was nothing to be done about such an inevitability. And she certainly wasn't fond of the man, felt no need to mourn his passing.

What did upset her was that screwdriver with its unmistakable dayglow orange handle. It was part of a set she'd bought for Jack on their fifth anniversary, and she'd never seen another like it.

The office walls were thin, inexpensive paneling over a wooden frame. In the confusion, they must have forgotten she was there, because when the police arrived and set up shop in the personnel office, they talked quite freely and audibly.

"Find anything?" A male voice, deep, unknown, bored but with an undertone of irritation.

"Sure did. I don't like it though." Another male, quieter, but slightly hoarse.

"You never like it. What've you got?"

"Two prints on the handle, recent ones. Real recent."

"God forbid we should get an easy one for a change. Why the funny face?"

Short pause. "The prints are funny, kind of blurry even though there's a good clean contact. And they're small. Real small."

"Small?"

"Yeah. Dan, I think these prints are from a kid. Either that or a midget."

Terry tuned out the conversation, realizing that despite their recent difficulties, Timmy still loved her enough to act on her behalf.

"But you should have asked me first," she whispered. "This time you've really been naughty."

Terry slid her hand down to the pocket of her jeans, reached inside, and pulled out the shriveled, nearly mummified item she carried there, interlacing her fingers with those of her son, being careful not to break any of them like she had the last time.

Timmy always liked it when Terry held his hand.

CONTINUITY PROBLEM

It was raining on the morning when I first arrived in Managansett. A lifeless rain with no wind, just a steady, thrumming downpour of oversized droplets that burst like miniature bombs as they landed. Visibility was so bad that I'd almost crept into town, struggling to follow the inadequately marked and badly maintained pavement. The road had narrowed almost as soon as I'd crossed the town line, unkempt trees crowding in from either side, the breakdown lane dwindling from functional to a symbolic gesture. There were patches of pre-dawn fog that hid the distance, and occasional gaps in the trees that were hard to differentiate from the road itself until the sound of my tires leaving the pavement and rolling across dirt warned me I'd gone astray.

I wasn't due to arrive until Tuesday evening, but my last assignment ended more quickly than I'd expected and the oppressive heat and humidity in the Orlando area had bothered me more than usual, so I'd packed up my things and hit the road, driving north with only a single, brief stopover in Emporia, Virginia, for a shower and a few hours sleep. I also felt a distinct if childish pleasure, as though I was a secret agent slipping into a foreign stronghold undetected and unsuspected. Some of the thrill evaporated after a near accident; some jerk driving a blue Lexus identical to my own popped up out of nowhere, and I ended up on the median strip, half turned around, shaking violently and sweating despite the air conditioning.

Technically the sun was up when I saw buildings in the distance and knew that I'd finally arrived, but the sky was full of angry clouds and it might as well have been night. The rain had eased slightly but still came down with a muted roar. I pulled over to the side of the road, probably unnecessarily; I hadn't seen another vehicle moving in either direction since well this side of Providence. Although I had already committed the directions to memory, I read through them again, angling the printout to catch the best light.

There had been a time when I had been able to pick out the plum jobs from a reasonably diverse selection, but those days were gone now. The fact that it wasn't my fault was little consolation. My track record was good, and all of my past clients had expressed satisfaction with the work I'd done for them. But the economy had softened and budgets were constrained, and even when potential clients knew that I could save them money in the long run, they were unable to justify expending funds for my services "in the present business climate". Owners, directors, stockholders, and senior executives invariably frowned when they saw "consultation fees" listed in a financial plan. "We have smart people working for us, don't we? Why do we need some overpriced hired gun?" I felt like a dinosaur somehow aware of its imminent extinction.

So here I was in Managansett, Rhode Island, on a contract that paid half my usual rate to design and implement an inventory control system for a company too small to invest in SAP or even one of its lower priced competitors, but too big to continue using spreadsheets and index cards. The contract was for four weeks, renewable, but I could probably rough out the design in a quarter of that time. Convincing people to develop and use a new tool would take much longer.

The rain picked up tempo as I edged away from the curb, so I didn't see much of Main Street as I passed through the town's tiny commercial district. Everything was closed, even the small diner where I paused, hoping for coffee, and few of the buildings were lighted. About a third of the streetlights were dark as well, all along one side of Main Street, so it was most likely a power failure of some kind. There had been some impressive lightning a few hours earlier, violent enough that I had considered stopping at a motel and finishing the trip in the morning.

My plan to pass through New York City after midnight to avoid the traffic on the George Washington Bridge hadn't seemed quite so brilliant as I fought both fatigue and the elements on the drive through Connecticut. I turned the radio on to keep me awake and got some kind of entertainment talk show doing a *Star Trek* retrospective. At that moment I might not have minded being beamed to my destination, although frankly I never understood why anyone would ever submit to such a thing. I mean, the guy who arrives is a copy, right? So the original is dead, isn't he?

My directions came from Google maps, which was a good thing since most of the streets had no signs identifying them. I used the mileage estimates and only had to correct course once, turning into a street so dark and tree covered that I'd mistaken it for a driveway. I finally did see some other traffic, two or three cars cautiously proceeding back in the direction from which I'd come, presumably the early risers off to work. After passing through several blocks of residential homes, the road took a sharp left and passed between two tracts of undeveloped land. There were no streetlights at all out this far from town center, and I had to slow down even further to avoid slipping off the side of the pavement.

But eventually I found the house, one of a pair that faced each other. Mine was the one on the right. The driveway was well maintained, though currently under about two inches of water, and I felt a surge of relief as I rolled up close to the garage and killed the engine. I took the flashlight out of the glove compartment and angled it up through the window, confirming the number over the door. It was indeed 333 Crescent Drive, my home for at least the next four weeks.

I sat for a few minutes, hoping for a lull in the rain, but if anything the drumming was growing steadily louder. "The hell with it!" I couldn't sit in the car any longer. I decided to make a dash for the door, which was protected by a small, overhanging roof. My feet were soaked as soon as they touched the ground and I twisted an ankle when I tried to pivot around the car door, slam it shut, and run for shelter all at the same time. Off balance, I fell to one knee, banging it hard enough to make my head spin. I swore more colorfully this time and staggered the rest of the way, then leaned against the door while I caught my breath. The few seconds of exposure had left me soaked and chilled.

I had just begun to collect my wits and breathe more evenly when I remembered that the key to the house was in my briefcase, which was currently resting in the passenger seat. At that point I was so tired that it struck me as wildly humorous, and I was laughing as I limped back through the rain, retrieved my briefcase, locked the car, and then returned to try the key. The lock was reluctant to turn but eventually acquiesced and I stepped into my temporary quarters just as the rain suddenly died away as abruptly as if someone had turned a faucet.

I glanced up at the suddenly lightening sky as I closed the door. "Thanks a lot," I said to no one in particular.

The lights worked, once I found the switch, which was mounted unusually high and further back from the doorframe than I expected. The windows were heavily draped and the hall light didn't extend very far, but I saw that I had a small sitting room to my left and a larger dining room to my right. The stairs to the second floor were directly ahead of me and there was another light switch there, located more conventionally. Now that I had arrived, I was more exhausted than ever, and all I wanted to do was sleep. I didn't have to show up at Eblis Manufacturing until Wednesday morning, which gave me almost four full days to settle in, unpack, and find my way around. But my first priority was sleep.

There were three bedrooms on the second floor and I picked the one with the private half bathroom. I stripped down to my underwear, which was damp with sweat rather than rain, and draped my sodden clothing over the shower rail, then turned down the covers and crawled into bed. There was a musty smell in the air, but the sheets were crisp and cool and I fell asleep almost instantly.

I'd like to say that I wakened refreshed and with my spirits much improved, but that wasn't the case. It was still overcast and drizzling, and I was disoriented, my bruised knee hurt, and when I got out from under the blankets I stubbed my toe on a wrinkle in the carpeting. My clothing hadn't dried and the suitcase was still out in the car. I actually considered making a run for it in my underwear; the driveway was pretty well shielded by trees and I only had the one neighbor. But I chickened out and put on my pants and shoes before venturing outside.

The rain fell softly and steadily and the air was full of the smell of wet foliage, partly pleasant, partly not. I retrieved the rest of my luggage and carried it upstairs, took a quick shower and put on some jeans and a turtleneck. There were two dressers in the room and I arranged the rest of my travel wardrobe into one of them and put my toiletries in the half bath. Someone had left a half tube of my brand of toothpaste behind, but I dropped it into the wastebasket. Settled in, more or less, I went downstairs to explore the ground floor.

The kitchen was adequate, the appliances old but in good condition. The oven needed cleaning, but I didn't plan to use it; the microwave was enough for me. There was a fair collection of pots and pans, and an idiosyncratic selection of groceries in the cupboards. The refrigerator was empty except for a jar of mustard and a six-pack of soda, but the freezer compartment had a fair selection of frozen dinners. A not particularly clean microwave sat on the counter beside a more reputable toaster. The furnishings in the other rooms were inexpensive and mismatched, but not outrageously so. There was a full bathroom downstairs, larger than the other, but showing more obvious signs of heavy use. The toilet was cracked, the faucet on the sink leaked, and the tub was discolored.

The house belonged to Eblis, my temporary employer. They used it for visiting VIPs, consultants, and the occasional company function. I would have preferred a motel room, but there were none convenient to the plant. I couldn't really complain. Eblis would be paying for my expenses for the next month and the house was certainly more than adequate.

Having completed my tour, I went back upstairs. I hadn't unpacked my medications – high blood pressure, high cholesterol, allergies. I put them in the medicine cabinet, then regarded myself in its mirror. Kevin Sirillo, aged thirty-six, a bit under six feet tall and only a few pounds overweight. Not a trace of grey in my dark hair, which was as thick and wavy as it had been when I was a teenager. Perennially single and currently unattached. Toni broke things off after insisting that I was too caught up in my own private obsessions, that I had stopped interacting with the world in general and her in particular except on the most superficial level. Everyone needs their own space, don't they?

I hadn't seen much of the town on the way in, and I'd already exhausted the scenery indoors, so I grabbed a windbreaker. The rain had all but stopped when I stepped outside. The ground steamed and the leaves were sodden and dripping, the earth spongy underfoot. On impulse I walked past the car and down the driveway, avoiding a few small pools of standing water, until I reached the street. The house directly opposite was bigger than mine, and better maintained. I heard the sound of wind chimes from somewhere out of my line of sight and then, very distinctly, voices from behind me.

From inside the house.

I'm not stupid. I hesitated at the front door until I was certain that what I was hearing was the tinny sound of a television set or radio. Then I unlocked the door and went back inside. There was a radio in the kitchen and a thin, male voice was predicting scattered showers throughout the day. I turned it off and looked around, but the doors were all secure and the house was empty. I assumed that it had been powered up all along and the local station had just resumed broadcasting.

My first stop was the diner I'd passed earlier, Monroe's, which was open now and which served reasonably good coffee, good enough that I drank three cups with my fried eggs and toast. I wasn't the only customer, but no one seemed very talkative, not even the ones who sat together, and I didn't even rate a curious glance. The waitress greeted me with feigned pleasure. "Nice seeing you again." Since I'd never been there before, her insincerity was obvious, but I didn't bother correcting her.

With considerably improved spirits, I drove slowly through Managansett after breakfast. There was a barbershop, a laundromat, a tailor, a couple of bars, a convenience store, and two more small diners that looked even less appealing than Monroe's. I passed a school and a library and a police station, but there was no movie theater and, as far as I could tell, no churches. I might not thrive here but I would certainly survive, and if I got too bored, Providence was only a half hour away.

I made a brief stop at the convenience store and drove back to the house where I noticed fresh, wet tire tracks in the driveway. Someone from Eblis had probably come out to make sure the place was okay in anticipation of my arrival. I parked and went inside, half expecting to find a note waiting for me. There was no message, but obviously I'd been right because there was fresh milk and butter in the refrigerator, a jar of instant coffee on the countertop, and a package of English muffins beside the toaster. Coincidentally, my unknown benefactor had exactly duplicated my own purchases.

I spent most of the rest of the morning reading and napping, then left for a mid-afternoon lunch at Monroe's. The waitress genuinely recognized me this time and was considerably more pleasant than she'd been earlier in the day, so I tipped her generously. After all, I expected to be a regular customer over the course of the next few weeks.

Although I had planned to spend the afternoon doing some preliminary work based on the information I'd been sent, my attention kept wandering and I finally turned on the television. Even with cable, the selection was terrible and I ended up watching some kind of science program dealing with cell degeneration and aging. The guest, a white haired woman with an irritating voice, said something about how every atom in our body is replaced within seven years and that in a sense we are not the same person throughout our lives but a series of distinct though nearly identical individuals. It reminded me of *Star Trek*'s transporters and I turned the television off, vaguely unsettled. The implication was that continued consciousness was an illusion, that the "self" we perceived at any given time was just the latest in a series of always slightly different personae. And the nearly infinite earlier versions of ourselves were what? Dead? Or does each continue to exist in a separate flow of time?

An engine started up in the driveway as I was making a fresh cup of coffee. Although I walked to the front window immediately, I saw only my own vehicle there and it was empty, but another was just disappearing around the near corner. It looked like another blue Lexus.

I considered visiting one of the local bars, but in the end, I compromised and went to the Loft, an oversized barn turned into a bar and grill. It was on the outskirts of town and I almost didn't find it, but just before I decided to give up and turn around I saw its lights through the trees. The menu didn't offer much variety but the food was good and the drinks weren't bad either. I had two Bloody Marys, and then an Irish Coffee for dessert. The waitress actually brought me three drinks, insisted that I had ordered another round, and went away mildly miffed even though I was quite certain it was her mistake.

I was feeling pleasantly sleepy when I got home, but my mood didn't last long. Someone had clearly been in the house during my absence. The television was on, a half cup of coffee sat on the counter in the kitchen, and I was pretty sure that some of my things in the bedroom had been rearranged. Nothing seemed to be missing, and after considering calling the police, I decided that it would involve too many explanations, and it was probably someone from Eblis anyway. And I was tired.

But I made certain that the locks were all engaged before I went to bed.

It was daylight when I woke up, but it seemed as though no time had passed at all. I showered and shaved, but felt uneasy, as though someone else was in the house, watching me. I picked out clothing almost at random, dressed hurriedly, and searched from attic to basement. I was alone. But there was a dirty dish in the sink that hadn't been there the night before, and when I touched the toaster, it was still warm.

I thought about calling Nicholson, my contact at Eblis, but it was Sunday and he certainly wouldn't be there. There might be a dozen people with spare keys to the house, and they weren't expecting me for another couple of days. But if someone had stopped by to check the place out, they must have realized that I – or someone – was living there. Why not make contact? Or call the police if they were suspicious?

I made coffee, noticing that there was a mug missing from the rack over the sink. I looked around but there was no sign of it. Thoughtfully, I took the cup I'd just made and walked out the side door onto the narrow little porch that wrapped around the corner, ending in the backyard. The rain had stopped and the ground was drying, although there was still an oppressive cloud cover. It was cool enough that I drank the coffee quickly and I had just decided that a second cup wouldn't hurt when I noticed something at the far end of the porch. The missing coffee cup was balanced precariously on the railing.

Inside, I found myself trembling violently. I told myself it was anger, and that was partially true. But I was also disturbed, disoriented, and slightly frightened. I considered going upstairs, packing my things, and moving to a motel in Providence, regardless of the long commute. I went to the bedroom and retrieved one of my suitcases, but the absurdity of the situation hit me then. Convinced that I was over-reacting, I decided to wait until I had calmed down and thought things through more rationally.

And the next thing I knew, I was sitting in front of the television, watching a college football game. I didn't know the score, or even who was playing, and when I glanced at my watch, I realized it was the middle of the afternoon. My immediate assumption was that I had dozed off in the chair, but then I saw the plate on the coffee table in front of me. I, or someone, had eaten lasagna for lunch. There were two soda cans, one empty, one half full.

Had I blacked out? Nothing like that had ever happened to me before. I stood up and began pacing nervously, trying to remember preparing the meal, eating it. After a while, I thought I had recaptured fragments of the experience, but by then I was trying so hard that I might have manufactured the memories without realizing it. So to clear my head, I decided to take a walk outside.

The Lexus was not in the driveway.

Once again I had the impulse to call the police and once again I hesitated. I went upstairs and found my cell phone, then walked slowly back down. Maybe I had just pulled up so close to the building that I hadn't been able to see it from the front window. Knowing this was nonsense, I went out the front door anyway, and there it was, parked just as it should have been. There was no way that I could have missed it from the window.

I walked slowly forward and touched the hood with my hand, to reassure myself that it was really there. It was solid, all right, but it was also warm to the touch. The engine had been running recently.

Although I made a cursory search of the immediate area, I didn't expect to find anyone. A pattern was emerging and either I was the focus of some clever but bizarre plot or my mind was playing tricks on me. Had I driven the car myself, during a brief blackout period? But if that was the case, why had I not seen it from the window?

After closing and locking the door, I dropped heavily onto the couch, my thoughts swirling chaotically. It was only a moment or so before I realized that the coffee table no longer held evidence of my unremembered lunch.

The dirty dish and fork were in the kitchen sink, the empty soda cans were in the trash.

Whatever is happening to me has been accelerating. In an effort to organize my thoughts coherently, I have written this account of everything that has happened – or at least that I can remember – since I arrived in Managansett less than forty-eight hours ago. I have no recollection of the transition, but when I finished writing the above I found myself wearing bathrobe and slippers, and I know that I was fully dressed when I started. There is also an empty soda can beside my laptop which I cannot recall fetching, or drinking.

The gaps come more frequently now. I reach for an object and find myself standing on the opposite side of the room. I glance at my watch, blink, and minutes have passed, once an entire hour. My surroundings seem increasingly unreal and the feeling that I am not alone approaches certainty. Objects in the room are moved without my intervention, but never when I'm observing them. It's like living with the invisible man, but is the cipher my unseen companion, or am I the one whose existence is fading?

I speculated at first that one of the earlier manifestations of myself was somehow lingering, interacting with the world just enough to skew my perceptions. But now I believe that it is I – or rather, this momentary "I" – who has overstayed my welcome. I keep looking around, expecting to see a bright light and an ethereal figure beckoning me to enter, but instead all I see is this cheaply furnished, ugly room and...

ECHOES

I had expected the cell to be squalid, but I hadn't anticipated just how unpleasant the conditions of my incarceration would be. Under ordinary circumstances I would be outraged at the indignity, but given the alternative, I can only view this as a mildly painful inoculation to ward off what might have been a much more serious malady.

The first time I experienced the echo, it was so transient that I imagine most people would have dismissed the phenomenon as just a trick of the light or a blurring of the vision. Fortunately, unlike most people, I'm acutely aware of conditions in my immediate surroundings at all times. I've never understood how someone could believe that there is a distinct line of demarcation between their body and their physical location. After all, the body is just the immediate, portable environment that contains the essential us. If I cut my hair or bleed or even if I were to lose a limb, that wouldn't diminish who I am. We don't have absolute control over our own bodies, any more than we do over the rest of our environment. I wouldn't be able to grow back that missing limb, and if someone should choose to stab me or if the police locked me up, they'd be demonstrating that at least in some respects they have as much control over my body as I do myself.

But I'm straying from my point here. The incident occurred just as I passed my first anniversary at Eblis Manufacturing, where I sat in a cubicle for eight hours a day and processed inventory transactions, filled in spreadsheets, prepared materials requisitions, and pretty much spent all my time pushing paper, or more properly, pushing pixels around the screen since most of my work was at a computer terminal. There were two other people in the same office, Dorothy Gingrich, who looked old enough to have learned the fundamentals of her job in ancient Rome, and Hector Racina, a quiet, lumpish young man who spoke very labored English. Both of them kept to themselves, which suited me just fine, and I don't think we'd exchanged more than a dozen words a week in the entire year that I'd been there.

Nor was Mr. Horty, my nominal superior, any more voluble. Once I had assured him that I understood the essentials of my job, he seemed content to let me fill in the gaps on my own, and from that point forward treated me – and my co-workers – as though we were simply pieces of office equipment with no personalities or opinions. His attitude also suited me perfectly, as it apparently did Dorothy and Hector.

But one day I received an email telling me that my annual review was to be held at 2:00 PM the following Monday and that I should report to Mr. Horty's office at that time. It was annoying, certainly, since I knew perfectly well that I was performing above the level which was expected of me. I had the lowest error rate in the department and the highest productivity level, and several of my suggestions to the software support staff had been implemented. I'd even received a commendation (by email) from Mr. Horty for my observations about the redundancies in the scrap reporting system.

The meeting started well. Horty waved me to a chair without looking up from the file folder spread open on his desk, presumably my personnel records. I was hoping for nothing more than a brisk "well done" or perhaps a "thank you for your efforts" or, if Horty was feeling particularly expansive, "you're an important asset in this department". But Horty was apparently in a rare mood of conviviality.

He called me Mr. Vardoger instead of Vincent, and the first thing he asked was how I liked working at Eblis.

"I've found it rewarding and professionally satisfying."

Then he wanted to know if I had any complaints.

"None whatsoever." Actually, the air conditioner was too loud and it blew directly down into my cubicle, Hector had a distracting habit of tapping his pencil against the side of his coffee cup, the lighting was not optimal, and the rest rooms could have been better maintained, but I wanted to help Horty along and get this interview done as quickly as possible.

"Do you have any suggestions to make about how we could improve things around here?"

"I've sent along a few ideas."

His eyes glanced up from the folder and met mine for the first time. "Yes, I see that noted here. How about your co-workers? Any conflicts there?"

"No, sir."

His eyes drifted away, contemplating something on the wall behind me, or perhaps in another place altogether. "Where do you see yourself two years from now, Mr. Vardoger?"

I was momentarily confused by his question, but realized he meant this on a metaphorical rather than physical level. "I have no plans to look for another job, Mr. Horty. As I said, I'm quite happy here at Eblis."

"Yes, but in what capacity?" He sounded mildly, unaccountably annoyed. "You're a young man, hard working and bright. You surely don't want to sit at a desk processing transfer slips and receiving logs for the rest of your life."

Well, actually, that seemed perfectly agreeable to me, but I could tell that Horty was looking for a different answer. "I'd be willing to serve in whatever capacity I'm suited for."

His eyes flashed and I had the strangest feeling that he was seeing me for the very first time. "So you don't want my job eventually?"

The prospect made me distinctly uncomfortable. It is difficult enough to be responsible for the actions of one's own body without having to worry about those of others as well. "I don't think I'm cut out for a supervisory position, sir."

He resumed his contemplation of my file and our eyes never met again during the course of the interview, which seemed to go on interminably. Every suggestion that I'd offered was mentioned and faintly praised, and Horty made a check mark in the file after each. I thought we were just about finished when he shifted position in his chair and moved on to what he termed "opportunities for improvement" in my performance.

It was all that I could do to sit in my seat while he made totally inappropriate or trivial suggestions. I should take the training course for our new order entry software, even though I would never have any reason to use it. I had made six transaction errors during the past quarter, out of over fifteen thousand entries, much better than Hector or Dorothy had ever managed to achieve. I needed to make a stronger effort to interact with my co-workers in order to develop team spirit and improve morale. There were a few other things, so inconsequential that I would be embarrassed to even note them here.

At last it was over. Horty said "thank you for your time" without looking up. I hesitated, then stood up, tempted to say something rash about how unfair and arrogant it was to turn what should have been a rewarding experience into an exercise in humiliation but thought better of it. As I stood, out of the corner of my eye and for just a second, I thought that I saw myself still sitting in the chair, leaning forward with a hint of aggressiveness, but as I half turned back, that secondary figure stood and turned and melted into me and my vision was completely normal.

I finished the day in a quiet rage, well below my usual productivity level, and I just barely caught myself before I made a significant transaction error.

The second time it happened, I was tempted to dismiss the phenomenon as the product of an overactive imagination. Fortunately, unlike most people, my imagination is firmly under control and I never allow it to interfere with my perceptions of the world. I am not a hypochondriac; if I seek medical help it is always because of an actual illness. Although I have a deep love of books, I do not read fiction; I have never understood why one would want to immerse oneself in another person's artificial reality. I rarely dream and do not confuse the lingering after effects with the waking world. I do not believe in ghosts, flying saucers, an omniscient god, conspiracy theories, the assertions of politicians, or any other fantasies. My beliefs and perceptions are thoroughly grounded in reality.

I was certain that what I saw was neither a mirage nor a delusion. Besides, I wasn't the only one who witnessed the event.

It was on a Saturday and I was running a few errands in downtown Managansett. I hadn't slept well the night before and was drowsy, so I decided to stop and have a cup of coffee. It was moderately crowded and I had to wait in line while four other people were served, but eventually I faced a young lady with her hair tied back who asked me "What can I get for you?" except she slurred it all into one word.

"A tall French roast, black." And then I watched as she filled a cup from an urn clearly marked "Decaf".

"That'll be two dollars," she said, another single word.

"I beg your pardon. I asked for regular. That's decaf."

She looked at me as though I'd grown a set of horns. "You don't want it?"

"I want a tall French roast, black. Not decaf." My voice, I assure you, was perfectly even and inoffensive.

"Why didn't you say so then?" But she set it aside and took a fresh cup as she turned away. And filled it with decaf again.

I'm not bellicose by nature. If anything, I'm too self effacing. Most mornings I would have meekly accepted what she offered and quietly decided never to do business there again. But I was tired, grouchy, and the memory of my humiliation at the hands of Mr. Horty had still not completely faded.

"Young lady, I asked for a regular coffee, not a decaf. If you can't serve your customers properly, I suggest you find someone who can." And I turned on my heel and stalked away, while the three people standing in line behind me turned their faces away, pretending not to have seen or heard what had just happened. I trust they had better luck with their own purchases.

But that wasn't the end of it.

Leaving my car in the coffee shop's parking lot, I walked across the street to the post office and purchased some stamps. When I emerged, I could see a small crowd gathered in front of the coffee shop, and as I crossed back to retrieve my car, I could hear someone shouting angrily. I had just reached the sidewalk when I noticed the young woman who'd so badly served me coming in my direction, waving her arms, her expression furious.

"You son of a bitch!" was the first thing I could actually distinguish, each word distinct this time. As she approached, I also noticed something altered in her appearance. The hair on one side of her head was plastered down against her skull and there was a dark smear over the same shoulder and the front of her uniform. I couldn't understand this or why she would have reacted so strongly to my earlier comment, or waited so long to display her rage, and I stood frozen, trying to interpret the situation so that I could understand it.

Had it not been for one of the other customers, an older man with a completely bald head wearing a sweat suit, I really believe she might have physically assaulted me. She was only two steps away when he caught her by the arm. "Miss, it wasn't him. I saw the guy run the other way, up toward Cannell Street."

She allowed herself to be stopped, but glared at me with undiminished fury. "I saw him! This is the guy!"

"No, it's not," said the man quietly. "They're dressed the same way and they look alike, but it wasn't him."

For a few seconds, my fate hung in the balance, and even when she turned and stalked back toward the coffee shop, her body language said she didn't believe what she'd been told.

"What was that all about?" I asked.

The bald man shrugged. "Some guy who looked just like you threw a cup of coffee in her face, then ran off." He looked at me closely. "You don't have a twin brother, do you? He sure looked a lot like you."

The incident troubled and excited me.

I own my own home, a little cottage on Vernon Street just a half mile from downtown Managansett. It was a pretty little place, in reasonably good repair, in an attractive neighborhood. On one side was an undeveloped triangular lot, too small and awkwardly shaped to build on, and that afforded me a welcome degree of privacy. On the other side, unfortunately, was the proverbial neighbor from hell.

Ted Kramer was a teamster currently in the second year of idleness following a road accident that left him, theoretically, disabled. He had a tall stockade fence around his backyard, but I knew for a fact that he'd recently built himself a patio, laying the concrete and doing the brickwork himself, and I wondered how long it would take the insurance company to catch up to him. There were two large apple trees on the side of his property that bordered my yard, and some of the branches extended well past the fence. It was a nuisance cleaning up the dropped, rotting apples before I could cut the grass, but even worse were the hordes of insects that were drawn to the fruit. I had broached the subject of trimming the branches back shortly after moving in, and Kramer had responded with an obscenity laden warning not to touch his trees. Although I had the law on my side, I had decided not to make things even more unpleasant by carrying through with my plan.

My consideration had not been reciprocated. The Kramers had frequent parties which were invariably loud and raucous, went on until all hours, and left a mess of debris that blew down the street and into my privet hedge. Sometimes his guests parked in front of my house, and on two occasions they'd blocked my car in the driveway. Kramer also had a pair of dogs which he frequently let loose and they left pungent evidence of their visits on my lawn and woke me up howling in the night. Agnes Kramer was no better than her husband, an overweight slattern whose hair seemed to be perpetually in curlers and who went out for the mail wearing a tattered bathrobe. She played the radio loudly (country and western) while sitting on the new patio in the evenings when they didn't have guests – and sometimes when they did. I hadn't spoken to either of them since the first month of our acquaintance and sincerely hoped not to do so ever again. Actually, I hoped that lightning would strike their house, or that the earth would open up and swallow it into a sinkhole, or that they'd drive off in their pickup truck one morning and just never come back.

It was late in the week following the coffee shop incident. I'd just come home from work to find the street in front of my house covered with damp, wet leaves and pine needles. The Kramers had raked their yard into the street, then run the sprinklers, which eventually washed much of the waste material down into the shallow depression in front of my property. Fuming, I got out of my car, started for the house, and promptly stepped into a particularly unpleasant dog mess. As I was scraping it off my shoe, I heard my neighbor's screen door slam and a moment later Merle Haggard's voice carried over the fence.

I rarely drink alcohol; I don't like the way it interferes with my perceptions. But I had half a bottle of brandy in a kitchen cupboard and I poured myself a small glass, rationalizing that it was to calm my nerves. I had barely sipped it when the doorbell rang and, before I could possibly have reached it, rang again. When I opened it at last, I was startled to find Ted Kramer standing on my doorstep. It was the first time to my knowledge that he had ever ventured onto my property, preferring to send his four legged emissaries instead.

He was wearing a torn, sleeveless tee shirt and had a can of beer in one hand. I felt almost physically repelled by him even before I saw the expression on his face, which made me take an involuntary step backward.

"Hey, Vardoger, I want to talk to you."

"I'm just on my way out," I lied. "What do we have to talk about?"

He pushed his way past me into my house, a violation of my physical environment that I found so offensive that it overwhelmed my nascent alarm. "Seems like you've got plenty of time to talk when it suits you."

I had no idea what he was getting at and told him so. If anything, this seemed to make him even angrier. Kramer was a big man, topping six feet easily, broad shouldered, running more than a bit to paunch but certainly not soft. He stepped toward me and I retreated again, determined to keep a small circle of my own space. "Someone's been calling the insurance people, telling them I'm cheating them out of money."

I'd fantasized about doing that very thing, of course, but I'd never followed through. "Well, it wasn't me. Would you please leave now?"

"Who the hell else would know I dug out the garden Monday afternoon? Someone would have to climb up and spy over the fence to see that, and the Nelsons next door are out on Cape Cod for the week."

"Then maybe someone came into their yard and watched you," I said with a trembling voice. "It certainly wasn't me. I would have been at work, remember?" But that wasn't true. I'd taken Monday morning off to have my teeth cleaned. I was still at the house until 10:30, but I hadn't spied on the Kramers and I hadn't called anyone.

My quasi-lie seemed to have penetrated, however, because Kramer looked less certain of himself, though no less upset. "You just better watch your step, neighbor," he said belligerently. To my great relief, he started toward the door. "I don't like busybodies and I don't like snitches. You keep your eyes off my property and your hands out of my business, you understand?"

I closed the door the moment he was outside. But I didn't slam it, as much as I wanted to.

Instead I experienced a burst of quiet rage more intense than I'd ever felt before in my entire life. I stormed from room to room, as if trying to reach a place where my memories of the conversation couldn't find me, but they always did. At times I talked aloud, berating myself for not standing up to Kramer, rehearsing what I should have said one moment and raging incoherently the next. I'm not sure how long this went on before I returned to the kitchen and the brandy, but sometime after that I had another reason to complain. The bottle was empty and I was still conscious. It all seemed unfair.

I knew what I wanted to do. I wanted to go next door, tear up the Kramer's garden, cut down their apple trees, strangle the dogs, slash the tires on their truck, and then burn down the house. If the Kramers were trapped inside, so much the better. Eventually the brandy caught up to me and I fell asleep on the couch, staring at the blank screen of the television.

Wailing sirens wakened me.

Initially I was disoriented by the sound, by the darkness, by the fact that I was not wearing pajamas and lying in bed. There were flashing lights close by, very close, and the sirens abruptly stopped, but the echoes seemed to be trapped inside my head and I kept hearing them for quite a while afterwards. When I tried to stand, I nearly fell. My head ached, my stomach rumbled, and one of my legs was all pins and needles. I waited until the room slowed to minimal rotation, then carefully walked to the bathroom and vomited efficiently and refreshingly into the toilet.

I'm not sure how long it was before I took interest in the outside world again. It might have been an hour or more because I fell asleep with my forehead pressed against the white porcelain of the toilet. When I next opened my eyes, it was just before three in the morning. There were still flashing lights outside and voices talking loudly, and at irregular intervals the crackle of a police radio. I washed my face, checked my appearance in the bathroom mirror, then walked to the front door and stepped outside. It must have rained earlier in the evening because the grass was wet and the lights reflected oddly.

The Kramers' house was a smoldering ruin. Two hoses were still playing on the ashes but it was clear that the fire was effectively out. I blinked, wondering if I was dreaming, and glanced toward the apple trees, half expecting to find that they'd been cut down. They hadn't. I came as close as the firemen would allow, joining several other neighbors, all of whom were talking in hushed tones. The Kramers' pickup truck was still there and its tires were flat, melted rather than slashed. There were three police cars and an ambulance, which had driven up onto the lawn and was now parked in the garden, the front wheels in the marigolds, the rear mashing down daffodils. The back of the ambulance was open and there were two stretchers on the ground nearby. No one seemed to be in a hurry.

Edith Neal, an elderly widow and chief neighborhood gossip from up the block, saw me and broke away from the group she was with. We weren't exactly friends because she'd spread some nasty stories about me a while back, but we pretended to be sociable when we met. "Isn't it terrible, Mr. Vardoger?"

"I'm not sure what happened, Edith. I was asleep."

She looked at me oddly. "How could you sleep through all of this, Mr. Vardoger?"

"I took some pills," I lied. "I have insomnia. Are the Kramers all right?" I tried to sound sincerely interested.

Edith shook her head. "Gone, the both of them. They just brought the bodies out a few minutes ago."

It was the next day before I heard the rest. The fire had started in the kitchen and speculation was that one of the Kramers had left a burner lit on the gas stove and that a stray breeze had blown a curtain into the flame. They had probably been overcome by smoke and died without ever waking. .

Edith made a point of stopping by to tell me the details. "I wonder why the dogs didn't raise a ruckus when the fire started. They were both sleeping in the house at the time. Something doesn't sound right to me. Those dogs barked if a fly flew in through a window or a car passed on the street. I say they were already dead when the fire started, and that means it wasn't an accident."

But the police apparently weren't seriously bothered by the inconsistency. I wouldn't have been either except for one thing. When I went back inside, I took off my shoes so that I wouldn't track water into the house. They'd been dry when I went out, of course, or I would have found evidence on the carpet or in the bathroom. There was no question at all in my mind; I hadn't set fire to the Kramers' house while sleep walking or in a drunken stupor. I hadn't left the house at all.

But my umbrella was sitting in the hall closet, and it was still damp.

The next few days were uneventful, but the following week – this past week – has been a complete disaster. One of the apple trees was damaged in the fire, and during a windy rainstorm the trunk split, depositing the bulk of the tree on my property. A call to the police was not helpful; the Kramers had no known relatives and the disposition of their estate – and responsibility for its liabilities – was unresolved. That same evening, another of my neighbors came home late, drunk, and sideswiped my car, which I'd parked in the street to avoid having it scratched by the fallen tree's grasping branches. I called a local tree service, who removed the debris on Thursday, but they carelessly damaged my lilacs in the process. Friday morning, Mr. Horty called me into his office and told me that because of low sales, they were being forced to reduce expenses, and even though my performance was outstanding, Hector and Dorothy had seniority so I was the one who would have to go. Arriving home, I found my front window broken with a note from still another neighbor saying his son had been playing baseball in the street and they would, of course, pay for the damage.

Earlier this evening I changed into a sweatshirt and jeans and sat in the front room with a fresh bottle of brandy, a full one this time, but even though I drank steadily, I remained conscious and reasonably sober, my fury burning off the effects of the alcohol. It was just after midnight when I felt a bit strange and hastened to the bathroom, assuming that I was about to become sick. The strangeness, however, passed within a few seconds and with no obvious resolution. Just to be safe, I remained in the bathroom, leaning against the side of the shower, trying not to be consumed by my thoughts. By my anger.

I wanted to smash Mr. Horty's face with a blunt object. I wanted to throttle Mrs. Neal for the unkind gossip she'd circulated when I first moved to Managansett. I wanted to throw the Wilson boy through a window like a baseball, beat Oliver Begley to death for having hit my car, and disembowel the ignorant lout who'd mangled my shrubbery.

The front door closed.

I always lock up when I'm in the house. It seems to me a rudimentary precaution. Nevertheless, I was quite sure of what I'd just heard and, under normal circumstances, I would immediately have started to consider concealing myself from whatever intruder had picked my lock or in whatever other manner gained entry. But the past week had drained all of the emotion out of me, and the brandy probably added another layer of indifference, so instead I boldly opened the door and stepped out to confront my mysterious visitor.

But there was no one there. As I mentioned, I live in a small cottage. There is no place that anyone could have been hiding. I was alone in the house. But the door had definitely closed. I walked across the room and discovered that it was not locked. My hand lifted and I almost turned the knob to secure it, but a flicker of motion out of the corner of my eye distracted me and instead I crossed to the front window and looked out onto the front lawn.

There were several people there, or rather, there were several of the same person there. He was wearing a sweatshirt and jeans and he looked a lot like me. He, they, could have been my twins, and they were all moving away from the house, dispersing now on their various missions.

I thought about Mr. Horty and Mrs. Neal and Petey Wilson and Oliver Begley and the landscaper whose name I didn't know and it occurred to me that I should warn them, but frankly there probably wasn't time to convince them that I wasn't nuts, and even more frankly, I felt a surge of fierce glee at the thought of what was coming to them, of what they had coming to them, and instead I climbed into my car and drove downtown and parked in front of Terry's Bar & Grille. The clientele there were notoriously unruly and it was not at all difficult to entice one of the older men into starting a fight. He was uncoordinated and clumsy and I managed to avoid any serious harm while prolonging things until the bartender had successfully summoned the police.

And now I'm sitting in this cell, only a few feet from my erstwhile combatant, and the officer who arrested me told me that I was in big trouble and maybe he's right.

But at least I have an alibi.

FOREVER IN MY THOUGHTS

Toni felt the touch of his eyes as they tracked her progress across the office. It wasn't the first time she had attracted admiring stares from a man, despite a body that was just a trifle too slender to be sexy, but they'd never previously affected her so strongly. There was a definite sensation of physical contact, a feeling of feather light pressure up one thigh, over her hip, moving higher.

She stopped and turned quickly enough to catch the new clerk, Evan something-or-other, abruptly dropping his head, pretending to be studying something on his desk. Toni's mouth twisted into a quick, unpleasant smile. Dream on, she told him silently. Evan was slightly overweight, not enough to bother her under normal circumstances, but with his pale skin, thin and undisciplined hair, narrow set eyes, and puffy cheeks, he appeared unwholesomely swollen rather than obese. And his lips were too full and wide for his face.

"Hey! Earth to Toni. Anybody home in there?"

She turned, blinking, found herself facing Marian Darby, her nominal supervisor and closest friend. "Oh! Sorry, Marian. Guess I was daydreaming."

"Not about him, I trust." Marian inclined her head in the new man's direction. "I still don't understand why Maggie hired him. His work experience is limited and he certainly doesn't add to the office decor."

"Probably works cheap. Didn't you tell me Maggie's running over budget?"

"So who isn't? Speaking of which, if you don't have a hot date tonight, would you be willing to put in some overtime?"

The conversation turned to the backlog of unfinished projects sitting on Marian's desk and, for the time being, Toni forgot about her new admirer. But twice more before the day ended, she jumped at a sudden, phantom touch, and on both occasions there was hasty movement from the other side of the office, as though he had turned his head away at that exact moment.

Toni spent the rest of the week researching old product cost standards in the records storage area of Eblis Manufacturing, the company where she had worked since high school graduation five years previously. As a consequence, it was the following Monday before she returned to her desk, and during the interim, she had completely forgotten about Evan.

She had just finished sorting her overflowing "In" box into three piles of successively lower priority when a vague uneasiness caused her to raise her head and look around.

The office wasn't quite right. It was still recognizably the same room, but it was somehow...simpler. The paintings on the wall were mere blobs of color, lacking detail. The row of filing cabinets was recognizable, but the labels on each door were simply white rectangles. All the desks except her own were clean and orderly, empty chairs tucked neatly in place, and when she glanced down, she realized that most of the paperwork she had just sorted was mysteriously gone. At the far end of the room, a pale moon glimmered in the darkness, even though she had arrived only an hour earlier, at eight in the morning.

"Sure gets lonely working here late at night."

Startled, she turned and found Evan standing beside her desk. Except that it wasn't quite the Evan she knew; he was still overweight and his clothes were wrinkled and threadbare, but he held himself with an air of assurance and his voice was deep and forceful.

"I don't mind it so much now that you're working here with me," she replied warmly, even as alarms were cycling wildly in her mind. What was she saying? What was happening here?

"Do you suppose anyone suspects? About us, I mean." Evan suddenly reached out and touched her shoulder, cupping it with the palm of his hand. A thrill of sexual tension heightened her senses even as her mind jerked with revulsion. Against her will, Toni turned in her seat, inclining her head back as his face descended and those too wide lips closed over her own...

"Toni, wake up!"

She blinked as the office suddenly became brightly lit and crowded once more. Marian Darby was standing at her side, frowning. "What is it with you lately?"

"God, Marian, I'm sorry. I think I fell asleep." She shook her head vigorously.

"Must've been one helluva weekend." Marian dropped a new set of reports on the desk, already turning away.

As soon as she was out of sight, Toni rose and went to the ladies' room where she washed her face so vigorously that she had to reapply her lipstick.

When she returned to the office, Evan was staring in her direction. She met his gaze levelly and he turned away almost immediately, but she thought that he was smiling as he did so.

It happened again during the afternoon, shortly before the day ended. Two of the three piles of work had been disposed of and Toni was feeling rather pleased with herself. Her back hurt from leaning over the desk, so she pushed her chair back and stretched her arms out, head back and eyes closed.

When she opened them again, she was no longer in the office. Or anywhere within the confines of Eblis Manufacturing for that matter.

Toni rose from the couch as though something had bitten her. Where was she? It was obviously someone's apartment, sparsely furnished, only a couch, floor lamp, and a television in the entire room.

"Here we go."

She spun on one heel, eyes widening as Evan emerged from behind a half wall that led to a tiny kitchenette. He held two wine glasses, one of which she accepted.

"Cheers!" He raised the glass to his lips and drained it, and she found herself doing the same. It tasted like grape juice.

"Why don't you sit down? You know how wine makes you light headed."

Toni knew no such thing; she had a remarkably high tolerance for alcohol as a matter of fact, and she wasn't convinced that this was really "wine" in any case. Nevertheless, she suddenly felt dizzy and half fell, half sat on the overstuffed couch.

Evan took his place beside her, much closer than was necessary.

"Are you okay?" He leaned forward, staring into her eyes.

Within her mind, Toni wanted to jump up and run from the room, preferably after telling Evan just exactly what she thought of him, but instead she found herself swaying slightly, teasingly. "I'm just a little bit tipsy," her traitorous lips formed words that horrified her. Tipsy, indeed. A ridiculous word. She might have gotten pissed, bombed out of her mind, or blown away, but never "tipsy". "I feel like I'm going to fall right off the edge of the world."

"I'd better hold onto you then." And his arms were suddenly around her and she was pressing her face into his chest while his hands moved from shoulders to waist and then to her buttocks. Toni wanted to struggle, scream at the top of her lungs, but instead leaned back, pulling Evan down on top of her as she raised one leg and wrapped it around the back of his thighs. He shifted his own weight, brought his left hand around to cup her right breast, bringing a surge of ecstasy so intense that she arched her back convulsively, closing her eyes as the sensation burned through her nerve endings.

There was a sudden sense of weightlessness as she fell to the floor.

Toni opened her eyes, blinking rapidly, convinced that they had slipped off the edge of the couch. Except that the apartment was gone. She had in fact fallen off her chair and lay there now, one leg folded painfully back, the other stretched out under the desk.

"Here, let me help." Several people were standing around and one, Bill Eversole, had extended his hand down from what appeared to be a nearly infinite distance. "Are you all right, Toni? You took quite a fall."

Obediently, she grasped his hand and let him haul her to her feet. Sharp pains lanced through her left knee protested and she rubbed the point of her right hip with one hand, still having difficulty understanding what had happened.

Across the office, Evan stared silently, a mischievous grin on his face that didn't disappear until after he had turned away.

Toni agreed to work late again that evening, even though Marian had to attend a PTA meeting and would be unable to keep her company. Determined not to think about the unpleasant experiences earlier in the day, she concentrated on the matters at hand and cleared up most of her backlog by a few minutes before eight. She was about to call the guard and tell her to come lock up when a thought occurred to her.

She rose and crossed to Evan's work area.

The desks all locked, but it was a simple mechanism she had learned to circumvent years ago when she lost the key to her own. The drawers were mostly empty, and what they did contain was primarily generic office supplies. But she did find a copy of his employment application, learned that his last name was Wade and that he lived right in Managansett, was twenty three years old, unmarried, a high school graduate, whose previous work experience was with several temporary placement services. She also found a wallet sized photograph of a prominent and scantily clad actress, three rolls of breath mints, and a paperback novel titled Lust in the Ashes, apparently part of a series about life after an atomic war.

With a vague sense of guiltiness about spying, she returned the desk to its previous condition and called the guard.

That night, Toni experienced the most realistic dream of her life. If it was in fact a dream.

Her first impression was that she'd been in an accident. She lay half buried in a pile of unrecognizable rubble, apparently unhurt although her clothing was so badly torn that she might as well have been naked. When she tried to stand up, she discovered that her left ankle was pinned tightly to the ground by a fallen beam of some sort.

"Can someone help me?" Her voice echoed off the half collapsed roof above; through several gaps, she could see bolts of lightning playing through a sky filled with roiling thunderheads, although no rain was falling.

"Toni? Is that you?" There was the sound of someone making his way through the wreckage and she turned to see Evan Wade stumbling in her direction. Despite the destruction through which he moved, Evan's clothing was neat and clean.

"Over here!" Her emotions seesawed between relief and revulsion. Her apartment building must have exploded, she realized; probably a gas leak of some sort. "My foot is caught."

He reached her side and crouched to examine her piniored limb. "No problem," he said softly, then placed both arms around the rough wooden surface. She saw his back tense as he strained to lift it and he whispered, "Pull your foot out now." When she had done so, he released the beam, which fell back with a crash and a small cloud of dust.

"What happened?" Toni sat up, rubbing her bruised ankle until she realized that what remained of her blouse concealed nothing of what lay underneath. And somehow she had forgotten to put on a bra that morning. Despite the hot, dry air, goose pimples formed on her exposed flesh.

"The damned idiots," Evan responded bitterly, turning to face her. "Just when it looked like the world was finally on the road to peace, someone decided to push the button."

"Oh God, no!" Toni raised both hands to her mouth, coincidentally allowing him a panoramic view of her bare breasts. "What'll we do?" But within her mind, Toni was struggling to control her own body. This is all nonsense, she thought. It has to be a dream.

"Don't worry," Evan said reassuringly, reaching out to pat her bare knee. "I'll make sure nothing happens to you."

Without transition, they were walking together along a street. Buildings on either side had been reduced to crumbling ruins, funnels of smoke rising into the still angry sky, scattered fires flickering here and there. Toni noticed that although she was barefoot, there was no sense of pain as she walked over the ragged, broken ground.

"We can shelter here for the night." He indicated a small office building whose roof had fallen in, but which was in much better condition than anything else they'd seen. The front door was missing, so they entered without hindrance, soon located an intact office with an undamaged couch. Evan found some candles in a desk and they were soon huddled together as darkness fell with unnatural suddenness. Throughout this transition, Toni felt stunned, allowing her body to play the part as it had been written for her without protest, convinced now that this was a nightmare she had conjured up from her previous hallucinations and the discovery of the apocalyptic book in Evan's desk earlier in the day.

But when his hands started moving over her body, the sensation was too real to ignore. Toni turned her head toward him, intending to shout obscenities, but was appalled to hear the actual words that emerged.

"Oh, Evan, I need you now more than ever. Can't you make me forget this horrible world?" Toni's mind wanted to vomit even as her body began to move rhythmically under Evan's. The remains of her blouse and his untouched shirt had disappeared by now, and he was moving his hands over her breasts -- breasts which she now realized had gotten a good deal larger during these past few hours.

"God, you're so good! Don't make me wait for it!" Toni did not live a celibate life, but never in her life had she uttered such banalities during sex. Nevertheless, Evan seemed to find her words stimulating, and he literally tore off what remained of her jeans -- she had apparently forgotten to put on panties this morning as well as a bra -- while his own pants seemed to slip back of their own accord. She had a brief glimpse of an impossibly long appendage before he slammed his body down into hers.

Her last thought before unconsciousness overwhelmed her was that no matter how hard she scrubbed, she would never feel clean again.

She woke in her own bed, alone, unsurprised to discover that the world was intact, that no nuclear war had taken place, and that her breasts were back to their normal, unexceptional dimensions. "You're losing your goddamned mind, Toni," she muttered aloud as she swung her legs over the side of the bed, then immediately doubled over in pain, both arms clenched across her abdomen.

Her thighs were bruised from just above the knees to just below the hips.

She almost literally ran into Evan Wade at work that morning, turning a corner just as he reached it from the opposite direction. Without thinking, she retreated, one arm half raised defensively. He smiled and apologized shortly, then moved on.

That evening, the dream took up where the last had left off. They were chased through the ruins by hideously deformed mutants, then became separated due to her stupidity rather than his error. Captured by the mutants, she had been stripped naked and tied to a cooking spit over a low fire, only to be rescued in the nick of time when Evan appeared, armed with an automatic rifle that never needed to be reloaded. After dispatching several score of the mutants, he freed her, for which she was so grateful that she made passionate love to him in the ashes of the fire, even though hot coals burnt her flesh.

The following morning, she discovered a dozen tiny blisters on her buttocks.

Her life fell into an uneasy pattern in the days that followed. Although there were no more incidents while she was awake, she dreamed of Evan every night. She was convinced now that he was somehow invading her thoughts, manipulating her imagination while she slept. From time to time, she found herself quietly weeping with frustration. There was no one she could talk to about the situation, not even Marian; what she believed to be happening was clearly impossible, and if she claimed otherwise she'd end up in an institution. Her work was suffering as well, and Marian had already warned her that Mr. Nicholson was unhappy with the situation.

Evan never approached her at work or elsewhere, confining his attentions to her dreams. At times she believed he was quite conscious of what he was doing; at others she wondered if he might be unaware that he was somehow dragging her into his own wish fulfillment fantasies. It was not a difference that mattered; the results from her point of view were identical.

Apparently Evan had tired of the nuclear scenario. During the days, or rather the nights, that followed, he rescued her from pirates, terrorists, and a psychopathic killer. They survived plane crashes in storm swept mountains, were shipwrecked on abandoned but bountiful islands, were trapped in a sunken submarine for days awaiting rescue, and thwarted an invasion of alien creatures who, despite their entirely inhuman appearance, had crossed the galaxy for the express purpose of raping human women. In every instance, she rewarded Evan's efforts with her body, the single element in her dreams which did not vary from scenario to scenario.

Through all of this, Toni sank into an uneasy apathy. After several nights of fruitless efforts to affect her own part in the minidramas of her mind, she had taken to disengaging herself as much as possible. Several people told her she appeared unwell, and indeed she moved with none of her previous easy grace. Psychosomatic or not, she wakened each morning with a fresh collection of bruises, even occasional scratches. All of this could have resulted from uneasy thrashing in her sleep, of course, but Toni was unable to avoid noticing that the injuries always coincided with those she had dreamed about, and always replaced those of the previous day.

She might have continued this apathetic acceptance indefinitely if Evan had not read the vampire novel.

Toni had gotten into the habit of walking by Evan's desk several times during the course of a day, trying to see what book he might be reading. The pirate dreams had occurred while he was reading afaell Sabatini, the shipwreck after Peter Benchley, and the psychopath coincided with his purchase of *The Silence of the Lambs*. So when she saw the dark cover decorated with two dripping fangs poised over a punctured planet Earth, she knew pretty much what to expect that evening.

She found herself in large wooden cage with a dozen other women, all of them completely unclothed, and even though she had managed to remain relatively detached during her recent dream experiences, their utter terror communicated itself to her. Nor was she unaware of the fact that each and every one of them bore an uncanny resemblance to herself; they might have been her sisters, if she had ever had any sisters.

"There's no hope for us now," one of her fellow prisoners was insisting. "They've taken over the whole world. There's no one left to fight them."

"It's not over yet," protested another. "There was time to create a resistance movement."

Several black caped figures appeared just beyond the limits of their confinement, one of whom opened a door on the side of the cage. One by one, the prisoners were pulled out into the dim light, where one or another of the vampires would seize hold of his victim, bend to rip out a throat with gleaming fangs, drain the blood until the woman's struggles ceased and her limp body fell to the floor.

Toni was the last to be taken and for once, her mind and body worked in consort, struggling against the powerful arms of the red eyed monstrosity that held her. The fangs were within an inch of her throat when the vampire suddenly jerked, eyes widening with surprise. The restraining arms fell away from her shoulders and Toni stepped back far enough to see the wooden shaft that had suddenly emerged from the creature's chest.

The room was a sudden pandemonium as archers systematically finished off the rest of the undead creatures. When they had all fallen and turned to dust, one of the rescuers rushed to her side. It was, of course, Evan Wade.

This time the dream Toni was so grateful that she rewarded him with something special. Oral sex.

And that was the straw that broke the metaphorical camel's back.

Toni was no prude. She'd lost her virginity at seventeen and hadn't looked for it since. During the years that followed, she'd slept with eleven men, on one occasion with two of them at the same time, and had even experimented with her own sex. She had tried mild bondage, in both roles, performed sex in a bathtub filled with jello, and had allowed a man to lick whipped cream from various parts of her body. But there was one act which she had steadfastly refused to even consider, despite frequent importunities, and once even in the face of a mild but definite physical threat.

The following morning she rose calmly, called Marian and told her she was too sick to come to work. After a long hot bath that made her feel no better, Toni dressed and drove to her uncle's house on Cape Cod. He was in Florida for the winter, but always left her a key so she could look in on the place from time to time. Behind the panel of a false closet, she found her uncle's collection of handguns and rifles, chose the revolver that he'd taught her to use while she was still a high school student, located the right ammunition in a drawer and loaded it. Satisfied, she replaced the panel and drove back to Rhode Island.

Although she had eaten neither breakfast nor lunch, Toni felt no hunger as she sat in her car in the parking lot behind the apartment building where Evan Wade lived. The clock on her dashboard moved slowly but relentlessly forward, and she became more alert when it passed five o'clock.

At seventeen minutes past, she saw him climb out of a battered Datsun and start toward the rear entrance. With one fluid movement, she opened the car door and slipped outside, the revolver concealed in her purse. She moved quickly across the lot at an angle, in order to intercept him just short of the entrance. As she approached, he caught the movement out of the corner of his eye, half turned in her direction. At that moment, she withdrew the revolved from concealment, raised her arm, and fired. There was a satisfying look of dismay on Evan Wade's face just before the bullet struck him in the forehead. His body flew back against the wall of the building, then slid to the ground.

She had intended to fire several more rounds, but two cars had just pulled into the lot, and Toni had no intention of being caught or identified. Hiding the weapon again, she hurried back to her car, started the engine, and pulled out onto the street before the newcomers could discover the body.

Marian told her the news early the next morning.

"Did you hear about poor Evan? Someone shot him in the head out behind his apartment building last night."

Toni made what she hoped was a suitable dismayed face. "That's horrible! Do they have any idea who did it?"

Marian shrugged. "If they do, they're not saying. Probably a mugging. There's no place safe anymore, I guess."

"Did he have any family?"

Marian shook her head. "Maggie said he was brought up in an orphanage."

"I suppose we ought to go to the funeral."

"Well, that would be a little premature. He's not dead yet."

Alarms began to ring inside Toni's head and she felt a return of the strange detachment that had colored the last few weeks. "What do you mean? I thought you said he was shot in the head?"

"Well, yes, he was, but he's still alive. In a coma, according to the radio. They don't know if he'll pull through or not. I called the hospital, but they said they wouldn't know anything until after he'd had a chance to recover from the surgery. I'll call again this afternoon."

The morning passed all too quickly. Toni regretted not having shot from ambush. She was quite certain that Evan had recognized her before the shot; she had meant for him to do so. That flash of awareness just before the bullet struck had been a small recompense of the weeks of humiliating sexual slavery, dream or not. But now he could identify her to the police if he recovered consciousness. She had returned the gun to her uncle's hiding place, but if he gave the authorities her name, she knew they'd be able to find it, registered or not.

At shortly after four that afternoon, there was news, both good and bad. The bad, from her point of view, was that Evan Wade's condition had stabilized, that the hospital felt confident he would not die in the foreseeable future, barring unforeseen complications. The good news was that, although he had intermittent periods of consciousness, he was totally paralyzed, could not even speak or blink his eyes, and the doctors believed it might be a permanent condition.

She left work that evening in a calmer frame of mind, if not entirely at ease. After an unusually heavy meal, she took one of her infrequent sleeping pills and went to bed early, determined to finally experience some untroubled rest.

Toni found herself lying on a bed of filthy straw in a dark room with a barred door. Even as her internal self collapsed into a pool of self pity, realizing that she was still subject to Evan Wade's unconscious desires, the door creaked open and three men entered, one wearing an elaborate clerical costume, the others outfitted as medieval men at arms. They lifted her to her feet and half pulled, half dragged her out of the room.

They passed along a narrow corridor to a wider, torchlit room, at the opposite end of which three heavily robed men sat at a long table. Her escort forced her past an array of devices she only vaguely recognized, a rack, a brazier of glowing coals, a strappado, a strangling post, a rack of whips and flails. Toni had never been particularly interested in history during her high school days, but she realized she had been thrust this time into the era of the Spanish Inquisition.

"You are accused of trafficking with demons!" The voice thundered across the room. "In order to save your soul, we shall use pain to drive the forces of evil from your body."

And just before the soldiers lifted her body onto the rack, Toni caught sight of the Grand Inquisitor's face, half concealed in the shadow of his cowl. It was the face of Evan Wade.

Toni suddenly realized there'd be no rescue this time.

TOOTHMARKS

That first night, Alex thought she had a mouse in her house. She was cleaning off the kitchen table after supper when one of the forks slipped and fell to the floor, and when she knelt to retrieve it, she saw the very faint but unmistakable signs of gnawing on the table leg. The light green paint had been chipped away to reveal a raw wound of underlying wood.

"Damn!" She knelt and let her eyes trail around the small dining room, then moved on hands and knees to check the antique sideboard, each of the dining room chairs, and the base of her hutch. They all seemed to be untouched.

She stood up and walked to the kitchen, surveying it critically. Yes, she was guilty of leaving dirty plates in the sink, and there was even a crust of bread that she hadn't thrown in the trash yet. It was her own fault if she was attracting rodents; she'd just have to be more careful about leaving food out.

And she'd buy a trap, or better yet, some poison, on her way home from work tomorrow. That should take care of it.

It was another frustrating day at work. Eblis Manufacturing had been caught badly overextended in inventories and short on cash by the latest mini-recession, was currently reorganizing under bankruptcy proceedings, and there was a hiring freeze as well as a prohibition against overtime. Which meant that salaried people like Alex Troth had to take up the slack by putting in extra hours at work and, in her case, by bringing paperwork home to finish in the evenings. She was so caught up in indignation that she drove right by the hardware store, but remembered it a couple of blocks later. Cursing, she swerved abruptly into a parking lot in order to turn around, and scraped her tire noisily against a concrete guide marker.

There was a long line at the register and the cashier seemed determined to make conversation with every customer. The price tag was missing from the mousetrap and he had to check with his supervisor before ringing it up, and then Alex realized she didn't have enough cash with her and had to wait while her credit card was verified. When she finally arrived home, it was dark outside and she was in a foul mood not helped by the fact that she stubbed her toe on the threshold as she entered.

She dropped her purchases on the kitchen table, then went back to the car and brought in the box of files she was currently reviewing. These ended up on the coffee table in her living room, right next to her laptop. She poured herself a glass of brandy, and by the time it was half gone, the edge was off her anger and she was feeling hungry.

"Not hungry enough to cook," she said aloud. The production review meeting had run through lunch, and there hadn't been time to eat before the staff meeting, so she hadn't run out for a sandwich until mid-afternoon. Tonight would be a snack night.

Alex arranged the files she'd be working on first and set the rest aside, then walked out to the kitchen. What was she in the mood for? Crackers and cheese? She had a nice bar of cheddar and some fancy crackers. There was also a stick of pepperoni, most of a half gallon of ice cream, and some left over salad. Salad seemed too virtuous and it was too cool a night for ice cream. Crackers and cheese then, and maybe some pepperoni. She opened the cabinet door and let her eyes rove among the boxes before selecting the one she wanted, then reached up and plucked it from the shelf.

A thin trail of crumbs fell across the counter.

Alex stood dumbfounded for the first few seconds, not actually comprehending what had happened. Then she slowly rotated the box and saw the hole on the opposite side, right near the bottom. Something had chewed its way into the box.

Outraged and vaguely disgusted, she threw the crackers into the garbage, tied off the half filled bag, and carried it outside to the trash bin. Back in the kitchen, she removed all of the other boxes from their resting places, discovering to her relief that they were all untouched, then examined the interior of the cabinet very closely. There was no mousehole, no obvious way that anything could have entered; it must have gotten in while the door was open.

Did that mean it was trapped inside the ravaged box? Had it been curled up among the crackers as she threw it into the trash? The very though made her skin crawl, and she wasn't about to go outside and check. But she spent the next half hour going through all of her other cabinets and cupboards until she felt reassured that nothing else had been touched, and that no small creature was building a nest among her groceries. She set the trap under the kitchen table and distributed the poison packets throughout the house.

Then she poured herself another brandy. She didn't get much work done that evening, and her stomach rumbled when she finally staggered to the bedroom.

The situation at work didn't improve. Two days later, there was a general layoff that included office staff. Without warning, Alex found herself having to manage with three rather than four clerks, and she would have to share her expediters with the sample department until further notice. It wouldn't have been so bad if some of the paperwork had been eliminated as well, but most of the managers were nervous about their own jobs and were demanding more reports to prove that they were busy and on top of things. Alex found herself ordering sandwiches at lunchtime so she could work at her desk, and most nights she didn't leave until dusk had already fallen.

Nothing showed up in the mousetrap and a week later she found toothmarks on the arm of her favorite chair.

"Goddamn it to hell!" She slammed her clenched fist against the wall hard enough to raise a bruise and make the pictures of her parents jump and clatter. Furious, she stormed out to the kitchen, glanced down at the still untenanted trap, and swore quite colorfully until she was out of breath.

The hardware store was still open, although they were already mopping the aisles when she arrived. She bought four more traps and an armful of poison, and glared at the cashier as he ran her credit card.

Her nightly ritual was set the following evening. She dropped the day's paperwork on the kitchen table as she entered from the garage, then made the rounds of the house, checking each trap and each bit of poisoned bait. There was never anything to indicate that they had been disturbed. Then she made a second circuit of the house searching for damage, starting with the kitchen cabinets, then the dining room, bedroom, living room, and the small second bedroom she used to store out of season clothing and other odds and ends.

It was three weeks before it occurred to her to try the basement.

She lived in a small house on the very edge of the developed part of Managansett, her tiny plot of land snuggled up against the woods that stretched north past the reservoir. It wasn't much more than a cottage, but she lived alone, assumed that she would spend her life alone, and rarely entertained guests. She was not an accumulator. If she wanted to see a movie, she rented it; when she was done with a book, she donated it or threw it out. She had no living family to clutter her life with unwanted gifts and none of her friends were close enough that they thought of each other at Christmas.

Most of her furniture came from her parents' home, which she'd sold following the accident that had killed them both. Alex told herself that they had sentimental value, but in her heart she knew that wasn't true. But they were familiar and comfortable, and by taking them she avoided the hassle of choosing new items of her own.

But she hadn't taken anything other than what she needed, so she didn't have much to store, and since the laundry room was attached to the kitchen, she had no reason to visit the basement on a regular basis. At time she forgot it even existed.

The night she went to the basement followed a particularly bad day at work. She'd fallen behind in her tallies and couldn't provide current production figures for several items during the staff meeting. That afternoon she discovered she had promised product availability based on a stale report of a lot that had actually already been finished and shipped. The deli had delivered the wrong sandwich at lunch and one of her clerks had given two weeks notice.

She made her usual survey immediately upon arriving home but it left her dissatisfied. Then she thought of the basement, although it actually took her a few seconds to remember that the door was located in the tiny foyer, known locally as a mudroom, at the back door. Having solved that problem, she grabbed a flashlight from the kitchen, opened the door, and toggled the light switch.

No luck. The basement remained as dark as ever.

She retrieved a lightbulb from under the bathroom sink and returned to the mudroom. With the flashlight illuminating the steps ahead of her, she descended, located the burnt out bulb, and screwed the new one in its place. Immediately soft yellow light fought a desperate battle to push back the shadows.

The house was nearly a century old and the basement was rough concrete and exposed wooden beams. There were cobwebs everywhere, and spiderwebs as well. A cricket chirped in one corner and at least three spiders regarded her dolefully. There were some rusting tools at the foot of the stairs, left by the previous owner, and she picked up a small pitchfork, using it to rake away the filmy obstructions in her path.

There was a disused coal bin to her left, the furnace and hot water heater to her right, a large empty space in between. A few cardboard boxes were piled against the far wall, items she'd taken from her parents' home but never used, and two relatively new filing cabinets under a slit window. These held all of her long term paperwork,old tax returns, the mortgage on the house, her birth certificate, a copy of her parents' will, and other odds and ends.

She made her way slowly around the basement, poking into corners with the light, checking the ceiling above her as well as the floor below. It was much dirtier than she remembered – she hadn't been downstairs in almost a year – but there was no nest, no droppings, no indication that her unwanted houseguest had built a lair beneath her feet.

With nothing to show for her effort, Alex was about to leave when she impulsively turned to the filing cabinet, opening and closing each door in turn. It was the third drawer that stopped her, the one that contained her job related files, copies of her resume, service awards, letters of commendation, a few project reports which she'd authored, and other memorabilia. They were still there, but they were unrecognizable now.

Each and every piece of paper in that drawer had been chewed into shreds.

The cashier at the hardware store recognized her this time. "More traps. You must have a real problem with mice."

Alex counterfeited a smile. "They don't seem interested in the bait I've been putting out. Can you suggest something better?"

He shrugged his shoulders. "I wouldn't know about that, but my uncle owns a farm up north and he says there's nothing better than a cat for getting rid of mice. They're mobile, they work cheap, and they never give up."

She thought about it but shook her head. "I'm not ready to share my living space right now, but thanks for the suggestion."

But she was starting to run out of places to lay her traps.

The following Friday was the worst day yet at Eblis. There was another layoff, thankfully sparing her department, but it was obvious that her people were going to have to cover for some of the vacant positions. She told off the purchasing agent when the wrong size copper coils arrived, then had to apologize when she discovered she'd entered the wrong material code on the requisition. At lunch she spilled coffee down the front of her suit, and during the afternoon her computer locked up costing her two hours work because she'd forgotten to reset Autosave in the program she was using. When her assistant, Lucy Dean, came by to pick up the latest priority list, she was staring at the wall in obvious distress.

"Are you okay?"

Alex let her head fall back and stared at the ceiling. "No, but I will be in a few minutes."

"Did something happen?"

"Nothing major, just a lot of little stuff. You know, I've had to deal with major crises in the past – when my parents died, when I lost my job at Eyre Products, when the Venture gift line was dropped. I think I'm pretty good under that kind of pressure. It gives me a challenge, a goal to work toward. It's the little things that get to me, though. Something minor here, another problem there. After a while they start to gnaw at you and when you turn to confront them, there's nothing there, but those little teeth are busy again behind you. How many little cuts does it take to equal a hemorrhage, Lucy?"

The younger woman looked distinctly uncomfortable. "I don't really know, Alex."

"No, I don't imagine you do." She shook her head back and forth and combed her hair with her fingers. "Don't mind me, Lucy, I'm just tired and grouchy this morning. The list is right here." She picked up the two page printout and handed it across the desk. "Can you make a copy for David?"

"He's out with the flu."

"Yeah, that figures."

That night she found toothmarks everywhere. A hole had been gnawed into the back of her couch, and the drapes were badly chewed. One of the kitchen cabinets had apparently been left open, and there was a fan of crackers and uncooked rice across the counter and onto the floor. A corner of the quilt on her bed had been shredded and feathers spilled from her pillow when she picked it up. The handle of her toothbrush was covered with bitemarks and her favorite sweater was lying on the floor in pieces.

The traps were all empty and the poison undisturbed.

On Wednesday, one of Eblis' biggest accounts filed for bankruptcy protection, which turned a very large receivable into a questionable asset. This particular chain of stores bought mostly customized items, so Alex stayed at work until nearly midnight, altering production schedules to convert some work in process to other, saleable items, and putting other lots on indefinite hold pending their customer's ultimate fate. She arrived home exhausted and emotionally drained, poured herself a drink, and decided that a truncated grand tour would be adequate this evening.

Nothing seemed to have changed until she reached her bedroom. Superficially it looked the same as always, but when she opened the closet doors, it was as though someone had thrown excelsior in her face.

Most of her wardrobe was mangled beyond recognition.

The following morning she took time off work to go to the animal shelter and adopt the largest, nastiest looking cat she could find. It sat quietly in the backseat on the way home, glaring at her so hard she could feel its eyes on the back of her neck. In one corner of the kitchen, she put down food and water and the brand new kitty litter bin she'd purchased. "Make yourself at home," she told the nameless cat, who was sitting disdainfully a few feet away. "Good hunting."

The cat did not come to greet her at the door that evening, which was just as well since she was in as bad a mood as ever. Nicholson had proposed merging his department with hers as a cost savings, which meant she'd lose staff as well as authority if the idea was adopted. She found a few new instances of gnawing, but they were small – the arms of chairs, the cover on her ironing board, the corner of the calendar hanging over the sink – and she might have missed them on earlier inspections. She turned on more lights than usual, but the house still seemed like foreign territory, and the darkness outside seemed to creep through the windows.

The cat was curled up on her bed, raised its head without welcome when she entered the room. The food dish was empty and there was no sign of a small corpse anywhere about. It occurred to her that if the intruder finally did eat some poison and then the cat ate the intruder, the cat might die as well, but that didn't bother her particularly. The cat was expendable and would be returned to the pound promptly if it accomplished its purpose.

She booted up her laptop, warmed some leftovers in the microwave, and started to work.

Two days later, she returned to find the kitchen in chaos. All of the cabinets had been opened, and there was food scattered everywhere. Not one cookbook remained unshredded. Bags of sugar and flower lay in misshapen pieces. Canned goods had rolled through the debris, and in some cases the labels had been chewed off making it impossible to identify their contents without opening them. The ruins of the calendar were in the sink, along with strands of torn curtain. The corner of one cabinet door showed deep toothmarks, and her plastic serving utensils were mangled almost beyond recognition.

The rest of the house seemed untouched, but Alex wondered how much longer that would last. The appetite of her unwanted houseguest seemed to be growing prodigiously, or maybe he'd invited in a few friends.

"Cat!" she shouted. "Where the hell are you? Why aren't you doing your job?"

She stalked him from room to room, looking under the furniture as well as on top of it. There was no sign of him. She even went down into the basement although the door was closed and latched. A second drawer of paperwork – her tax returns this time – had been shredded, but there was no other change since her last visit.

Back on the first floor, she checked the rear door and all of the windows. The catfood was untouched today and the water dish full. She made another fruitless circuit of the house. The attic was a crawlspace, and she'd never even poked her head up into it. She didn't see any way the cat could have gotten up there. There was no fireplace, no broken window, no torn screen.

She was out of brandy so she drank warm beer, three of them, sitting at the kitchen table and staring at the wreckage. When the beer reached her bladder, she stirred herself into rising and walked somewhat unsteadily to the bathroom. With one hand fumbling for the zipper on her hip, she lifted the toilet seat cover, then jumped back with a sharp cry.

The cat was in the toilet bowl, half floating in red fluid. Something had chewed through its throat.

When Carlson called her into his office the following week and told her that in view of the shrinking volume of sales, the company no longer needed a separate full time production scheduler for giftware, she nodded and thanked him, then cleaned out her desk in a daze. All she could think of was that now, at last, she could stay at home and watch for the enemy.

"I'll get you now," she whispered under her breath. "I'll watch for you and wait for you and when you stick your furry little head out, I'll rip it off."

It's possible that she was more audible than she thought, because the security guard escorting her watched her very closely until she left the property.

Alex spent most of the next day sitting in her living room, not doing anything except listening. The television was off, and the book she'd been reading was sitting on the corner table. She waited to hear the scurrying of feet, the grating of teeth, or the squeak of marauding rodent glee. Nothing happened. She stirred herself twice, once to eat cold leftovers right out of a Tupperware container, once to use the freshly sanitized toilet.

The sun dropped below the horizon and she stayed where she was without turning on any of the lights. Traffic outside thinned and then died away almost entirely. Crickets serenaded from outside the windows and a dog barked down the street. Inside the house, the only sound was Alex's heartbeat and the clicking of the mantelpiece clock, whose mahogany finish was marred by toothmarks.

Sometime after midnight she nodded off to sleep, and in the morning when she woke, stiff and uncomfortable, something had chewed arcane patterns in the rug. Alex stood up and examined the damage dolefully, then chuckled lightly and went out to the kitchen, tracking through the mess that littered the floor. She'd brought home fresh groceries the day before, but hadn't even bothered to put them away. Now they, and the paper not plastic bags that had contained them were torn and ruined. She scooped up a bowl of cereal from a pile that looked relatively clean and ate it with her fingers.

It was three weeks before the neighbors called the police, and three hours before the police showed up at the house. Alex's car was in the driveway, but no one answered the doorbell and the phone was apparently off the hook. Actually, the cord had been gnawed through. The two patrolmen walked around the periphery of the house, peering in windows, and only acted because there was so much obvious destruction inside that they suspected violence. They came in through the back door, slipped and slid through the rotting food that covered the kitchen floor, and found Alex lying in front of her bed.

One of the officers bent to check her pulse and she reared up and closed her jaws on his wrist. It took both of them to subdue her, and both were bitten several times in the process. By the end of the day, Judge Reinhart had officially placed her in the custody of the Sheffield Clinic while they searched for her next of kin. They never found any, and Alex eventually spent most of the rest of her life in a room even smaller than her tiny cottage in Managansett.

Her house was sold to cover some of the expenses, but only after it was thoroughly cleaned. None of the furnishings were salvageable and even some of the woodwork had to be replaced because of the toothmarks.

"She must have gone completely nuts," Lucy Dean told her co-workers. "My brother-in-law worked the case and he said everything in the house was all chewed up."

"Did she keep some kind of animal in there with her?" asked David Sucher.

"No, that's just it. They said all of the toothmarks were human, every one of them. She must have spent weeks or even months doing it. She chewed up just about everything in the house."

INSPIRATION

Lisa Stone left the stage while the final notes of her closing song were still echoing, allowing the security people to hustle her through the wings and along a preplanned route to the side entrance where a car waited. The precautions were more show than effect; if anyone actually meant to do her harm, there were too many opportunities to actually prevent an attack. And if Ted Troia's theory was correct, the conspiracy against her did not involve a physical threat. At least not directed toward Lisa.

In any case, it was virtually impossible to shield her if she persisted with the concert tour. Rock stars, like politicians, actors, and other celebrities, sacrificed security along with privacy when they attracted the public's attention. After writing scores of interviews and articles, as well as six biographies, two of them authorized, Ted felt very little sympathy for the rich and famous. But Lisa Stone was different.

Ted left the theater on his own, took a taxi back to the hotel where Lisa was staying. He smoked a cigarette outside, since she disliked the smell of tobacco, before entering and taking the elevator to her floor. The security men nodded when he stepped out of the elevator and let him pass without comment, recognizing him, smirking among themselves. Ted pretended not to notice.

"Oh, there you are Ted. C'mon in. I thought you'd gotten lost."

"Heavy traffic." He closed the door behind him, tried to hide his disappointment when he realized they weren't alone. Dean Campbell, her business manager, was sitting at the far end of the suite.

"Dean's not too happy with me. Seems I'm being fiscally irresponsible again."

"You DO pay me to look out for your financial interests, you know. It's not really fair to complain when I'm just trying to earn my salary."

"Who's complaining?" Lisa switched to her innocent waif look, and Ted marveled at how well she could manage it. Thirty-five years old, but still looked twenty, at least until you were very close. And very few ever had that opportunity. "I value your opinion, Dean, but that doesn't mean I can't make my own decisions, or that we'll always agree."

Ted shook his head, uncomfortable, and crossed to the wet bar, started to mix himself a drink. An oversized Elvis Presley puppet - marionette actually - sat on the counter, Lisa's official mascot and good luck charm.

"Maybe you can make her see reason, Ted." Dean had tried more than once to recruit Ted as an ally, a role he had so far resisted. "She wants to do the Chicago concert for free."

"Not for free," Lisa protested. "I just want the money to go to charity. It's not as though I need it."

Campbell shook his head. "Your cash flow projections for the next several months don't look good. Even with the concerts, you're in an earnings trough that won't see an upturn until your next album is ready, and you just told me that won't be for at least six months."

"I need to write the songs," she said mildly.

"All the more reason to bank the money while you can." Campbell wet his lips with his tongue, looked toward Ted for support. "Lisa, your net worth has been steadily declining, even though your last five albums have all gone platinum. Do you have any idea how much money you've given away?"

"Dean, I'm tired of arguing about this." There was a sudden hint of steel in her voice, and Ted recognized the erosion of Lisa's patience. "I have plenty of money to live on, comfortably, even if I retired right now, which I don't plan to do. You've known me long enough to understand my reasons. So let's drop the subject."

For a second, it looked as though Campbell might persist, but instead he nodded, then quickly stood up. "All right, boss. Whatever you say. I'm too pooped to argue about it. In fact, I'm calling it a night. Catch you tomorrow."

Ted waited until Campbell was gone before speaking. "He has a point, you know."

Lisa threw herself down onto the couch, arched her head back. "God, Ted, not you too? You of all people should understand why I give the money away, why I have to."

"I know that you feel guilt about your success, and that you've been trying to buy absolution for imaginary sins for most of your career. That doesn't mean I agree."

She sighed. "Mix me a drink, will you?"

He already had. He crossed and handed it down, then eased onto the couch beside her. Lisa sipped slowly, her eyes closed, waiting for the neat brandy to burn its way down to her stomach.

She wasn't a particularly beautiful woman, and her singing voice wasn't good enough to raise her above the crowd. Indeed, her first album had done well only because of the hit single, "Old Magic", and the second foundered so badly that her career might well have ended before it was truly launched.

If her kid sister hadn't been killed, Lisa might have ended up as a waitress or a hairdresser.

It sounded callous phrased that way, but it was still the truth. Lisa and Kari had been very close; their parents had died in an airline disaster and Lisa had been largely responsible for raising her sister. They'd stayed together, even while Lisa was on tour.

The mutilation murder had been particularly gruesome; rumor had it the girl had been literally torn apart. Profoundly shocked, Lisa had shut herself off from the world for months, emerging finally with the score for "Kari's Song", still one of the most frequently played singles in rock history. Two months after its release, Lisa signed a contract for another album, but with the stipulation that her share of the proceeds would go to help finance rape crisis centers all over the country.

"It was my last gift to Kari," she explained to Ted during one of their early sessions. "To make up for all the things I might have done for her if she'd lived." But Ted had sensed the truth even then, that Lisa felt guilty, probably because she'd stayed late at a party instead of returning to the apartment that evening.

"If you'd gone home, you would have been just another victim," he'd suggested later, after they'd grown more intimate. "You shouldn't feel any responsibility."

"You don't understand. It's not a rational thing, but that doesn't make it any less real."

If they'd ever caught Kari's killer, Lisa might have been able to set aside the pain, but the police had never even had a solid lead.

The Elvis puppet had been Lisa's last gift to her sister, and she kept it with her constantly in honor of Kari's memory.

"Hey, Ted! Where are you?"

He came to himself, realized he'd been drifting among his thoughts, felt the warmth of her hand on his arm. "I'm right here," he said, and proved it by leaning forward into her embrace.

But later, lying beside her in the oversized bed, Ted couldn't sleep. Although he hadn't really convinced anyone else, Ted was convinced that he had detected a pattern in Lisa's life, one that pointed to the presence of a sinister enemy, relentless, ruthless, and clever enough to have escaped detection. An enemy that had followed her ever since her teenage years in Managansett.

Everyone else dismissed it as a tragic string of coincidences.

"Kari's Song" quickly became one of the most popular rock singles of all time, but its companions on the album of the same name ranged from so-so to forgettable. A followup album barely made gold, and the recording company delayed and eventually canceled the next. Lisa was reduced to doing backup vocals for bigger names, like Brian Sparrow.

Financially, Lisa was self sufficient, having banked the proceeds from a brief but popular concert tour, but her career as a major voice in rock appeared to be over. She became romantically involved with Sparrow, and after a brief, hectic courtship, the couple married in a secretive ceremony. Their daughter, Kelly Marie Sparrow, was born ten months later, and Lisa announced her retirement from the music business.

Three days after their third anniversary, Brian Sparrow was killed in an automobile accident. It was hit and run; the other driver was never identified although the vehicle, stolen earlier that day, was found abandoned a few hours later.

Lisa retreated from the world, renting a chateau in Switzerland to keep the public at a distance, quietly converting all of her late husband's holdings to cash and donating the proceeds to a wide range of charitable organizations. Shortly after the last of the money was gone, Lisa returned to public view by debuting a new song at a benefit concert. "Death Is a Dream" wasn't quite as successful as "Kari's Song", but the story of a young girl and her ghostly lover was the hit of the show, and resulted in a new record contract.

Restless, Ted slipped out of bed, careful not to disturb Lisa. They'd started sleeping together only a few weeks earlier, much to the surprise of both of them. The earliest interviews had not gone well, and Ted had almost backed out of his agreement to ghostwrite her autobiography. There'd been a tension between them that had seemed to be simple incompatibility; it had taken a while for them to realize it was sexual, and even longer to do something about that realization.

And now they were lovers, and Ted was wondering what might happen when the book was done, when he no longer had an excuse to follow her around the country. He didn't like thinking about it.

The light over the bar was still on and he poured himself a glass of white wine. "Someone hates Lisa enough to commit murder, old buddy, but she won't believe me. What are we going to about it?"

Elvis remained silent.

"Yeah. I can't think of anything either. But we can't let anything bad happen to her. We just can't."

The barriers had started to go down while Lisa was discussing her personal tragedies. Apparently she'd never really talked to anyone about the deaths before, and there was some psychological transference involved. For his part, Ted had come to realize that there was a real person behind the facade of glitter and lights, that the stage show of self assurance and strength was largely an act designed to disguise a deeper vulnerability.

"You've known her a lot longer than I have. How do I get through to her that she's in danger?"

Elvis didn't have an answer for that one either.

Chicago was not a roaring success, probably because of what Ted privately thought was a mediocre selection of songs. He would never admit it to Lisa, but too much of her music sounded alike to him, rock muzak, monotonous lyrics, simple riffs and strings of melody strung together almost randomly. When Lisa was inspired, she was one of the best, but most of the time she was just another hack song writer.

Something disturbing happened in the hotel that first night.

Lisa was depressed by the way things had gone during the Friday night show and was worried that Saturday would be even worse. Ted knew the signs well enough to distance himself, and slept in his own room that evening.

By two in the morning, he realized he wouldn't be able to sleep. Rather than waste time turning restlessly in bed, he got up, booted his laptop, and began editing the draft of Lisa's autobiography in process. It was the chapter dealing with her daughter's kidnapping.

This was the most difficult part of the book, for both of them. They hadn't yet met at the time it happened, but like everyone else in the country, Ted had followed the twenty-four day ordeal in the papers and on television news. Lisa had offered to pay any amount of money, of course, but the kidnapper had never responded, just kept mailing the twelve year old's severed fingers, one every two days.

Then, on the last day, the head. They never caught the kidnapper, never even found the rest of Kelly Marie's body.

Ted pushed his chair back and stood up, unable to separate his emotions from the words he was reading. Much of the story had been reconstructed from contemporary accounts, necessarily since Lisa still had difficulty speaking about that period of her life.

He dressed quickly, small angry movements, and left the room. The elevator arrived quickly, brought him to the lobby, where a sleepy but uninterested counter clerk nodded as he passed by.

It took almost an hour to walk off the tension.

When he returned to his room, Ted knew something was wrong as soon as he opened the door. It was dark inside and he was quite certain he'd left at least two lights on. He swung the door wide, letting the subdued hall light illuminate the interior.

And the wreckage.

Hotel security replaced the smashed light fixtures quickly but city police refused to allow Ted to examine what remained of his belongings until an evidence team had gone over everything thoroughly. Not that there was anything worth salvaging.

His clothing and few personal possessions had been savaged almost beyond belief. Not one item, not even a sock, was worth saving. Each article of clothing had been torn into strips, along with towels, sheets and blankets, even the shower curtain. His luggage had been crushed flat, the electric razor shattered and dropped into the toilet. Worst of all, his laptop was a total loss, along with all the work he'd done on the book since his last backup, nearly a week earlier.

Two hundred dollars in cash that he'd left on the dresser had been ripped in half and dropped on the floor.

The hotel couldn't explain how anyone could have gained access, since the door lock was functioning properly. Ted had left one of the outside windows open, but he was on the nineteenth floor and there was no balcony.

"I don't understand it," admitted the investigating officer from the city police. "A thief who went to the trouble to get a passkey would have taken the cash at least, probably the computer as well. This destruction...it's just crazy."

They gave him another room for the balance of the night, but he didn't get any sleep there either.

Lisa knocked on his door at nine the following morning. He let her in, surprised that she had broken precedent by coming to him, noted with some satisfaction that one of her bodyguards had posted himself outside the door.

"Ted, I just heard what happened. What's going on?"

He shrugged, too tired to think clearly and not really wanting to talk about it. "Just one of those things. Don't worry about it; everything's replaceable."

She stepped close, wrapped her arms around his back, pressed her cheek against his chest. "Things like that scare me. Too many of the people close to me have had awful things happen to them. If you're right that there's someone behind it all, I don't want you to be next."

"I'm hardly important enough to be a target." But maybe he was. It hadn't occurred to Ted to connect the savaging of his hotel room to the string of violent attacks in Lisa's past until now. Was it possible?

"You're important enough to me. I've needed someone I could talk to about things for a long time. But if I've put you in danger..." She didn't finish the sentence.

"I thought you didn't believe my theory." Lisa had consistently refused to accept that someone had been stalking her for over two decades, had agreed to tighter security arrangements only after considerable protest.

"I don't, but I'm not foolish enough to overlook the possibility that you're right." She drew back, stared up into his face. At that moment, without her makeup, her expression unguarded, Lisa appeared both attractive and vulnerable, and Ted felt a surge of emotion that was almost painful.

Christ, he thought, that's all I need. Fall in love with an aging rock star with deep rooted psychological problems. Spend the rest of my life following her from one concert stop to another, living in hotel rooms, snatching snippets of time to write whenever her schedule allowed. It sounded terrible. It sounded wonderful.

"Well, if you can write a hit based on the trashing of my hotel room, it'll be worth it." He regretted the words as soon as he said them, but he was tired and his internal censor wasn't on the job. "Kari's Song" and "Death Is a Dream" had both been megahits, but "Part of Me Is Part of You", released a year after Kelly Marie's death, had surpassed both within weeks of its release. If Lisa had been willing to keep even one tenth of the money it had earned, she would have been a very rich woman. But as before, she immediately donated virtually the entire proceeds to charity.

Ted felt her body stiffen and spoke quickly, hoping to divert her attention. "Hey, as long as we're both up at this ungodly hour, why don't we do actual breakfast in a real restaurant? No room service."

Some but not all of the tension dissipated. "I thought you didn't think I should be out in public places like that."

"Hey, at this time of the morning, no one'll believe it's really you. Particularly if we find some greasy spoon no self respecting rock star would ever be caught dead in." He bit his tongue when the last few words came out, but Lisa didn't seem to notice.

"All right," she unwrapped herself from around him, sounded considerably more cheerful. "You're on. But what about Rambo?" She cocked her head toward the door, beyond which the bodyguard was no doubt prowling restlessly back and forth.

"Send him on an errand," Ted answered recklessly. "What the hell, you only live once."

Saturday night's audience was considerably more enthusiastic and they moved on to Detroit in higher spirits. Then Milwaukee, Toledo, St. Louis, and Atlanta. Lisa's reviews were not good, audience reaction was generally polite, but often restrained, and Ted knew she was unhappy even before she admitted it openly.

"Maybe you were right; maybe I should cut this tour short."

Ted knew it wasn't security problems that were bothering her. Lisa was not like most rock singers he'd met. The money was almost incidental, and she was generally embarrassed by fulsome praise. But she was deeply devoted to her music; it was important to her that what she created meant something to people, that it touched them on some level. In rare bitter moments, she complained that her reputation rested on three very sad songs, not the more exuberant singles like "Fire Up Your Love", "City Girl", "Hot Spots", or "Traffic Jam".

"Why don't people like happy songs?" she'd complained more than once.

"Maybe because most people aren't really happy. You've shown them how to take the bad parts of their lives and turn them into something beautiful, and they respond to that transformation."

"But music is supposed to be uplifting, not depressing. A way to escape from all the bad stuff."

"You can't really escape unless you're willing to face the unpleasantness first." He'd been mildly drunk at the time and felt as though he were being profound. Later, sober, he wasn't so sure. But Lisa had seemed satisfied with the explanation, or at least she hadn't pursued the subject any further.

They were spending a few days incognito at a quiet inn back in Managansett, her home town, just west of Providence, where Lisa's next concert had been booked at the new Civic Center. The band and most of the rest of the entourage were elsewhere, visiting family, getting laid, or just taking a therapeutic break. The room adjoining Lisa's was occupied by two bodyguards; Ted was across the hall.

He'd already reconstructed the material lost when his laptop was trashed, and had used much of this current layover to probe for additional material. With any luck, he'd be able to start the final draft by the end of the year, well ahead of schedule.

"Ted, I'm going away for a day or two."

"What? Where?"

The two of them were eating in the inn's dining room, the bodyguards sitting at a table just out of earshot. She reached over and pressed her fingers against the back of his hand, reassuring.

"Don't worry. I'm flying out to California to talk to some people about a video. No big deal. One night and I'll be back."

"I could go with you. There's nothing pressing here..."

She shook her head. "No, I'd rather you didn't." He must have displayed the dismay he felt because her face softened. "It's nothing to worry about, Ted. I mean, I still feel the same way about you I always have. It's just that I...I want to get away, just for a day or two, and get some perspective."

"We haven't made any commitments to each other," he answered slowly. "You're certainly free to do what you want." It sounded stiff but he couldn't help being resentful.

"Ted, stop it. I don't like it when you play the hurt lamb. If you don't realize how I feel about you by now, then you're a lot denser than I think you are." She turned away, and her eyes were bright with unshed tears. "It's hard for me to talk about this, Ted, hard for me to feel...affection for people, or to admit it anyway. Whenever I've had something like that in my life, it's always been taken away."

He felt immediate remorse, reached out to take her hand in his own. "I'm sorry, Lisa. I'm just being foolish. You're taking Arnold and Rambo with you, aren't you?" The bodyguards' real names were Nathan Moore and Lester Wade, but Ted and Lisa had rechristened them.

"I suppose I ought to."

"No supposing about it. Have a good time."

"Now I'm feeling guilty about leaving you here by yourself."

"Nonsense. It'll give me a chance to turn my notes into real copy. It's hard to work when you're here." He grinned boyishly. "Too many distractions."

Her flight out to the coast was early the following morning.

Ted did spend most of the day working, and when he turned off the computer that evening, he tossed the last of his handwritten notes into the drawer where he kept odds and ends. It was after nine, he hadn't eaten yet, and the dining room was too formal for his mood. Instead, he walked to the nearby downtown area, found a small, not particularly clean diner, and had one of the best bowls of chili he'd ever eaten. After that he visited a dimly lit bar, drank more than usual, but what the hell, he wasn't driving and he didn't have to get up early in the morning.

It was after midnight when he finally returned to the inn.

The front desk was unoccupied, the dining room closed, and only the night lights were on. Ted climbed the stairs on unsteady legs and almost tried to let himself into the wrong room. With a self deprecating laugh, he found the right door, worked the lock, and stepped inside.

He turned on the lights as the door clicked shut and then something slammed into the side of his head and he fell into darkness.

When Ted opened his eyes, the nausea hit him even before the pain. The taste of bile was strong and bitter, and his head throbbed angrily. And that wasn't the only place where it hurt. There were lines of fire around ankles and wrists, where they'd been tied to the arms and legs of the chair in which he sat.

The gag in his mouth didn't help much either.

He was still in a motel room, his own in fact. The new laptop was right where he'd left it on the small desk, and his replacement luggage was visible in the rear of the open closet. There was no one in sight, nothing out of place.

Except that Lisa's Elvis doll was lying on the bed, propped up against the pillows.

Ted made a brief attempt to wrench himself free, gave up almost immediately, afraid he'd faint from pain. And that's when the puppet moved.

It had to be some kind of trick. Ted blinked frantically, as though to clear the impossible sight from his vision. It did no good. Elvis climbed down from the bed, walked slowly but purposefully forward until he was standing directly in front of Ted.

"How are you feeling? I was afraid I might have hit you too hard, that you might have a concussion."

Ted didn't answer, couldn't have answered even had he not been gagged. The puppet's jaws moved in coordination with the words, but the voice was not Presley's, not even male.

It was Lisa's voice.

Elvis...Lisa...whoever it was, must have seen recognition in Ted's eyes, because the wooden head nodded. "Yes, it's me, Ted. I know this is all hard to believe, but it's true, and it's important that you understand why this is happening. Otherwise it'll all be for nothing. Remember the lines of 'Old Magic', my first hit? The bit about 'sacrificing everything for love'? Well, that's what I did. You remember I told you about how I'd never had a pet when I was a kid? Well, that was a lie."

Elvis - despite the voice he couldn't think of it as Lisa - moved to the desk, began pulling open the drawers and emptying them, books, newspapers, magazines, loose papers, spilling them all onto the floor.

"Just before they died, my parents bought me a kitten, and when they were gone, it was the only thing I had left besides my sister that I really loved. But I wanted to write songs, needed to, you know, and while I was doing research so the incantations in 'Old Magic' would be authentic, I found something I could use, something that would let me funnel all the hurt and anger and emotion into the song. The only catch was, I had to sacrifice something I really loved in order to create it. The choice was Kari or the kitten, so it was really no choice at all."

Elvis kicked the papers around the room, then crossed to the dresser, out of Ted's line of sight. When the puppet returned, it was carrying something in one hand. Ted's lighter fluid.

"I thought having help with that one big hit would kind of kick start my career, that after that I could emake it on my own. But things didn't work out. I needed another inspiration, and there wasn't much to choose from. You know I've never been very good about making friends, and when it came down to it, Kari was the only thing left in the world that I really valued. The only thing I could give up that would truly be a sacrifice."

Elvis began spraying the lighter fluid around the room, elongated arcs dark on the paper, less obvious on the blankets, curtains, wallpaper.

"Brian wasn't as hard but Kelly was even worse. And back in Chicago, when I was so down I was ready to just give up, I realized how much I loved you and I thought you could help me. But you weren't in your room and at first I was so furious I couldn't even think, but afterwards, I was glad you weren't there, because I still loved you and I didn't want to have to live without you. I'd already given up so much, you see."

The lighter fluid was almost gone now, the last few drops trickling out.

"But the way I see it, I've given each of them a kind of immortality. Their songs will still be played long after we're all dead and gone, maybe forever, you know? It's my final gift to them, in return for what they've given me. They were the inspiration for all my greatest hits."

Elvis threw down the empty container, then raised his other hand. Ted's cigarette lighter, bright red against the pale, painted wood.

"Just as you'll be for my next. I really do love you, Ted. I just thought you'd like to know. It wouldn't work if that wasn't true."

And then Elvis flicked the Bic.

INTRUSIONS

Anne looked back at the photograph of herself, where it rested against the base of the lamp, and shuddered, her stomach churning.

The burglar must have gotten in through the sliding doors from the balcony. She'd left them open overnight. It had been hot and muggy when she went to bed, lying nude on top of the sheets, so exhausted that she doubted anything would wake her before morning.

Nothing had.

She needed to call the police, she realized, and check the rest of the apartment, find out what was missing. The bastard had used her own camera, which she'd left sitting on the dressing table the night before. It was gone now.

Maybe she should have listened to Mickey, let him move in with her. But she hadn't wanted to give up her independence, and despite his assurances that there'd be no change in their relationship, Anne knew instinctively that they'd be crossing a line into unexplored territory if their clothing shared a closet, their books nudging each other on the same shelves.

No, she wouldn't change her decision, not just yet. But maybe she'd invite him to sleep over for a few nights. It wouldn't be the first time. Nothing permanent, just a chance for her to regain her sense of security, or as much of it as was possible under the circumstances.

Anne stood up from the bed warily, elated to discover that her legs would now support her weight. She'd nearly fainted when she spotted the photograph, interpolated the implications, collapsed as though someone had broken all her strings.

"Good looking boy." Ben Dardenian was examining the collage of photographs mounted on the wall with evident interest.

"My brother Jimmy," Anne answered impatiently.

"Looks to be about twelve, thirteen?"

"Fifteen, actually. He was small for his age. Can we get back to my problem?"

Detective Lieutenant Dardenian lowered his head and turned to face her. "You say nothing else was taken?" The policeman sounded skeptical, and Anne couldn't much blame him.

"No, as far as I can tell, the camera's the only thing missing. There was even some paper money lying in plain sight on my dresser, and he left that as well."

The detective blinked, scratched his forehead idly. "Do you have any ex-boyfriends who might want to scare you, Miss Ketteridge?"

"No, none at all. I've been seeing the same guy for six months, officer, and everything's fine between us." More or less, she thought.

He nodded, but perhaps only to himself. "Well, there's nothing more that we can do here. I'd be less than honest if I told you there was any real chance we'll arrest anyone. We've found some prints in the bedroom that aren't yours, but they look to be pretty old."

"Probably Mickey's." She blurted it out before realizing what she was saying, covered her embarrassment with bluster. "He's the guy I've been seeing."

"Probably so then." The detective did not allow himself to look uncomfortable, or censorious.

She didn't call Mickey until after they were gone, and when she did he insisted on coming right over.

"Are you all right?" He glanced around the apartment as though suspicious that the lurker might still be about.

"I told you, I'm fine. Just a little...I don't know...disconcerted. I mean, he came in while I was here, sleeping." She hadn't told Mickey about the photograph.

"You're lucky you weren't raped. I'll bet you left the sliding door open again." Her expression confirmed his suspicion. "How many times have I told you..?"

"At least a zillion. All right, point conceded. I did something stupid and got off easy. Let's give it a rest, all right? I already went through all this with the police."

And suddenly she was in tears and Mickey was holding her against his body and then he was carrying her into the bedroom and their clothes went away as if by magic. It had been two weeks since the night she finally allowed herself to be maneuvered into bed, and Anne still felt awkward and embarrassed and uncomfortable. She whispered into his mouth and ears and her fingernails made long shallow scratches down the curves of his shoulderblades as she tried to convince herself that she was lost in pleasure. But her eyes kept straying over his shoulder, toward the sliding glass door to the balcony.

Mickey left early the next morning, a quick stop at his place before reporting to work at Eblis Manufacturing. Anne knew he was planning to return that evening, probably with a change of clothing, expecting to be asked to stay. She wasn't sure how she felt about that.

Everyone seemed strangely aware, as though they knew of her victimization, although she'd told no one and it hadn't been important enough to make the newspapers. Mickey stopped by on his way to the purchasing office to see how she was doing and she smiled and brushed him off as quickly as possible. She stayed close to her desk all day, finished documenting the latest round of systems changes, and left a few minutes late to avoid the crowd.

There was a message on her answering machine. Probably Mickey, she thought, touching the replay button.

"I like your body." It was a husky voice, muffled. "I'd like to see it again. Maybe do more than see it."

That was all. Anne rewound and let it play through a second time. Not Mickey; he had a deep growl and the slightest hint of a lisp. But who then?

"Just some nut," she said aloud, wiping the message, trying to convince herself.

"Detective Dardenian called today. Our prints were the only ones they found, so whoever it was must have worn gloves."

"Doesn't sound like they're going to catch him." Mickey sounded bored.

"I guess not."

Although she'd decided to send Mickey home, Anne had weakened and agreed to let him stay. Two weeks ago, life had seemed so much simpler. Then Mickey had gently invaded her body, and some unknown had almost as gently invaded her home. Neither place seemed entirely hers any longer.

"Just until we know he won't come back," Mickey'd argued.

Anne noticed that for all his attempts at reassurance, he brought up the subject of the burglar at every opportunity, a fresh weapon in his armory of reasons for moving in.

Wednesday she came home to find another message on the machine. When it turned out to be a sales pitch, she laughed weakly at her over reaction. "You're really spooked, girl." But as she had done every day that week, she checked to see that each room was empty before actually relaxing.

There was something stuck in her typewriter.

It was a piece of stationery with an odd texture she'd never seen before, and the message was brief and clear. "I've seen you with that man. He's not right for you. Someday I'll teach you what it's like to be really loved."

Mickey stayed a fourth night, but this time they didn't make love. He'd fallen asleep on the couch while watching a movie, and Anne quietly turned off the television and the lights, grateful for the respite.

Around midnight, she felt him climb into bed, and rolled away, bunching up her pillow. After a few seconds, his hand touched her hip, moved down her buttocks, a single finger tracing the cleavage line. Then he was touching her between the legs and Anne opened her mouth to protest that it was late, that she wasn't in the mood, but before she could find the right words a wave of sensation made her shiver with anticipation. For once, he'd managed to avoid his usual fumbling and touch her in just the way she most wanted.

Anne moved her legs, making room for him, pressing her face into the pillow and concentrating entirely on the electric surges within her body. With surprising ease he brought her to the brink of orgasm, hesitated until she turned her head and told him not to stop. And then she was arcing her back and shuddering with the intensity of the release.

She hadn't quite subsided when he leaned over in the darkness and whispered, "Was it as good for you as it was for me?"

It wasn't Mickey's voice.

Anne rolled violently away, fell off the edge of the bed and hit the floor with stunning force. Elsewhere in the apartment, she heard footsteps, hoarse shouting, the words incoherent.

She managed to get to her feet just as the overhead light came on. Mickey was standing in the doorway, eyes blurred by sleep, his hair comically disarrayed. Across the room, the sliding door to the balcony was open about eighteen inches.

"What's going on?" Mickey blinked and stared at her.

"Someone was in here!" Her voice was a brittle croak.

His expression became more alert, but Mickey's eyes betrayed his doubts as he looked around the room. "You were dreaming, Anne. It was probably just the curtains blowing." He crossed to stand between her and the balcony.

"The wind didn't blow the door open; it was closed when I came to bed." Her skin was covered with goose pimples and she quickly put on a robe.

"Maybe you just thought it was. We were up pretty late."

Anne shook her head. "Not that late. And I know this wasn't a dream." She didn't specify how she knew, but she still felt aftershocks from her orgasm.

"Well," he sounded doubtful, but he walked out onto the balcony. "I wouldn't want to jump down there in the dark, but I suppose it's possible." They were only one floor up. For long seconds he stared out into the night, then came back inside and closed the door. "I think from now on you'd better keep this locked."

By Friday, it looked like Mickey had already decided he was staying permanently and Anne dreaded the inevitable conflict when she told him otherwise. He wouldn't get violent or even overtly angry; instead, he'd try to "reason" with her, citing the financial advantages as well as the safety reasons, insisting that they had something good, open and honest and "not superficial" until he wore her down by persistence rather than logic.

Anne invariably ate in the company cafeteria, usually a fancy salad of some kind. But today she was restless, and although there was no evidence that anyone other than Mickey knew about her recent misadventures, Anne still felt uneasy in crowds, as though she were suddenly being excluded from the subtext of conversations.

So she decided to go out for lunch.

Every morning, she stashed her bag in the same desk drawer, where it stayed until she went home. It was there now, but when she reached the parking lot, she stood frustrated, fishing around for her keychain.

"Got a problem?"

She looked up, disoriented. It was Mickey.

"Saw you from the loading dock. Anything wrong?"

"No!" She saw his surprise at her intensity, realized she was not behaving normally. "No," she continued more quietly. "I just wanted to go out for something and I've lost my keys."

"Maybe you dropped them."

"No, they probably fell out in my desk. I'll just have to go back..."

He interrupted her, waving his own keyring. "Take my jeep. Go ahead. I'll catch up to you later."

"All right. Thanks."

Her keys were sitting on top of her desk when she got back, which was surprising since she'd never left them there before. "This business is really getting to you," she mused, and thought no more about it.

Sunday afternoon, Mickey said he was going back to his place to get some more clothes.

"You know, I'm feeling a lot better now. You don't have to babysit me anymore."

His eyes shifted speculatively. "It's no problem, Anne. I think we're ready for a stronger commitment and..."

She stepped close, placed upraised fingers across his lips. "Don't, Mickey, don't say it. Maybe you're right, maybe it's time for us to take the next step. But not right now, not this weekend. Let me think about it for a while, let's both think about it, and then we'll talk."

Surprisingly, when Anne dropped her hand, Mickey nodded. "Okay, I guess this isn't the time to make a big change. I'll call you." And a few minutes later, he was gone.

Anne spent the rest of the day rearranging the furniture in her apartment. She hadn't planned to do it and rarely indulged impulses, but the need to reassert her control over her environment was irresistible.

She remembered to lock the balcony door before falling into bed.

The morning was cool and clear, a fresh breeze stirring the hedges around the apartment building. Wearing just her robe, Anne walked out onto the balcony, drinking in the daylight, feeling better than she had in two weeks. A few cars were already missing from the parking lot, and Anne realized that she had to get going if she was going to make it to work on time.

A shower improved her spirits even further, and afterwards she walked into the kitchen, toweling her hair, poured herself a cup of coffee from the freshly made pot, and started making breakfast. But when the toast popped, she didn't react, didn't move.

She just kept staring at the half empty cup of coffee from the fresh pot she hadn't made.

This time Detective Dardenian was openly annoyed. "Look, Miss Ketteridge, you just told me that not even the boyfriend has a key. There's no sign of forced entry, nothing is missing, and as far as I can see, no crime has been committed. Maybe you put the coffee on before you went to bed last night..."

"I don't drink coffee at night, not in this weather."

"...or maybe you made it this morning before you were completely awake."

Anne could see this was going nowhere. "All right, all right. I'm sorry I bothered you. Just go if that's what you're going to do."

He hesitated, then walked to the door, paused with his hand on the knob. "Have you considered taking a vacation, getting out of town for a while?"

"I'm not overworked and I'm not having a breakdown."

"I never said you were. But if someone really is playing games, he might lose interest if you were out of reach for a day or two."

She thought about it, nodded. "I have some vacation coming; I'll think about it."

"You do that. And have the locks changed, just in case."

It was an hour later when Anne noticed that a new photograph had been added to the collage. It wasn't extraordinary in itself, an angled shot of the bedroom showing how she'd pushed the two dressers together and shifted the vanity table to the opposite side. Except that she'd only moved the furniture last night and certainly hadn't taken the photograph.

She no longer even owned a camera.

Mickey's forbearance proved to be short lived. Wednesday he showed up after work, announcing his intention to take her out for supper.

"Is that a new lock I saw?"

"Yes, I had the super fix it yesterday. And a deadbolt for inside."

"Good idea. I heard you asked for some time off."

"I'm going up north for a couple of days. Packed and loaded the car this morning."

Supposedly it was to be a short evening, but Anne was reluctant to return to her apartment alone. Mickey sensed how she felt and was clearly delighted. His subsequent lovemaking was vaguely desperate, as though he measured his virility by the amount of sweat produced. Anne was distracted and disheartened, fearing her growing dependence on a partner she now realized was shallow and obvious. Her pretended orgasm wasn't even a good act, but he accepted it as sufficient excuse to roll over and doze off.

Anne took a quick shower, realized it was only ten o'clock. Mickey was sprawled across the bed, leaving room for her only if she curled into a ball. Briefly she considered the couch, but realized she wasn't really tired. It was still nice outside, the sky clear, and impulsively she threw on a halter top and jeans, then slipped quietly out of the apartment, working the deadbolts quietly for fear she'd wake Mickey.

He'd insist on accompanying her if she went for a walk, and she really wanted to be alone just now. It felt strange the moment she stepped outside, knowing there was someone in her apartment while she personally was absent. She'd never left Mickey alone there before.

How did I get into this mess, she asked herself. My life was going just fine, good job, no entanglements, no problems. Mickey had been just as patient and courteous after they'd spent that night together, but their relationship was fatally altered, and she was no longer certain of its shape or texture.

Anne had difficulty putting her dissatisfaction into words. Mickey was considerate, undemanding, and seemed determinedly monogamous. He'd never lost his temper, or said a harsh word, or denied her anything she'd asked. His sexual tastes were conventional if somewhat strenuous, and he even took the garbage out without being asked.

There was something wrong between them, though, and Anne had no idea what it could be.

It was nearly midnight when she realized she was lost. Standing at the corner of two dimly lit residential streets, she chose one at random, surprised herself by emerging only a few blocks from her apartment building. There was an entire world lying just outside the limits of her experience, she realized. Against such a scale, her own life and its problems seemed trivial.

There were flashing lights in the parking area when she rounded the building. Many flashing lights. An ambulance and at least two police cars. Another arrived as she was crossing toward the main entrance.

A uniformed officer stepped out of the shadows. "Excuse me, Miss. You can't go in."

"But I live here. What's happened?"

"There's been some trouble. We'll be out of the way as soon as we can. If you'd like to speak to the sergeant over there," he gestured toward one of the flashing cars, "he might be able to help you."

When she told the sergeant her name and room number, his face changed. "If you'll wait right there a second, Miss Ketteridge, I'll tell the lieutenant you're here."

And that's when she knew that something had happened to Mickey.

She identified the body before they took it away.

"We found his wallet inside your apartment. Can you confirm that this is in fact Michael Grant?" Ben Dardenian was all business now.

"Yes, that's Mickey." He looked smaller somehow, lying there.

"The way we figure it, the perpetrator rang the bell. The victim was probably half asleep when he answered the door. His assailant was waiting with a knife. Death was almost instantaneous, no defensive wounds, no sign of a struggle. And the murder weapon's missing."

Anne squeezed her eyes shut, turned away to hide her face, ashamed she felt no tears.

"One of your neighbors works second shift, came home and spotted him lying halfway out of your apartment. Where were you this evening, Miss Ketteridge?"

She explained that she'd gone for a walk.

"About what time would that have been?"

"Ten, or just after."

"Under the circumstances, was that really a smart thing to do?"

Anne's temper flared. "The police department implied I was imagining the whole thing. I guess I just decided they were right."

Dardenian had the grace to look uncomfortable. "All right, I guess I deserved that. But if you'd told us about the other incidents, we might have looked at things more seriously." She'd just described the telephone message, showed him the note and the mysterious picture.

"Do you have any family in the area, Miss Ketteridge?"

She shook her head. "No, I'm an only child and my parents are both dead."

"A friend you could stay with for the night? We're going to be going over the site here until dawn at least, and you look like you're ready to collapse."

"There's...there's a motel just down the road a way. I'll take a room there."

"We'll need a rather lengthy statement from you...tomorrow."

"I understand that."

"Will you be all right? I could have someone drive you over."

It took two tries before she could speak. "No. Thank you. I'll be fine." Everything she'd need was in the trunk of her car.

Dardenian wasn't present when she gave her statement the following day, but another detective told her it would be all right to return to the apartment. "Sometimes the evidence team leaves kind of a mess," he added apologetically.

A considerable mess as it turned out. After carrying her bags back into the apartment and unpacking, Anne spent the entire afternoon cleaning surfaces covered by fingerprint dust and some sticky gelatinous substance. Too tired to cook, she ate a late supper at a small diner across the street, then walked home quickly, keeping to the well lighted areas.

She had just closed the door to her apartment when strong hands grabbed her arms from behind.

"Welcome home, Anne. I've been waiting for you."

She let her shoulders slump, then twisted violently, pulling free. One hand stabbed at the light switch as she turned to confront her attacker.

He was shorter than she by an inch or so, but about the same age, sandy haired, rather good looking.

"Who are you?" It was suddenly important that she know his name, more important even than escaping.

"It hasn't been that long since we were together, Anne. Don't tell me I've changed that much."

There was in fact something familiar about him. "Oh my god! Jimmy?"

"Got it in one, Sis. I'm surprised you didn't guess sooner. I told you we were meant for each other."

Anne's eyes strayed to the door but he was already moving toward her and she felt that same weakness that had come over her the first time, back home in Managansett, when he'd lured her out into the woods to see his secret place and then tried to make her do terrible, unthinkable things with him. When he tore open her blouse it was as though she'd slipped back through time, and the walls of her apartment lost their texture, the wallpaper fading into a chaos of vines and brambles. She'd fought him then, but she had no strength to do so now, and when he carried her to the couch, she was hoping he'd touch her the way he'd done the night he slipped into her bedroom.

And then she felt his hand between her legs and his fingers inside and he was touching her in such a wonderful way that all the menace of the situation just seemed too trivial to be concerned about, and she threw her head back against the couch and let the sensations steal her will.

The doorbell rang.

Jimmy was instantly motionless. A few seconds passed, and the bell rang again. Anne dazedly sat up as he withdrew, still feeling waves of pleasurable anticipation.

"I have to answer the door," she whispered.

Jimmy shook his head.

Whoever it was knocked this time, and then a familiar voice, Detective Dardenian's. "Miss Ketteridge, we know you're home. It's very important that we talk to you."

Jimmy kept his voice low. "If you tell them I'm here, I'll make you pay, Anne. You know I can do it, don't you?"

She nodded. "Wait till I'm out of sight, then let them in." And he moved silently across the room, eased the closet door open, and slipped inside.

"Just a minute. I'm not dressed." Her torn blouse went under a cushion and she pulled a fresh, though wrinkled replacement from her ironing basket. Walking was difficult, her body throbbing as though Jimmy was still with her, still inside, still touching her just the right way.

"May we come in?" A tall, redhaired woman in a police uniform stood behind Dardenian. Her pocket identified her as Curtis.

"Certainly. Make yourselves comfortable. Can I get either of you anything?"

"I think not." Dardenian sat on the couch; Curtis moved to the adjoining chair but remained standing.

Anne felt distanced from reality, as though she'd had a bit too much to drink, that moment when she believed she was acting normally but suspected otherwise. She sat facing the detective.

"Do you have any news?"

"In a way." Dardenian looked uncomfortable. "Miss Ketteridge, I spent the better part of the day tracking down your family history." He raised a hand when she started to speak. "Let me say what I have to say first. Although I didn't realize it until recently, you weren't entirely truthful to me."

"I know I should have told you everything that has happened sooner, but..."

He waved aside her excuses. "The first time I was here, you identified the boy in the picture there," he nodded toward the collage, "as your brother. But later you said you were an only child."

"It wasn't a lie, exactly. Jimmy was adopted and he was only with us for a year before he died."

"Why do you say he died, Miss Ketteridge?"

Anne's face remained blank, uncomprehending.

"The official reports simply say that he disappeared. The case was never solved and they assumed he ran away."

Anne spread her hands. "Well, we all assumed that he'd been killed. I mean, what else could have happened to him?" But he hadn't died, she realized. Mickey had died though.

"A lot of things actually, but I think you're right, Miss Ketteridge. I think James Tattersall, your adopted brother, died the day he disappeared. And I think you know that because you killed him." Dardenian leaned forward, his eyes glittering. "Just like you killed Michael Grant."

Anne shook her head, stunned. "But you saw the photographs, and I told you about the telephone message..."

"We only have your word for it that the message was real, and you could have typed the note yourself."

"But I didn't."

"We used a warrant to search your car, Miss Ketteridge, and found something interesting in the trunk. Do you know what it was?"

Anne blinked, shook her head. She was trying to think clearly, but the shooting surges of pleasurable pain between her legs hadn't gone away. If anything, they'd grown more intense since she'd sat down and crossed her legs.

"A camera with a shutter timing attachment, perfect for self portraits. Two more nude photographs and a nearly full box of stationery. Not to mention a bloodstained knife. I'm afraid I'm going to have to ask you to come with us, Miss Ketteridge."

Anne stood up, her palms pressed together. "But I didn't do anything. It was Jimmy. I don't know where he's been all this time, but he came back and he killed Mickey and he's hiding in that closet right this minute."

Both officers involuntarily glanced toward the closet, but the door remained tightly closed. "Let's check it out." Dardenian sounded fatigued rather than anxious.

Curtis nodded and drew her weapon. She approached the door cautiously, then pulled it open so violently that it flew from her hand and hit the wall with a crash. The small space was filled with off season clothing, all hanging neatly in garment bags. There was no space left for a human being to have hidden.

But there was something else in the closet as well. Huddled on the floor was a polished human skeleton, the bones crudely wired together.

"See? I told you it wasn't me." Anne smiled at Dardenian, shifting her body as it shivered toward the brink of an orgasm.

Officer Curtis crouched, used the barrel of her revolver to lift one of the arms. A wire was broken and it ended at the wrist socket.

Anne clenched her thighs and threw her head back as the rush became too powerful to resist. Dardenian stared at her with wide eyes, as though he feared she was in the grip of an epileptic seizure. He was hovering over her when she finally settled back, a smile of contentment transforming her.

"Jimmy always loved me," she said quietly.

KINDRED SPIRITS

I've never been lucky when it comes to neighbors. I have always minded my own business, even turned the other cheek in the face of minor provocations, but to no avail. It has been this way for as long as I can remember.

Old Mrs. Anderson who lived next door when I was a kid wasn't really a witch, although I and my playmates thought so at the time. She was just an unpleasant old woman who hated kids and noise and disorder and of course I was a kid and noisy and disorderly. It's part of the job description. She shouted at me when I walked past her house, complained to my parents when I played too loudly, and accused me of sneaking into her yard at night and looking in through her windows. Even my parents were relieved that day when she was found at the foot of her staircase with a broken neck. My father joked that someone had probably pushed her and my mother pretended to be offended although she almost certainly shared the sentiment. Mrs. Anderson hadn't much liked adults either.

I wasn't interested in college, though in retrospect that was probably a mistake. I used my savings to buy myself a used trailer at a park on the outskirts of Managansett. It was what they used to call a granny flat, ample for a bachelor or even a young couple just starting out. I was inordinately proud of having my own place, but some of the luster faded when Arthur Melby moved in next door.

Melby – no one ever used his first name – was a Hell's Angel wannabe. He had a beat up Suzuki motorcycle that you could hear coming from half a mile away, invariably wore a torn tee-shirt under a black leather jacket, didn't shave and rarely washed, and there was a variety of crude tattoos competing for space on his increasingly ample body. Melby played his music too loud, threw empty beer cans into my lot, swore incessantly and for no apparent reason, and christened me "Beanpole" Bailey despite my attempts to remain civil and neighborly. It was uncomfortable standing downwind from his trailer which had accumulated a skirt of crumpled beer cans, cigarette butts, and miscellaneous trash. Complaints to the park manager did no good because he was Melby's uncle. He just spread his hands and told me that there was nothing that he could do about it.

It became so unpleasant that I had been considering selling my trailer and looking for an apartment but then the cops came and handcuffed him when he swore at them. It wasn't long before they found his drugs and took him away. I never saw him again, his trailer was sold for scrap, and things started to look up. Unfortunately, the government saw fit to draft me toward the end of that year and I found myself in the Army. I won't dwell on the various objectionable bunkmates I shared quarters with over the course of the next two years. Their unpleasant natures differed only in details, and every single one of them snored or talked in his sleep or had other unpleasant habits. Fortunately I somehow avoided reassignment to Viet Nam and spent most of my time in Korea working at a supply depot.

I wouldn't want you to get the wrong impression. I'm not some kind of recluse or misfit. I do enjoy being with other people. I work in a crowded office and I fancy I'm as popular as anyone else. I trade jokes and opinions about sports and politics, I occasionally go to lunch or out for drinks with my peers, and there are two or three whom I genuinely consider friends. I don't date anyone at work, but that's a matter of personal policy, and I have from time to time entertained young ladies in the usual manner. It is true that none of my relationships have lasted long – the thought of marriage frankly frightens me – but each has ended amicably. Well, except for Doris. She persisted in blackening my name after I broke things off and I might have had a serious problem with her if it hadn't been for her accident. I even visited her at the nursing home once but the nurse told me she probably wasn't even aware that I was present.

After my discharge I briefly rented an apartment, a dreadful year during which my nerves suffered terribly. The people above me had unusually active children, who seemed more inclined to jump up and down than to actually walk across the floor, and they gave parties once or twice a month, which lasted into the small hours. The neighbor to my right was not particularly sociable but he never infringed upon my rights and we even exchanged pleasantries from time to time. The elderly man on the other side was a very different matter; he was forever imploring me to run errands for him because his health was "not as good as it might be." He died in his bed not very long after I moved in and I frankly felt considerable relief, but it was short lived. The next tenants were another young people with kids – a particularly obnoxious boy who drew stick figures on my door with a crayon - and I knew I'd have to move.

I rented a house as soon as I was able, though the word "house" implies an inappropriate grandeur. It was a converted carriage house, one large sitting room with a kitchenette in the back and a tiny bathroom. I slept in the loft. Its greatest asset was its isolation; I literally could not see another dwelling place from any of the three windows, nor could I ordinarily hear anything except infrequent distant shouts. It was in excellent repair and spacious enough to allow me to unbox all of my books and arrange them on makeshift shelving.

Alas, my landlord – who lived in the main house up the road – added a pair of large dogs to his household and belligerently refused to confine them. Although I was never actually attacked, I was frequently accosted by one or both while outside working in my small garden. They would bare their teeth and growl menacingly until I slowly backed away or, on more than one occasion, pitched stones at them until they retreated. There were similar complaints from others in the neighborhood, which had no more effect than my own, and peace was only restored after the dogs succumbed to a piece of poisoned meat.

Although there were probably a dozen or more suspects in this "crime", my landlord decided quite arbitrarily that I was responsible and evicted me peremptorily. Fortunately, my mother had passed away that summer and had left me enough in her estate that I could finally afford more sumptuous quarters.

My house on Burnell Street was even more convenient to my job at Eblis Manufacturing. I could walk to work if the weather was clement almost as quickly as I could drive when it was not. Real estate values in Managansett had not escalated as dramatically as elsewhere in the state so the house came with a good sized yard, nearly an acre – most of which was covered by brush and small trees. This provided welcome insulation from my neighbors on either side, and the land behind was undeveloped and likely to remain so. The elderly couple who lived across the street were pretty much housebound and dependent on aid workers who visited daily, and I carefully refrained from making their acquaintance. It seemed a nearly ideal situation for me.

And so it remained for the next six years. The woman across the street died at last and her husband was subsequently moved to a nursing home. I eyed the FOR SALE sign on the front lawn with considerable apprehension, and briefly entertained the possibility of buying the place myself. Unfortunately, I'd just replaced my roof that spring and I'd upgraded the electrical service the year before, so my savings were not up to the task. I could have applied for a mortgage, of course, but I had so far managed to live my life debt free and was loathe to bring this freedom from care to an end.

The sign remained there for six months, during which time I only once saw anyone visit the property, though others may well have done so in my absence. My trepidation had lessened considerably. The house was, after all, in serious need of work. The paint was peeling, a few shingles were missing from the roof, the windows were old fashioned, and the porch was positively unsafe. With each passing day it became a less attractive proposition to any prospective buyer. There was a growing possibility that it would simply remain empty for the foreseeable future. My simmering anxiety dissipated and eventually I stopped worry about it entirely.

And then one day the following spring a SOLD sticker was superimposed on the now fading sign. Mrs. Carlyle had come into my life.

Anita Carlyle was a competent, determined, energetic, and industrious woman. She was also acerbic, nosey, brazen, and tasteless. I did not know any of this immediately, of course, and in fact it was another two months before I even saw my new neighbor, although I imagine she must have visited the house while I was at work from time to time. I was in no hurry to make her acquaintance. A succession of contractors descended upon the property, rebuilding the porch, clearing the chaotically overgrown yard, and carrying out various repairs and improvements inside. There were plumbers and carpenters and electricians, oh yes. A new furnace was installed along with central air conditioning. The roof was replaced by the same firm I had employed, after which aluminum siding covered the elderly clapboards.

It was admittedly unfair of me but I was predisposed to dislike my new neighbor simply because of the inconvenience she caused. There was constant noise from across the street – even on the weekend – and on more than one occasion my driveway had been partially blocked by service vehicles. I began to imagine the worst – a large family with troublesome teenagers who would throw toilet paper into my trees, race their cars down the street, play loud music until all hours, and possibly even vandalize my meticulously arranged gardens. It was a great relief to hear that the new tenant was a recent widow with no children but I still dreaded the day she would move in.

I consoled myself with the possibility that she was an elderly woman who might be confined to her bed. An invalid whose keepers discouraged visitors would be best. I wished her no pain, of course, merely a wasting disease that left her relatively comfortable but immobilized and uninterested in social interactions. Even if her health was not seriously impaired, she might prove to be a pleasant but distant person whose presence would in no way disturb my way of life. But Mrs. Carlyle was in fact only in her early thirties and looked even younger, a petite woman whose advent on Burnell Street was as calamitous as the fall of a meteor might have been.

The moving van was just leaving when I arrived home from work that terrible Friday. It had been dreary and overcast that morning so I had driven the short distance to the office where a particularly hectic day had left me tired and irritable. The van's driver was singularly incompetent. Even with the assistance of his co-driver, it took nearly ten minutes to back out of the driveway into Burnell Street proper. Admittedly it is a tight fit because of the stone walls that line the road on both sides, but a proper professional would have analyzed the situation and acted optimally. I was in a foul mood when I finally pulled into my own driveway and I stood for a while at my front window, glaring across the street. A meal and a brandy soothed my nerves, however, and I admitted to myself that I was being irrational. Resolving to give Mrs. Carlyle the benefit of the doubt, I retired to my library, planning to finish the history of the Napoleonic Wars I'd been reading even if it took until dawn to do so. It nearly did.

I was wakened from a sound sleep by the grumbling of a lawn mower. It had been a very warm evening and my bedroom window was open. I rose and closed it, which reduced the unwelcome noise by about half, and glanced at my alarm clock as I stumbled back to bed. It was barely 7:00 AM! While I certainly wouldn't fault anyone for maintaining their property in good condition, there was a town ordinance specifically prohibiting any such activity for another full hour.

I was of half a mind to stalk across the street and inform my new neighbor of her transgression, but I remembered my resolution to give her the benefit of the doubt. So I put a CD of harpsichord music by Bach into the player and allowed it to drown out the muted rumblings. I was asleep again within minutes.

We didn't actually meet for several more days, although I noticed her working outside from time to time, or sitting on her newly refurbished porch. She invariably reclined with her feet up on a settee, drinking something from a tall glass, listening to the radio, whose volume was enough to make my teeth ache. Country and western, I thought. Even rap would have been preferable.

At the same time I could not help but notice that she was not unattractive. She wore her hair long and dressed well enough to complement her figure without being strident about it. I allotted her points for that, but her balance sheet was still well into the negative. As far as I could determine she had no visitors and, I was pleased to note, frequently absented herself in the evenings. She clearly had independent means rather than regular employment and I have to confess that this struck me as quite unfair. I would have abandoned my job at Eblis in a heartbeat if it had been within my power to do so.

I was introduced to Anita Carlyle by our mailman, after a fashion. I found one of her letters mixed with my mail a few days after she arrived. If it had been a routine flyer, I would have tossed it out with my own, but the return address was a law firm so I reluctantly trekked across Burnell and rang her doorbell. Her expression was guarded at first, but relaxed once I had explained why I was disturbing her. She became so effusive then that my defenses were breached and I found myself accepting her invitation to come in for coffee. It was, as I feared, made from instant rather than fresh brewed, but I put a brave face on it and the encounter was on balance reasonably enjoyable. She had a tendency to dominate a conversation and was extremely opinionated even on the most trivial matters, but I had no reason at that point to think that this would impinge upon my own life in any serious fashion.

The clues were all there, but I failed to realize their significance until sometime later. For one thing, she already knew my name, marital status, employer, and my fondness for books and gardening. "Mr. Winslow, down at the convenience store, told me all about you," she confided. Winslow was a notorious busybody who gossiped with his customers incessantly. His brother was the plumber who had installed an outside faucet for me.

Winslow had obviously found an appreciative listener in Mrs. Carlyle. She regaled me with stories about our neighbors, some of whose names were unfamiliar to me. The older Lombino girl was pregnant and dropping out of high school. James Nicholson's wife had refused to press charges after he broke her nose and blackened both eyes. The Venturas and the Nelsons had stopped speaking to one another after Jeff Nelson made a drunken pass at Frieda Ventura. There was more, but my threshold for scandal was low. I began to search for an excuse to make my escape.

Despite some lingering reservations, I returned to my own house somewhat reassured. Mrs. Carlyle appeared to be excessively loquacious and uncomfortably inquisitive but otherwise unobjectionable, and I was confident I could keep her at arm's length as necessary.

My confidence took a hit when she knocked on my door the following morning. She was holding a plate of freshly baked scones so despite being at a particularly enthralling part of the novel I was reading, I had no choice but to invite her in. Fortunately, I had just brewed a pot of coffee, a special blend of my own concoction, and I felt confident her visit would be an abbreviated one. I even managed not to wince when she told me the coffee tasted odd and that I might want to give the pot a thorough cleaning.

What did not escape my attention was that nothing escaped hers. Our eyes rarely met because hers were in constant motion. I could almost sense the way she was cataloguing my possessions, evaluating their cost, noting the state of my housekeeping, and conducting an ongoing analysis of my tastes and preferences and thus of my character. I had the odd sensation that I was suddenly naked. Throughout this process, we talked, or rather, she talked and I listened. Having decided that I was not a repository of fascinating details about our neighbors, Mrs. Carlyle was clearly more interested in the sound of her own voice than in whatever information I might divulge. I eventually took advantage of a brief pause and mentioned the ordinance against using a lawn mower either early or late in the day. With no visible reaction to my rebuke, she suddenly remembered that she was expecting a telephone call and made her exit. I felt genuine delight at this small tactical triumph.

My pleasure was not to last. The following week I received a visit from the town manager's office. Mr. Gettling was sorry to disturb me but there'd been a complaint about my gazebo. "There's a height limit for outbuildings unless you have a variance, Mr. Bailey. And I was unable to find one when I went looking for your building permit. And that's actually an even more serious matter. It seems, unless I'm mistaken, that you never actually applied for a building permit."

I had built the gazebo myself three years earlier. I'm more than a fair hand at carpentry and I was quite proud of my accomplishment. It was in fact rather taller than it needed to be, but I'd wanted to hang wind chimes high enough that they wouldn't brush against my head when I passed beneath them. The gazebo was not even visible from the street, surrounded completely by poplars on two sides and a Japanese maple on the third.

"We could issue the building permit retroactively, of course, but because of the requirement for a variance, we'd have to post a notice. If any of your neighbors objected, it would almost certainly be denied, and since there's already been a complaint, there's not much chance."

"So what are my options?"

"If I were you I'd apply for a permit to reduce the height by eighteen inches. That addresses both problems and leaves your neighbor with nothing to complain about." The man's sympathies were clearly on my side but neither he nor I had much choice at this point. I didn't bother to inquire about the origin of the complaint, since I knew that he would feel obligated to keep that information confidential.

"All right. I'll take care of it this afternoon."

There was actually no question in my mind about which of my neighbors was responsible for this outrage. Mrs. Carlyle was the only new person in the area and, belatedly, I realized this was probably her response to my veiled complaint about her lawn mowing. I felt almost physically ill after Gettling had gone, my hands shaking so badly that I spilled coffee on my pants. It was only after showering and donning fresh clothing that I felt my self control returning.

I filed the request for a building permit after lunch, then spent a considerable portion of the afternoon at the registrar's office reviewing the book of ordinances for the town of Managansett. There were quite a lot of them, far more than I would have expected for such a small, rural community. I remarked on this to one of the clerks who nodded resignedly. "Everybody who gets elected to the town council for the first time has some hobby horse he or she is riding and most of them manage to get things added to the code. Mostly no one remembers them after that." I took a good many notes.

Mrs. Carlyle's house was situated quite close to the road, almost abutting the sidewalk. The former residents had not owned a car, at least not while I was living across from them, and they had neither driveway nor garage. One of the construction projects completed before Mrs. Carlyle had taken up residence was the paving of a foreshortened driveway that led straight in from the street. It was at least a foot or so shorter than it should have been and her massive Lincoln's rear bumper was thrust into the street even when she pulled forward far enough to nudge the porch. I took a photograph and anonymously forwarded it to the chief of police with a brief, typed note of explanation.

Two days later I could hear the ensuing argument even from the far end of my house. The police officer was firm but polite while Mrs. Carlyle expostulated heatedly that she had a perfect right to park in her own driveway. "What do you expect me to do? Park on the street?" Which was no solution at all, as we all knew, because street parking is banned from midnight to 6:00 AM daily. I smiled to myself and went outside to do some gardening. When I next looked across the street, Mrs. Carlyle's Lincoln had been pulled up onto her immaculate lawn. Three days later a new, longer driveway was installed alongside the house, at the cost of several lovely lilac bushes, my only regret in the affair.

Lest you think that my personal animosity toward Mrs. Carlyle had colored my perceptions of her, I should point out that I was not alone in my reaction. James Nicholson was nearly arrested for trespassing one evening when he began pounding on her door and shouting threats. It seems that she had somehow learned more sordid details about his recent marital problems and had been telling everyone in town the unsavory – and rather perverted – details, perhaps even elaborating slightly in the process. Two teenage boys were arrested for throwing eggs at her windows after she'd reported them for clandestine smoking. Mrs. Wilcox, who runs a tiny yarn shop on Main Street, banned her from the premises for reasons unknown. One of the local police officers confided in me that he and his fellows wished she had never moved to town. "When she's not complaining about someone, someone is complaining about her."

On my personal front, attack and counter attack followed inevitably. She complained that the little shelter I'd built for my garbage cans was too close to the street. It was, but only by three inches. I was able to move it without too much difficulty. I complained about the sign she'd erected above her door. She had christened her house Gormenghast, as though it was some great English manor, but there was an ordinance against exterior signs in residential areas and she had to take it down.

There were other battlefields as well. Both of us were proud of our gardens, possibly our only common ground, no pun intended. But one morning I woke to find that someone had trampled through my flower beds, quite destructively, and when I realized that only the most labor intensive and vulnerable plants had been targeted, I knew she was responsible. That night I considered a retaliatory strike, but I could not bear the thought of despoiling a well tended garden, even hers, so I switched to an alternative tactic. A midnight drive to one of the farms on the north side of town netted me a burlap bag full of fresh manure, which I quietly distributed across the surface of her porch. Her shout of dismay the following morning woke me, but for a change I did not mind the disturbance.

Then came that dreary morning when I discovered that all four of my tires had been slashed during the night. Since I had no intention of abandoning my comfortable home I came to the inevitable conclusion that Mrs. Carlyle must go.

The situation offered me several advantages. Mrs. Carlyle lived alone, had never had an overnight guest insofar as I was aware, or a daytime one for that matter. Nor did she have a burglar alarm. She was not physically prepossessing and even someone of my relatively slight build should be able to overpower her with little difficulty given the element of surprise. There would be no shortage of suspects if foul play was suspected. I could personally name four people who would have happily pushed her in front of a train, starting with James Nicholson.

It would be better, of course, if it was made to look like an accident. No one had ever entertained the possibility that I might have sneaked into Mrs. Anderson's house as a child and pushed her down the staircase, and I was never forced to lie convincingly about what I'd been doing at the time, although I have no doubt that I could have carried it off. I considered poisoning Mrs. Carlyle – that had worked quite effectively for me with those objectionable dogs years earlier – but somehow I couldn't see her inviting me over for coffee again, or accepting my invitation for that matter. If I'd known where Arthur Melby was keeping himself, assuming he was out of jail, I might have tried hiring him to do the deed for me. I'm sure I could have contrived to do so without implicating myself, and then it would have been a simple matter to make an anonymous phone call turning him in, as I had done when I noticed that he kept drugs in his trailer. But I did not know anything of Melby or anyone like him. I would have to do this myself.

I also had to consider method. It would not do to suffocate her in bed, as I had done with my elderly neighbor at the apartment building. An autopsy would be inevitable for such a young woman. It had been a simple matter to sabotage the brakes on Doris' car, but I couldn't be certain of the results if I did the same to Mrs. Carlyle's Lincoln. My next thought was to make it look like a botched burglary. She was wealthy enough to be a plausible target. On the other hand, what if she owned a gun? If so, she would certainly know how to use it and I did not relish the possibility of being shot as an intruder. Alternatively, she might be made to disappear. There were several dirt roads leading into the nearby woods which offered multiple sites for clandestine disposal of bodies. It was turning cold but the ground wasn't frozen yet. If I chose that option, it would have to be soon.

I decided to employ a feint. I would call upon Mrs. Carlyle and propose a truce. Assuming she let me into her house, I could evaluate the possibility of a staged accident and at least partly allay her suspicions of me. There might even be an opportunity to settle things on the spot.

Having made the decision, I called to see if she was home. Before our breach, she had given me her number, somehow having learned my unlisted one. Her voice betrayed wariness, but she agreed. "But not right now. I'm quite busy. Why don't you come over this evening, around eight?"

I prepared for our encounter with great care. It was cold enough to justify wearing light gloves and if I contrived not to remove them, there would be no question of fingerprints. I found an old clasp knife in a drawer, carefully washed it and wiped it clean, then slipped it into my pocket. I was confident that it could not possibly be traced back to me. There would doubtless be plenty of blunt instruments on the scene should I need one. If my chance came tonight, I would be prepared to take it; if not, I would be armed with intelligence for another time.

Mrs. Carlyle must have been watching for me because she opened the door before I touched the bell. I followed her inside, noting the gleam of excitement in her eyes. This must all be some elaborate game for her, I thought. She relieves the boredom of her life by stirring up people around her. Unable to elicit love, she settles for hatred.

I pretended mild contrition and suggested that we had both over reacted and behaved like children. I thought at first she was going to agree with me, but to my surprise she laughed. "Mr. Bailey, you disappoint me. I've found our little competition very entertaining and I never would have believed that you'd surrender so easily." She poured me another cup of her execrable and this evening unusually strong coffee.

"It's not a question of surrender, just accommodation."

She shook her head. "Nonsense. You're just like my second husband, Bert." She must have noticed my surprise because she nodded. "That's right, my late husband wasn't my first. He was my third, in fact. I'm three times a widow."

My expression must have been comical because she laughed. "You're so easy, Mr. Bailey. Not much of a challenge at all."

I felt momentarily out of my depth. This was not at all similar to the scenarios I had rehearsed in my mind. "Perhaps I should go." I started to rise but she spoke up quickly.

"No, I'm sorry. I shouldn't tease. I'm afraid I have a tendency to aggravate people unnecessarily. Please forgive me. At least stay long enough to finish your coffee."

I would have preferred to pour it down the sink, but I masked my revulsion by taking another sip. It was so bitter it made my nose wrinkle. "So shall we call it even and start over?" I said at last, not meaning a syllable of it. There was a heavy candlestick near at hand, which would easily crush her skull. The clasp knife was a hard pressure against my thigh. Her windows had strong, ropelike sashes that could easily become strangling cords. I could think of half a dozen ways to kill her.

I can be very observant when I wish to be. I had already noticed that the ground floor windows were not locked and the curtains were all drawn closed. Should I strike now, ransack the house, bury some "stolen" articles in the woods, and wait for someone to investigate? But I was beginning to feel a bit light headed. I hadn't done anything like this in so long. Was I still up to it?

I finished the coffee by surreptitiously pouring it into a potted plant and set down the cup. "I shouldn't take up any more of your time."

She looked momentarily perplexed. "All right then, but would you do me a small favor before you go?"

"If I can." I stood up and felt slightly dizzy. All thought of killing her this evening had fled. My normal calm self confidence had abandoned me.

"It's the new furnace. Something seems to be wrong with it. Would you mind taking a look?"

"I'm afraid I know next to nothing about mechanical things." I wanted to go home and lie down. "Perhaps you should call a technician."

"Just please look at it. As a sign of our new friendship."

It was hardly friendship by any criterion, but it was easier to agree than to argue. It was less easy to negotiate the narrow staircase to the basement. I was feeling distinctly sick. I must be getting too old, I thought. My nerves aren't as steady as they once were.

I was halfway down the staircase when she hit me. It was the same candlestick I'd considered using on her a short while before.

Fortunately the constricted staircase interfered with her aim and the blow caught me on the shoulder rather than on the head, but it was still sufficient to send me toppling down to the basement floor. Mrs. Carlyle followed.

"Yes, you're just like Bert. He turned his back on me at the wrong time too. He was quite surprised when he 'fell' off that balcony. It wasn't very hard, just a little push and some play acting to avert suspicion. I was on the stage when I was younger, you know. Henry was more of a challenge; I had to get him good and drunk and roll him and his car off a cliff to get rid of him. And Tommy was almost happy to go, I think. He's the only one I miss sometimes, but he did go on about money all the time."

I looked around for a weapon, but I was so weak that I could barely rise to my knees. "Maybe this way is best," she said. "The poison should finish you soon and you're light enough that I can drag you home. I used weed killer, the same brand you use on your garden. Everyone will think you got tired of your miserable life and took a quick exit. I shall tell them how depressed you've been of late. It will be quite tragic, I'm sure."

She was quite near, towering over me, and just before I gave in to despair I remembered the clasp knife. I fumbled in my pocket, found it, gathered what remained of my strength, and lunged upward, willing my legs to lift me from the floor, bringing my arm up in as steady an arc as I could manage.

Mrs. Carlyle was quite surprised. The blade went up through the underside of her chin and presumably into her nasty, scheming brain with surprisingly little resistance. She stood upright for a few seconds more, then toppled to the floor without saying another word, for which I was profoundly grateful. I followed her to the floor a moment later, all of my strength expended, and almost immediately lost consciousness.

I woke to the realization that Mrs. Carlyle had muffed her fourth murder attempt. Happily her coffee tasted so terrible that I had barely sipped at it and had not imbibed a fatal dose. I was lying in a pool of vomit and sharp pains lanced through my abdomen every few seconds, but my head was clearing. I could hear voices and for a few seconds I thought Mrs. Carlyle was still alive, but her body was very close and cool to the touch.

I tried to get up, but my legs would not work; I could not even crawl. I lay back, trying to gather my strength, and listened to the voices. One I failed to recognize, but the other was unmistakably that of James Nicholson, who worked two doors away from me at Eblis. I could only hear snatches of the conversation, but both men were clearly drunk and there were several references to the "bitch", whose identity was self evident. At first I had no idea what their purpose might be. Nor did I care. Until this paralysis passed, external events were of no concern to me. Or so I thought.

But finally I realized what they were doing and I tried to sit up, failing utterly, falling back with a sigh of despair.

They were setting fire to the house.

LEAVE ME ALONE

When Aimee telephoned to tell me she wanted to break it off, she was also standing right beside me, her naked body still covered with sex sweat.

Yeah, I know that sounds crazy. How do you think I felt? Look, let me tell it to you from the beginning and maybe it'll make more sense. If it does, let me know, because I could use some enlightenment myself.

I met Aimee almost by accident. She was coming out of the Supramart at the corner of Walsh and Main. It's not a convenience store I use often; I live on the opposite side of Managansett and there's an IGA less than two blocks away. But I was in the neighborhood and the milk had gone sour that morning, so I figured I'd just pop in and pick up a half gallon on my way home.

This strikingly attractive woman was coming out as I entered, and she flashed me a smile that almost stopped my heart. Not that she was conventionally beautiful, mind you. Her face was a little too wholesome, Cheryl Tiegs with a hint of Kellie Martin. I was currently between involvements and, frankly, not in the mood for one. My brief liaison with Valerie Grant had put the fear of God into me. I mean, I'm fairly adventurous in bed, but that girl was pure poison. Bruises and scratches are one thing; contusions and a dislocated finger are something else entirely.

Anyway, I echoed the smile but without thinking about it, bought milk and a newspaper, and walked back to my car. When I spotted her a couple of spaces away, standing beside an elderly Volkswagen and looking distinctly lost, I almost shrugged and pretended not to have noticed. But chauvinist pig that I am, I couldn't reconcile that with my self image as a latter day knight errant, so I stowed my package inside and crossed half the distance separating us.

"Is something wrong, Miss?"

She bit her lip, hopped up and down nervously on one foot. "My tire's gone flat and I don't have a spare."

Her voice was husky, promising depths I suddenly felt the urge to explore. So easily we are trapped by our own vanity.

"There's a garage about six blocks down. I could drop you

and the tire off."

For a few seconds I thought she was going to turn me down, but she didn't. "If it wouldn't be too inconvenient, I'd really appreciate it."

Josephson's Garage was closed though, and by the looks of it hadn't been open in some time. The windows were boarded up and grass was sprouting through the blacktop. I told you I didn't get to this part of Managansett often. I told Aimee the same thing; that was her name, Aimee Harrison.

"Look, the nearest I can think of is the Shell station out on Route 13."

"But that's way the other side of town. I couldn't ask you to do that."

"No problem. That's where I'm headed anyway. I live up behind the new mall."

But the Shell station was swamped and wouldn't promise anything for at least three hours.

"I'll just walk over to the mall and get myself some supper. Thanks for the ride, Ray."

It was an exit line, but I'm stubborn. With a false and exaggerated Down East accident, I intoned, "You can't get theah from heah."

She blinked a question.

"There's a security fence all along this side. You'd have to walk up onto the highway and down the off ramp. Let me drive you by."

"You've already done more than..."

I raised a hand. "This is turning into a sitcom. Look, even better, why don't you have dinner with me? There's a nice restaurant down the road. I'll drop you back here afterward."

I expected a refusal, either angry or embarrassed. She surprised me.

"Ok, you're on, but only if I get to pick up the check."

I thought about it, decided not to push my luck. "You're on."

We didn't retrieve her tire until almost noon the next day.

Sex with Aimee was splendid. Splendid. Now there's a word I never use in ordinary conversation. But in this case it seemed totally appropriate. She was small, not much more than a hundred pounds, but solid, no tan lines, no misleading advertisements. And enthusiastic beyond anything in my experience. Somehow she managed to act as though each variation we tried was new. A perpetual virgin, always surprised, always receptive. We slept together five out of the next six nights, and the miss was my fault, a late evening session closing the books at Eblis Manufacturing.

Saturday night she brought over a pair of handcuffs and we experimented with them, first on me, then her. I'd been this route with Valerie, but where she'd terrified me, Aimee just turned me on. We made it together twice in just over an hour and when I got my breath back I staggered toward the bathroom on wobbly legs.

"First dibs on the shower," I croaked.

"No fair. You didn't have to get the cuffs off."

But the phone rang and I swerved to answer it. "Hello?"

Giggling, Aimee sprang off the bed, tried to slip past me to the bathroom, but I snaked an arm out and caught her, dragged her to me. I felt the heat pouring off her skin even through the double layer of sweat that insulated us.

"Ray? Is that you?"

"Yeah, it's me. Who's this?"

"I'm sorry to do it this way, but when we're together I don't have the nerve. We've had fun, Ray, honestly. But we can't go on this way. I have...other commitments."

I was pretty confused. "Valerie?" It didn't sound like Valerie, voice or tone, and we'd split a month ago anyway.

"Who's Valerie?" It was like stereo, the same voice and words coming from the phone and from the body still snuggled up next to me.

I felt pretty strange, I don't mind telling you.

"Who is this?"

"It's Aimee. Who the hell were you expecting?" That from the phone.

"What's going on, Ray?" This from the woman I'd just made frantic, awe inspiring love to.

"Look, if this is some kind of a joke..." I was thinking of Valerie again. She was famous for the dirty tricks she'd played on her lovers, leaving them abandoned in remote areas without their clothing, that sort of thing.

"I'm there with you now, aren't I? Make this the last time,

Ray, please? It was really good, you know, and I'd like it to end that way."

I hung up.

"Who was that?" Aimee was still pressed close, but I could sense a retraction in her skin, which felt ten degrees cooler all of a sudden.

"A joke, I guess. And not a particularly funny one."

It wasn't a joke.

The next time was even more unsettling.

Almost a week had passed and I'd put the incident out of my mind, my conscious one anyway. We were still sleeping together regularly, sometimes at my crackerbox development house, sometimes at her apartment. The landlady, Jeri Kaplan, was a high school classmate of mine and if she objected to my overnight stays, she never gave any indication.

It was Sunday. We'd made love twice in the evening, and around three in the morning Aimee woke me up with her mouth and we made it three. She wasn't an early riser, but I couldn't stay in bed after the sun came up, and since she doesn't have cable and I lusted after the news as well as her body, I tiptoed out and walked to the parking lot, figuring I'd go pick up the paper.

She was leaning against my Hyundai, waiting for me. Aimee, that is.

"How the hell did you get down here so fast?" I was smiling, a shit eating grin gracing my face no doubt, no sense of alarm.

"I asked you to leave me alone!"

I must have looked pretty stupid then. I mean, the comment and the angry tone seemed to come out of nowhere and I didn't connect it with the strange phone call. At least, not until some time later.

"Aimee? I don't understand..."

"I know what you're after!" She stepped forward, face inches from mine, reached up to grab her halter top and pull it sharply down. Aimee's full breasts tumbled free. Yes, Aimee's breasts. There were scratches on one of them I'd put there myself the previous evening. Things had gotten pretty rough the second time.

"This is all you ever think about, isn't it?"

I glanced around hastily but we were alone.

"Aimee, someone might see..."

"What? Are you embarrassed? I would have thought you'd like people to know you've been screwing me. Are you ashamed of me as well?"

I shook my head, confused. "I don't understand what's going on. I thought you liked me."

"It was fun, but it's over, get it? I want you to go away and never see me or talk to me again." There was such livid fury in her face, I was more terrified even than when Valerie Grant tied me to the rear bumper of her van and then started the engine.

"Can't we...?"

"No! Just go. I don't want to see you when I get back." She adjusted her clothing and stalked off, headed toward Main Street.

I guess I must have stood there a minute or two, no longer, just until she'd turned a corner and disappeared from sight. Then I shook myself, went back inside, climbed to the second floor and let myself in with the key Aimee'd given me.

She was still asleep in bed, naked, her breasts uncovered. The scratches were still there.

"Aimee, do you have any family around here?"

"Who? Me? No, Mom and Dad are retired and living in Florida now."

"Brothers and sisters?" Twin sister, I was figuring.

"Not anymore."

I raised my eyebrows. "I beg your pardon?"

"Had a brother. Died in Vietnam. No sisters. Always wanted one but Mummy told me to wait and have my own kid instead. She never really enjoyed having a family, I guess, just did it because it was kind of expected of her."

"So you never had a twin?" There, it was out.

Her face changed, but it was laughter. "God, no! I think Mummy'd have hanged herself if there'd been two of me. I was pretty wild in my teenybopper days."

She wanted to make love again but I begged off, telling her quite truthfully that I didn't feel well.

"Not this morning, dear, I have a headache," she pouted, but accepted my refusal with good grace otherwise.

Monday morning I called Dan Scofield. Dan and I are old school chums; in fact, I think he dated Jeri Kaplan a couple of times. Anyway, he'd worked for the *Providence Journal* as a reporter for a while, they went into private investigations. Not your Raymond Chandler type; more a super accountant with a nose for the figures that weren't supposed to be found.

Anyway, we were good enough friends that he'd do me a favor without asking any unnecessary questions.

"She's not local?"

"No. Comes from Taunton, originally, or so she says."

"You don't believe her?"

I didn't know the answer to that and told him.

"All right, give me a day or two."

I almost begged off seeing Aimee that night, but when I started making an excuse, she sounded so crushed that I relented. We had a late dinner, made love at my place, but I dropped her back at the apartment house just before midnight.

Dan called me at work the next afternoon.

"She's legit. Born in Taunton in 1970, second child to Ed and Joan Harrison. Brother Tom was two years older, helicopter pilot, died in Vietnam. Graduated Taunton High, spent two years at Amherst, finished up at Boston College. Works the helpline for Blake Computer software in Providence, moved to Managansett two months ago."

"Nothing...peculiar in her background?"

"It might help if I knew what I was looking for."

"If I knew, I wouldn't be asking you."

"Right. No, nothing. Three parking tickets, one unpaid. No arrest record."

"Anything medical?"

"Like, venereal disease? AIDS?"

"No, more like psychological."

"Medical stuff is hard to get, Ray. Nothing turned up the first time. I'll look a little closer if you want."

"Yeah, please. Thanks a lot, Dan. I owe you."

I spent that night at her place, still tense but Aimee seemed to accept that it was a sex thing. She played the submissive, figuring I needed reassurance that I was in charge, but all it did was make me wary. Too wary to concentrate.

"That's the first time this has happened."

"Yeah, well, sometimes the spirit is willing but the flesh is weak."

"Well, we don't want to wear it out, do we? Want to try again later?"

I said yes, meant no, but we did, and this time she swept away all my reservations in a flood of ecstasy.

The following Saturday things took a scary turn. Saturday Aimee tried to kill me.

Her Volkswagen was in the shop. Bad fuel pump was the major complaint, and the parts had to be ordered. We had a picnic lunch at Roger Williams Park, went to an open air concert, then made love daringly just off one of the main footpaths. The danger of discovery added an extra thrill and it was one of the best times we'd had yet.

It was hot and we dozed for a while, then collected our senses and our scattered clothing and walked back to the car.

"Damn! I can't find my wallet."

Aimee was poking around in her purse, lips thin with annoyance.

"Well, I keep telling you not to tuck it in the side pocket. Forget pickpockets, the damn thing could fall out if you swung your arm the right way."

"Yes, master." We'd used that phrase the night before and it had been infinitely sexy. Right now it was laden with sarcasm.

"Okay, I'm insensitive, inconsiderate and I'm also sorry. When was the last time you saw it?"

Back at our trysting place, of course, a good ten minute walk away. I'd make better time without her.

"Look, take the car keys and go start the engine, and the air conditioner. I'll be back as soon as I can."

Despite the heat, I half walked, half jogged back along the roadway, cut past the Temple of Music, and entered the maze of footpaths on the far side. Fortunately I remembered our route quite well, and even more fortunately I found Aimee's wallet almost immediately.

Then something hit me on the side of the head.

It hurt like hell and I staggered away, one arm instinctively raised. The second blow caught me on the elbow and numbed the arm from wrist to shoulder. I staggered a few steps before turning to face my attacker.

Aimee had one hand raised, a fist sized stone cupped in the palm.

"I keep telling you and telling you to leave me alone but you don't listen!" Her face was a caricature of fury, chin wet with spittle, eyes hard and bright, lips curled back from her teeth. She was wearing the same cutoff jeans and white tee shirt I'd seen her put on that morning. The corner of one hip pocket was slightly torn.

"Put the rock down, Aimee." My voice shook. I was scared, scared shitless. Her face said she could kill me, and then her voice said the same thing.

"You touch me again, you come near me again, you even look in my direction one more time and I'll tear your fucking heart out, you understand?"

"Sure, kid, sure." I retreated slowly, my good arm ready to fend her off, the numb one pressed against my side. "Anything you say."

"Don't patronize me, you goddamned asshole!" And with that she swung the rock in the general direction of my nose.

I'm a pretty big guy, one eighty, solid. I don't work out regularly but I lead an active life, and like I said, Aimee wasn't much more than half my size. Even so, she almost scored a home run. The rough edge of the stone slid past my cheek, close enough to draw blood. I grappled with her, twisted away from a kick aimed at my balls. Aimee hooked a leg behind my ankles and we both went over, but I half turned and managed to come down on top.

It knocked the wind right out of her. She was still gasping for air when I got back to my feet. There were speckles of blood on the front of her shirt, but it was my blood, from the scratches on my cheek.

She was crazy, I figured, split personality or something. And dangerous. I started to run.

It wasn't a jog this time. It was a headlong rush, fueled by absolute terror. What the Christ had I gotten myself into? All I could think about was getting back to the car, driving away, maybe calling the police. But could I call them? What would I say, that I was terrified by this minx of a girl? How much could I prove?

The car was where I'd parked it, and the engine was running. Aimee was sitting in the passenger seat, bare feet up on the dashboard, letting the cool air blow into her face. She smiled when she saw me and leaned across to open the driver's side door. She wasn't even breathing hard, but there were specks of dried blood on her shirt.

"Did you find my wallet?" she asked sweetly.

There was a message on my answering machine when I got back that night, so I called Dan Scofield. "What's up?" My voice sounded thin with strain.

"Found something. Might not mean anything, but you never know."

"Found something what?"

"Aimee Harrison's high school boyfriend was murdered during their senior year. Beaten to death with a shovel in his back yard."

"Do they know who did it?"

"Nope, never even had a hot lead."

"There's no way..." I licked my lips, tried again. "There's no way Aimee could be involved, is there?"

There was a long silence that said, "So that's the way it is", before he answered. "She didn't do it, if that's what you're wondering about. At the time of the murder, Miss Harrison was in Rhode Island Hospital recovering from a leg she broke falling off a horse in Lincoln Woods."

I let out a breath I hadn't realized I was holding. Relief? Or something else.

"Is that it?" I was ready to hang up.

"Not quite. You know she transferred from Amherst to BC?"

"Yeah, I remember you telling me that. She mentioned it too, some time back. Said her parents couldn't afford the tuition after they retired."

"Well, maybe. But it might have had something to do with Todd Grolier."

"Who's he?"

"Glad you asked that question. Todd Grolier was Miss Harrison's beau, or at least he thought so. Told a lot of people he was going to marry her. The lucky lady, according to reports, was less certain but didn't deny the possibility."

"So what happened to Mr. Grolier?"

"Another good question. Todd Grolier was found in his dorm room one morning with his throat cut and another portion of his anatomy...um...disconnected."

"And do we know who was responsible this time?"

"Nope, still unsolved. And the answer to your next question is, no, Miss Harrison could not have been responsible, not personally anyway. She was in the hospital again."

"Another broken leg?"

"No, a heart attack. Her father's. She flew to Pensacola the day before her boyfriend got croaked and didn't come back until the day of the funeral."

I felt less than reassured.

Later that night, I thought I had it all figured out. The sensible, movie plot answer was an unsuspected twin sister, stalking her sister's lovers, perhaps out of jealousy for a life she might have had and lost. That was so much bullshit. Sure, that would explain how Aimee managed to be in two places at the same time. But it wouldn't explain the identically torn pocket, the scratches I'd seen on her naked breast, or the spots of my own blood sprinkled across her shirt.

Did you ever hear of doppelgangers? They're a kind of evil twin, myth stuff, or at least that's what I used to think. Not anymore. It took a while to convince myself because I've never believed in UFO's or ghosts or any of that crap, but I mean, how can you deny something when it sticks itself right in your face? And maybe babies weren't the only way sex could lead to the creation of a new life.

So Aimee had this doppelganger, and if I kept seeing her, it was going to kill me. I liked Aimee a lot, but I liked living even better.

"Tomorrow," I told myself. "Tomorrow I call and break it off."

But that was too late. A couple of hours later, I killed Aimee Harrison. Sort of.

No, I'm not confessing to a murder. Not exactly. There has to be a human victim, right, and besides, it was self defense. I took a shower and was on my way to bed when she came at me from the kitchen, brandishing my biggest carving knife. If she hadn't stumbled on a throw rug she might have gotten me too. I was so stunned, I don't know if I could have done anything to save myself.

But when she staggered and fell against the wall, I saw my chance. Two quick steps and a kick, just like I'd learned in my brief stint as a karate enthusiast. Designed to dislocate a kneecap and bring her down. It did too, but she tried to lunge forward and disembowel me as she fell. I danced back and she fell on the knife, drove that big blade right through the bottom of her jaw and up into the skull cavity.

There was a hell of a lot of blood, but she stopped moving right away.

I must've stood there for a while, can't really remember. All I could think of was that Aimee was dead. If I killed her evil twin, the original would die too. Isn't that the way it's supposed to happen?

The telephone brought me back to myself. It was Aimee.

"I just woke up and I feel terrible, all sick inside and a headache like you wouldn't believe. Anyway, I guess I was dreaming about you because I was convinced you were in some terrible trouble so I just had to call."

"I'm all right." My voice sounded small and far away. "Just tired. I'll call you...tomorrow some time."

When I went back to the hall, the body was gone. All the blood too. Just my knife, next to the crumpled rug.

Aimee and I dated a little less often for a few weeks after that. I kept waiting for the doppelganger to come back, but I guess it was good and dead because nothing ever happened. At Christmas we flew to Florida to spend the holidays with her parents, who treated me like a teenager and refused to take our relationship seriously. We even had separate bedrooms and had to sneak off to a motel a couple of times even though she'd given up her apartment and moved in with me back in Rhode Island.

We never made any explicit plans, but by the spring our friends were asking if we were going to set a date, and one night I asked Aimee to marry me and she said yes. We decided on a June wedding.

That should have been it. Monster vanquished, hero and

heroine live happily ever after. But around the middle of April, Aimee started acting strangely.

For one thing, her moods kept changing unexpectedly. We'd go off to work with big plans for the evening, and when I got home she'd be sulking in her room and refuse to speak to me. Other times she'd break into tears for no good reason, or accuse me of hating her, spying on her, persecuting her. I dismissed some of this as nervousness; hell, I wasn't too easy with the idea of marriage myself. I'd been on my own for ten years and didn't relish putting myself in someone else's power.

But then she started accusing me of saying and doing things that I hadn't done, calling her at work, threatening her. If the doppelganger was the result of some really weird kind of schizophrenia, what might sudden paranoia lead to?

So last night I came home late, really late. I'd been out drinking, trying to get some courage out of the bottle I guess. See, I'd decided this wasn't going to work. We just weren't good for each other. I wanted to break it off, as friends if possible, and I was going to let her stay at the house for as long as it took to find another place.

The house was quiet when I got home, but Aimee always went to bed early. The light was flashing on the answering machine, so I punched the button and went out to the kitchen to make myself a bicarbonate.

It was a man's voice, full of anger and hatred, and the call was meant for Aimee. He called her a lot of things, filthy things, and threatened to kill her. I left the glass of water on the counter and walked back to the living room, shaking with dread. I couldn't place the voice, but it seemed vaguely familiar, and I believe you when you say it was my voice even though I know damned well I never made that call.

Aimee was in the bedroom, lying half on the bed, half on the floor. She'd been strangled and then someone had used one of my quartz bookends to cave in her skull. Several times. And no, I didn't touch the body or anything in the room, even though you say you've found some of her blood on my shirt.

But I didn't kill her, didn't touch her, didn't go beyond the threshold of the door. I just stood there, listening to the last few words of the recorded message.

"I warned you and warned you but you just wouldn't leave

me alone!"

PEEPER

When Artie saw the young woman standing on the opposite side of the counter, he knew he'd be using the last of his writable dvds.

"Can I help you?" He let the curtain swing back into place, concealing his living quarters from what passed for a lobby.

She glanced up, then away, not meeting his eyes for more than an instant. Probably in her mid-twenties, he judged, a trifle short but a real looker. "I'd like to rent one of your cabins."

Artie nodded, smiled in what he hoped was a friendly but not too familiar fashion. It wouldn't do to let this one get away; she was nearly perfect, straw colored hair cut to shoulder length, face a trifle babyish but with a clear complexion. He preferred them a bit taller and the pleated blouse concealed the stars of the show, but he was confident she would not disappoint.

"We do have one vacancy as a matter of fact. Just had a cancellation called in this morning." Which was not true; Artie almost always held Cabin One for what he thought of as his Special Guests.

"How much would that be?" She was already opening her shoulderbag.

"Well, I usually get fifty dollars per night," he started, but when he saw her eyes grow wary, he hurried on, "but I can shave that down some if you're staying longer."

Her bag remained open, one hand inside. "I was really planning to look for a place further north tomorrow, over the New Hampshire line somewhere."

Artie shook his head slowly. "You're not going to have much luck this time of year, Miss. Foliage peaks the next couple of weeks, you know. Normally I'm booked solid by now, but I had that cancellation. Makes no difference to me," although it did, "but if I was you, I'd stay here and take day trips to wherever it is you want to go."

Her eyes had grown thoughtful, but she wasn't convinced. Artie felt he had the hook in her mouth, all he had to do was jerk the line a bit. "Listen, frankly, Cabin One could use a little work. Business has been so good, I haven't wanted to shut it down and

make the repairs." He raised a hand to divert her question. "Nothing
major, believe me. You can check it out first if you want. The
bathroom fan's kind of noisy," it was best to establish that fact early,
"and the paint's peeling off the ceiling in a couple of places. It's the
smallest of the cabins, too; I blocked off part of the back to store
tools and stuff in. I tell you what; you stay a full week, two hundred
fifty. Less than that, we work out something in between." He
struggled not to sound too anxious.

The seconds stretched before she nodded and produced a
wallet. "I'll take it for tonight, anyway, and if it works out, I'll stay
the week. Do you take Master Charge?"

The card identified her as Debby Goldman of Derby.
Connecticut.

"Here you go, Miss Goldman." Artie opened the door and
allowed her to enter first. Although he'd offered to carry her bag,
she'd politely refused. He followed, flicked on the cabin lights. The
sun was just beginning to dip toward the horizon, but already long
shadows from the pine trees scattered among the cabins had imposed
a counterfeit dusk. The large front room boasted a small but
complete kitchen to the left, a table and four chairs to the right.

"It's a propane stove. If you run out, give a yell and I'll patch
in a new tank. Bedroom and bath are through here."

He led her into the bedroom, fitted with a double bunk bed
and a small bureau. The ceiling was heavily stained and some of the
paint had fallen away. "Water damage," he explained. "The roof
leaked some last year. I fixed it up so it won't happen again, but
never got around to repainting. I can take care of it someday while
you're out, if it bothers you any."

"No, that's all right." She sounded uncertain, and he turned,
but she immediately looked away. A shy one, he realized.
Sometimes that was good, other times it wasn't.

"Bathroom's through here." He brushed past and hit the
switch he had rewired, turning on the lights and the overhead fan. A
ragged vibration grew as the fan came up to speed, then settled into a
steady but obvious hum. "It's out of kilter, but the screws have
rusted in place and it's going to be a bitch to fix. I'll have to get up
there pretty soon though."

"That's all right; I just won't turn it on."

Artie shook his head. "Can't do that unless you want to stay in the dark," he explained. "Lights and fan are on the same switch. It was that way when I bought the place; I don't know why." Which was doubly a lie.

"Isn't it awfully bright?"

Artie shrugged. "It used to be bigger, but I cut off the back end when I put in the storeroom. That's it just the other side of this wall." He rapped his knuckles against the mirror that faced the sink and shower beyond. "I don't use it often, but if you hear something moving out there, it's just me rummaging around for light bulbs, toilet paper, or something."

"I suppose it's okay." She was either genuinely uncertain or wanted leverage to negotiate the price. She needn't have bothered; if there had been a practical way to offer the cabin at no charge to keep her there, Artie would have agreed without hesitation. "I'll let you know tomorrow morning if I decide to stay longer."

"No problem, and we'll adjust tonight to the lower rate if you stay on." He turned the bathroom light off and followed her out to the front room. "Here's your key; if there's anything you need, I live in the main cottage there, and I leave the front door unlocked. Just ring the bell on the counter."

"I'll be fine, thanks."

Outside, Artie moved quickly back to the main building, rounded the counter and disappeared into his private quarters. He slept in the first room, a tiny cubicle now that he'd moved the interior walls, making space for the workroom, his secret retreat. Fumbling with the chain that held the key suspended against his chest, he unlocked the door and slipped inside.

The far end of the windowless room was dominated by a big screen television set, on top of which sat a VCR. To the right, a bench stood covered with electronic equipment, two more recorders wired in tandem, a tape splicer, a collection of small tools, and some empty fast food containers. The left wall was concealed by floor to ceiling shelving, the resting place of Artie's collection of video tapes. A few of these he had purchased, but most were ones he had recorded, each neatly labeled, all female names, arranged alphabetically.

Remaining only long enough to grab an unopened blank tape from the bench and slip it inside a paper bag, Artie carefully

relocked the door. Outside, he forced himself to walk calmly to the
storage room. The key unlocked this door as well, and Artie stepped
inside, reached up to yank the pull chain of an overhead light before
closing and locking the door behind him.

Superficially, the storeroom was exactly as he had described
it. He bought toilet paper and light bulbs in bulk, and cartons of
each were piled up in one corner. Most of his tools were here as
well, a few cans of paint, extra shingles, glass bottles filled with
nails, pillows and other bed clothing, and so forth. Artie selected a
few supplies to carry back with him, just to provide an air of
legitimacy to the trip, and placed them in front of the door, so that he
wouldn't forget them. Then he turned to the real purpose of his visit.

A large pine wardrobe stood flush against the inner wall.
Artie opened the door, then carefully moved the linens stacked
within to reveal the rear end of the very expensive video camera he'd
installed four years previously. The lens of the camera was cradled
in the circle he'd cut from the rear of the wardrobe, held firmly
against the piece of one-way glass in the bathroom of Cabin One.

He slipped a virgin disc into the console.

Sitting in his room several hours later, Artie felt the familiar
frustrated impatience that plagued him whenever one of his Special
Guests was in residence. The camera was rigged to start recording
whenever the bathroom light was on, its own small operating sounds
completely masked by the noisy fan. Much of the footage he
acquired in this fashion was unusable, since many people drew the
shower curtain while bathing. He had recorded countless hours of
primping, tooth brushing, hair combing, and similar private, but
uninteresting activities, in order to acquire the occasional prize.

Sometimes there were surprises. Earlier this year, he'd taped two
women doing lines of coke, apparently choosing the bathroom since
it was only part of the cabin which had no windows.

Artie rose and crossed to the window, staring through the
darkness toward Cabin One. The lights were on but the blinds were
closed.   "Come on, Debby," he whispered into the darkness.
"You've been sitting in your car all day. A shower would be real
nice, wouldn't it?" He wished it were warmer. During the summer,
people took a lot more showers, and they didn't rush to get dressed
afterwards either.

Artie rarely rented Cabin One to anyone but unaccompanied females, although sometimes if the wife was good looking enough, he'd let a couple stay there. He had to be especially careful with those tapes, though; half the time it'd be the guy who showed up, and Artie erased those scenes right away. It would be bad enough to be caught with this stuff, but for anyone to think he was queer as well would be humiliating. Once he'd caught a couple screwing in the shower, standing up, with the goddamn curtain open and everything, but even though it was a real good sequence, he erased it. Just in case anyone might think it was the guy he was watching. There'd been some lesbian stuff a couple of times, and that was okay, he supposed.

A shadow moved behind the cabin window, left to right, and a few minutes later the lights went out.

Artie woke as the first threads of sunlight filtered in through the pine canopy. He showered quickly, in the murky half light of early morning, his own nakedness an unpleasant but unavoidable necessity, then dressed for the day before putting on the morning's pot of coffee. Half a box of not quite stale donuts would do for breakfast. He'd bought them in Managansett center three days earlier.

When Debby Goldman emerged from her cabin nearly two hours later, Artie was conveniently nearby, collecting fallen pine cones quite unnecessarily in a bushel basket.

"Good morning," he greeted her cheerfully, carefully keeping his eyes away from the considerably tighter halter top she was wearing today. "Did you decide whether or not you'll be staying on?" It wouldn't do to sound too eager, but the thought of having her leave before he'd gotten a good tape was unbearable.

"I want to check on some things first but I'll let you know by lunchtime if that's all right."

"Sure." He waved one hand deprecatingly. "Take your time. Just stop by the office and let me know."

She even smiled as she slid into the driver's seat, but what really thrilled Artie was the expanse of tanned thigh visible as her short skirt rode up on one hip.

The car had barely pulled out onto the main road before Artie was cursing the trembling that interfered with his efforts to unlock the storeroom door.

It was at once a promising and a frustrating tape.

Artie had spent a great deal of time adjusting the camera to get just the right angle. The field of view included most of the shower stall, particularly the end furthest from the showerhead itself, where most people entered and exited. The sink was just visible at the left, so that anyone standing in front of it would show up as well. The toilet was off screen; Artie was a fastidious pervert, not interested in the dirty stuff.

The first time Debby had entered, she had moved immediately out of his field of vision. Artie recorded the counter readings so that he'd know where to cut out the extraneous stuff with his editing oftware. She left the light on when she returned to the front room, so Artie fast forwarded. Then she returned, without her blouse but still wearing a bra, to remove her contact lenses and place them in a container beside the sink. The angle was poor, but Artie was pleased to see that her figure was as good as he'd hoped. This time she turned the light off when she left.

He had no way of judging how long an interval passed before the next sequence. She was wearing a fluffy pink bathrobe this time, barefoot, the hem of the robe just above her ankles. Her hair was slightly mussed, as though she'd been lying down. At first, Artie suspected it was a morning sequence, but she didn't have the puffy faced look that most people displayed upon waking.   She crossed to the right, just remaining visible as she reached up to take a bath towel from the shelf he had built above the toilet. She unfolded it, examining it critically for several seconds. It was white with dotted outlines suggesting pine trees.

"Don't worry, I washed the damned thing," he whispered.

With a small shrug, Debby turned and walked to the shower, the towel idly thrown over one shoulder. She reached inside the curtain, obviously adjusting the mix of hot and cold water; steam was visible at the edges of the curtain when she turned away.

With what appeared to be a single fluid movement, she dropped the towel onto the counter beside the sink, opened the shower curtain, let her robe slide from her shoulders and fall to the floor, and disappeared into the cubicle. Artie considered himself an authority of sorts on human behavior in the bathroom, and he immediately diagnosed Debby Goldman as inhibited and insecure.

The speed with which she had disrobed and concealed herself behind the curtain told him she was uneasy with her own nudity.

Fortunately, Artie could freeze each frame during playback. Unfortunately, even advancing the action frame by frame, he couldn't see much. There was a suggestion of one naked breast beneath a raised arm, obscured by a billow of steam and the blur lines of her movement. He was pleased at the implied modesty, although disappointed at the paucity of good material. The action returned to normal speed, and he waited to see if he'd fare better upon her emergence.

If anything, it was even more disappointing. One dripping arm and part of her face were visible around the edge of the curtain as she snared the towel. When she stepped out of the shower, it was wrapped around her body, tucked in tightly, and even the revealed length of tanned thigh and calf disappeared quickly as she donned her robe. With a passing glance in the mirror, she swept past and out of view.

There was nothing further of interest on the tape. If she had used the bathroom again this morning, she must have left the door open and relied on natural light.

Artie pressed rewind, then stood and walked nervously around the room. It was a nervous habit, but one he invariably indulged after each first viewing, as though the energy he had accumulated while waiting to see what his hidden camera had captured exceeded the catharsis of revelation. After several circuits of the room, his heart slowed to something like normal and he began to breathe normally.

When he played it again, he found a few brief shots he had apparently missed earlier. He hadn't noticed how tightly the slacks clung to her buttocks as she bent over the sink, or that she had unsnapped the back of her bra so that the cups shifted enticingly. The fleeting glance of a bare breast was more distinct than he remembered. Oddly enough, there was an even better profile shot as she entered the shower, her right breast quite clearly defined under a raised arm; he hadn't noticed it all the first time.

"You ought to watch out, Artie," he chided himself. "Next thing you'll be erasing good footage."

Thoughtfully, Artie left the disc in his computer and set off to make his rounds.

He had just finished changing the linen in Cabin Seven when Debby Goldman drove in. Artie walked over to her car with studied casualness.

"How'd it go?"

She was bent half forward, removing a nondescript package from the back seat, and Artie struggled to keep his eyes from tracing the outline of her bottom.

Straightening, the package clutched to her body, Debby gave him a half smile, this time making eye contact. "You were right; everything north of here is booked. If your offer is still open, I guess I'll be staying."

Artie struggled for the right degree of professional pleasure. "We'll be happy to have you, Miss, for as long as you'd like to stay."

"I'll be here through the end of the week anyway. Do you want my card again?"

He shook his head. "Don't worry about it; we'll take care of everything when you check out. You need anything, give me a yell."

Nodding, she turned away.

It was the middle of the afternoon before Artie caught up enough to return to his inner sanctum. He set an open can of beer down on the bench and selected the new file. Sitting down, he forced himself to take long calming breaths, then started the playback.

Debby crossed from left to right, then returned, crossed to the sink, removed her contact lenses, then exited left.

Artie hit pause, confused. It was the same sequence he had viewed that morning, the same sequence which had been archived behind a locked door throughout the day. Except that it wasn't.

When he had watched this morning, Debby had been wearing slacks. This time, as she crossed to use the toilet, she had been wearing bra and panties only. It wasn't something he could have missed; that was exactly the sort of detail on which he concentrated. And hadn't she left the room once before returning to remove her contacts?

Something was very wrong.

Sweat prickled on his skin despite the relative coolness of the day. Artie picked up his beer and finished it, to give his mind a temporary focus. His racing thoughts slowed toward an uneasy equilibrium.

"You son of a bitch," he whispered. "You're losing it, man. Either you're crazy now or you were crazy this morning." With slow, deliberate movements, he replayed the file. It had changed slightly once again.

"Son of a bitch!" Artie wanted another beer, but he was afraid his legs wouldn't support him. Instead, he unpaused the file and let it play further.

Debby returned for her shower as she had earlier, the fluffy pink robe covering her from knee to throat. She examined the towel critically before shrugging and tossing it over her shoulder, then bent to adjust the water temperature. When it was to her liking, she moved to the opposite end of the tub, dropped the towel onto the counter, let the robe slide to the floor, and stepped behind the shower curtain.

The profile shot of a single breast was still excellent, and despite his growing anxiety, Artie could not resist freezing the picture. He hadn't noticed earlier that she had turned her head, glancing back into the empty bathroom, an amused expression etched across her face.

Upon emerging, she fumbled briefly for the towel before wrapping it around herself and leaving the room. During the fumble, she revealed some quite interesting portions of her anatomy, some of the best footage on the tape. Under ordinary circumstances, Artie would have been delighted. There was only one problem. He was absolutely certainly nothing remotely like those images had existed when he'd viewed the recording earlier in the day.

He closed the file with a sudden rush of revulsion. There was a cold fire burning in his gut and thoughts were racing around so quickly he couldn't grab hold of a single one. Was he losing his mind? Hallucinating? Some weird kind of amnesia?

Or could someone have sneaked in and altered the recording? Perhaps while he was out fixing up the vacant cabin. But why would someone do such a thing, and how?

As a counterfeit calm took hold, Artie retrieved a second beer from the kitchen. It might be a conspiracy, he thought. Despite all his precautions, someone had learned of the camera in Cabin One. They had enlisted Debby Goldman, if that was her real name, in a plot to embarrass him, for purposes yet to be revealed. Blackmail?

"All right, you bastards!" He sat down and restarted the recording. Fear of exposure was slowly turning to a purging sense of rage.

Debby used the toilet, then crossed to the sink and removed her contacts, then threw her shoulders back and stared into the mirror, examining her face and torso critically. She used both hands to raise her naked breasts slightly, as though displeased with their almost imperceptible sag. Apparently satisfied, she turned and left the room. She hadn't been wearing a bra.

The rest was unchanged except that this time she left the shower curtain partially open, providing tantalizing but unsatisfactory glimpses.

Artie finished the second beer before rising. Either he was losing his mind or something infinitely strange and frightening was happening. The beer proved an inadequate anaesthetic, and he retrieved a half empty bottle of brandy from his bedroom, not even locking the door this time. After all, what was the use?

He replayed the recording repeatedly while the sun faltered and failed for the day. On each pass, there were subtle change, the cumulative effects becoming more and more erotic. Under ordinary circumstances, Artie would have been moved to a state of very extreme excitement, but the dulling effect of the brandy and the utter impossibility of what he was seeing numbed more than his mind.

When Artie finally fell asleep, or passed out, Debby was unclothed throughout the tape. She showered without closing the curtain, toweled herself dry facing the camera, and masturbated before leaving the room.

He woke to nearly complete darkness. The computer screen showed only his desktop. His mouth tasted sour and his stomach made gassy sounds of displeasure. Initially, he couldn't remember the previous evening's discovery.

Recollection came with a rush. "Bullshit," he mumbled, then groaned as a spike of pain lanced through the top of his head. He stared at the screen, half convinced he had dreamed the entire incident, his mind affected by the alcohol. It would be a simple matter to resolve, of course; all he had to do was play the tape again.

His body refused to move.

"Bullshit!" he repeated, more determinedly this time. Overcoming his lethargy, Artie selected the file and clicked on the play icon.

Static flickered across the screen, then was replaced by the familiar interior of Cabin One's bathroom. A completely naked figure passed from left to right, was off screen briefly, then returned, crossed to the sink to stare into the mirror briefly before exiting to the left. The picture jumped, then resumed, with the same person entering again, still unclothed, choosing a towel. After turning on both faucets and adjusting the mix, the figure swept back the curtain, set the towel aside, and took a protracted, languorous shower. Later, the damp towel discarded, the subject of the film masturbated in front of the mirror.

It was an almost exact replay of the last version Artie had watched. Almost. The one slight deviation was that on this occasion, the subject of the clandestine film was not Debby Goldman. In fact, it was a man.

Ordinarily, Artie would have stopped the tape immediately. The idea of watching a naked man under any circumstances made Artie uneasy, and in this context it would ordinarily have filled him with a panicky revulsion bordering on nausea. But there was one other matter to be considered.

The naked man was Artie himself.

It was, of course, impossible. Uneasy with his own nakedness, Artie bathed infrequently, always late at night, with only a dim light to dispel the darkness. He had never showered in Cabin One, would not have performed as the recording indicated in any case, and his masturbations, though frequent, were always hurried and clandestine, concealed almost from himself.

The irrefutable evidence seemed to mock him.

He turned off the computer, staggering slightly. When he felt reasonably steady, he turned, walked through the front room, swept aside the curtain, strode around the counter, and out through the screen door into the cool night air.

Darkness engulfed the grounds, the night sky obscured by a cloud front which concealed all evidence of moon and stars. The thick pine scent was cloyingly sweet and Artie's stomach churned anew. He shook off a wave of lightheadedness and glanced toward Cabin One.

There was a light on in the front room.

Unsteadily, almost unwillingly, Artie weaved his way across to the front door, raised one fist and knocked.

There was no answer.

"Fuck it." He fumbled in his pocket and withdrew the master key, let himself into Cabin One.

Everything was quiet inside.

There was no indication that the cabin was tenanted. The bedroom light was off, the table was bare and clean, none of Debby's personal possessions were in sight. Caution penetrated Artie's alcoholic fog and he called out hoarsely.

"Miss Goldman, are you there? I...I heard a funny noise and I thought there might be some trouble."

There was no reply.

Artie let the door bang shut as he stepped deeper into the room. "It's me. Artie, from the office. Is everything okay here?"

He remembered now that he hadn't noticed her car parked out front. Could she have moved out after all, without telling him? Emboldened, he crossed the room, hesitated at the door to the bedroom before reaching in and turning on the light.

It was unoccupied, the two bunks neatly made, closet door standing open, empty. There was no indication that Debby Goldman was staying here, or had ever existed.

Somehow her absence staggered him anew and he stumbled across the room, allowing himself to drop to a seat on the lower bunk. Had he imagined the entire thing from start to end? Did the recording really exist of did its images exist only within his failing mind? Or had he been drugged into performing those obscene acts for some mysterious purpose?

Artie shook his head, immediately regretted the act. A wave of soporific numbness robbed the last of his strength. With a low noise that might almost have been a sob, he lay back on the bed, closed his eyes, and let the darkness become all.

It was full morning when he stirred, diffuse sunlight piercing two small windows. He was displeased to discover that he had fallen asleep fully dressed, and discarded the sweat soaked garments immediately, letting them fall to the floor.

Artie strode naked into the bathroom, noting once again the annoyingly ragged vibration from the fan. While urinating, he realized he had never removed his contacts the previous evening. He did so now and set them down beside the sink before returning to the bedroom and setting out the clothes he planned to wear.

Returning to the bathroom, he selected a towel from the shelf over the toilet, opened it for inspection. The last time he'd rented a cabin, he'd found ants in the linens, and had made a point of checking ever since. After adjusting the water temperature, he opened the shower curtain and stepped inside. Mild claustrophobia had bothered him since childhood, so he left the curtain partway open, enough that he could watch his own image soap and rinse in the full length mirror on the far wall. He had never watched himself like that before and found the image oddly stimulating.

He masturbated into the towel before leaving the bathroom.

With his luggage loaded into the trunk, Artie went to the small office. Debby Goldman was seated behind the counter, looked up from her reading as he entered. She smiled with the same odd expression he had noticed while checking in, a knowing look, as though she could pierce every material or metaphysical armor to skewer his inner being. It made him distinctly uncomfortable, in a frustratingly indescribable fashion.

"Checking out, Mr. Rossiter?"

"Yes, I think so." He dropped the key onto the counter. "What do I owe you? We never did settle the price for the second night."

"Nothing," she shook her head. "Don't worry about it. It's been a pleasure having you."

Artie suppressed an illogical feeling of uneasiness that troubled him because it seemed to have no source. The woman had neither said nor done anything to elicit such a powerful aversion and she was actually quite good looking in an immature sort of way.

"Yes, well, I'll be going then."

As he was stepping through the door, she called after him. "Please come back again, Mr. Johnson. I'd be happy to hold Cabin One for you anytime."

He made no response.

Debby waited until her recent guest had pulled out of the driveway and into traffic before rising from her seat. It was time to review the file recorded by her clandestine camera and see what was to be seen. Artie Rossiter looked good enough in his clothing that she was anxious to see what lay underneath.

A PERFECT LUST

"Do you believe in true love, Alan?"

He glanced up from his meal. Lori was doing the fawn act again, eyes all soft and glowing. "No," he snapped irritably. "There's what, six billion people in the world? What're the chances of any one individual finding his or her perfect lover?"

"Well, maybe things are, you know, arranged so that we get a chance to meet them, but it's up to us to recognize perfect love when it happens."

"That kind of nonsense only happens in your romance novels, Lori." He caught the waiter's eye, silently demanded the check. The purpose of this meal was to get himself laid, not intellectually stimulated.

Alan Cramer didn't believe in perfect love, but it wouldn't be long before he believed in perfect lust.

Lori dressed and left his apartment without showering, perhaps sensing his lack of interest even as the last convulsions died away and he sank limply on top of her. He was pretty sure her orgasm had been faked. It didn't bother him that he hadn't adequately satisfied Lori's passions; most of the essentials of sex take place in the head, he believed. The body was just the tool for externalizing them. If she'd failed to get off, it was because of a deficiency in her imagination, not any lack of performance on his part.

He showered after she was gone, toweled himself dry, not surprised to discover he was already partially erect again. It was still early, just after nine. He ran his eyes down the shelf full of videotapes beside his bed, trying to decide which fantasy to feed tonight. He imagined himself fondling Jennifer Connelly's breasts, or lying with Jennifer Aniston's long tanned legs wrapped around his body, or doing Sandra Bulllock doggie style, or getting a blow job from Winona Ryder.

His staff stayed at half mast, as he'd known it would. Lately there was only one actress who turned him on, Jamie Daniels, just right at five foot six, one hundred twenty five pounds, with shoulder length silky blonde hair, an ample but not grotesque bust, and long, slender legs that were just as sexy in a pair of blue jeans as they were uncovered.

He had dvds of everything she'd ever been in, starting with her brief appearance in the low budget horror film, *Chopped Liver*. That had won her a good supporting part in *Rogue Moon*, and from there she'd leaped into prominence, playing against Matt Damon in Stephen King's *Finders Keepers*, and Kevin Kline in the psychothriller, *Deadly Designs*, for which she'd received an Oscar nomination.

Alan's only regret was that she had never done a nude scene, though she'd come close a couple of times. The brief chest shot in *Chopped Liver* was a body double and her striptease in *Dark Design* stopped at PG-13. He ran his finger along the shelf of movies until it reached the slasher film, two copies, one never opened. He'd only bought the second because it was a reissue, with a good shot of her face on the cover that hadn't been part of the original packaging, an attempt to capitalize on her later success. He peeled the cellophane back with a fingernail, held the box up close to his eyes. His bow quivered.

"All right, Jamie, it's you and me again tonight." He slipped disc into the player, powered up the television, and carried the remote back to the bed. *Chopped Liver* was an unimaginative horror film, a small town butcher disposing of his victims as specials of the day, with ample footage of nude teens boffing one another. Alan liked it only because Daniels never again was cast as the complete innocent, and he found that image incredibly appealing. She appeared toward the middle of the film, the shy cheerleader who finally got up the nerve to sleep with the captain of the football team but ended up as virgin hamburger. Alan used the fast forward button to skip all the dull parts, then let it slip back to normal play as the first of her two scenes approached.

He knew the dialogue word for word, the boyfriend pledging his love, Daniels tempted by his flattery, but uneasy about "going all the way". The jock pretended to be hurt, made a great show of surrendering to her wishes, and that counterfeit vulnerability pushed her over the edge. The scene ended with her unbuttoning her blouse.

Alan used fast forward to skim through the strangling of another teen and the impalement of his girlfriend, then slowed for the last bit he was interested in.

There. Daniels was in the bathroom, dressed in just her bra and panties, examining herself nervously in the mirror. Past her shoulder, the jock was just visible sitting on the edge of the bed, and a dark shadow wrapped a cord around his neck and pulled him out of sight. She heard a noise, turned and called his name, hesitated, then moved tentatively forward, her face alternating between a smile and a frown. Was he teasing her or had something happened?

At this point, two arms were thrust into sight from off camera, catching her by the upper arms, dragging her through the doorway and tossing her onto the bed. The rest of the scene was shot from the killer's point of view as he strangled his latest victim. Then the breast shot, the body double here, as Darwin the Butcher prepared to cut a few choice steaks.

That's what was supposed to happen.

But instead she turned back to the mirror. Daniels tentatively reached up and slipped one bar strap off her shoulder, then the other, holding her arms raised to cover her bosom, then lowering them just enough to reveal the top halves of her breasts. Alan sat up abruptly, stunned, and grimaced at the pain of his sudden full erection. "What the hell?"

There was a muffled sound from off camera and she hastily rearranged her bra. The scene then resumed its usual course. With a shaking hand, Alan pressed the stop button, then climbed out of bed and picked up the discarded box.

There it was, in very small letters, right at the bottom. "Director's Cut: Five full minutes restored to the commercial version for this release including previously unseen footage of Jamie Daniels." Only a few seconds mattered to Alan, this one wonderfully extended scene.

He replayed that four minute segment of the tape a dozen times, feeling himself growing harder with each reprise, so hard that it felt like all the blood in his body had rushed to that one spot, leaving him so lightheaded that he thought he'd faint. And then his back arched in a series of spasms so intense that he might have worried about hurting himself, had there been any portion of his consciousness left over to consider that possibility.

Alan had no idea how much time passed before he was aware of the world again. *Chopped Liver* had ended and the screen was blank, so it must have been at least half an hour. He struggled to sit up, still woozy, his skin stinging where the semen had dried in streaks. There were stains on the bedclothes as well, quite a wide spray in fact.

Naked, he staggered to the bathroom, steadied himself with one arm on the doorjamb, then continued forward, swept the shower curtain back.

There was a woman lying in the bottom of his bathtub. No, not just a woman. The woman. It was Jamie Daniels.

Alan sat down on the toilet bowl, stunned, convinced that he was hallucinating, that in a few seconds his vision would clear and he'd be alone, staring at a suggestive stain or an odd arrangement of shadows.

She didn't go away. In fact, she moaned softly and began to move.

Suddenly aware of his nakedness, Alan hastily retreated to the bedroom, threw on the first pair of pants that came to hand, not even bothering with underwear, then a pullover shirt from his top drawer. Drawing a deep breath, he moved back to the bathroom, stuck his head cautiously inside.

"Hello?"

There was a rustle from the tub, then an answer. "Who are you? What am I doing here?"

It was her voice, all right; that thready undertone was unmistakable.

"Umm, my name is Alan, Alan Cramer. This is my apartment, Miss Daniels. Would you like to...come out of there and sit down?"

She stayed where she was. "This is a kidnapping, isn't it?" Now her voice sounded frightened.

"No, nothing like that. Actually I'm not sure just what happened. I'm as surprised as you are."

"Really?" It was half query, half sarcasm. "I can go then?"

"Sure, any time you want. The door's not locked, not from this side."

"Would you mind...standing away from the door?"

He thought about it, nodded pointlessly, then answered. "Right. I'm just going to go sit on my bed until you're gone."

Seated, he waited while at least two full minutes passed. "It's all right, Miss Daniels. You can come out."

She did so this time, craning her head to locate him first, then moving directly past him to the hallway. She hesitated there. "I can really go? This isn't some kind of trick?"

"Believe me, I'm just as confused about this as you are."

Her eyes didn't believe him, and she disappeared into the hall. Alan waited a few seconds, heard the door open, but it didn't close. Another minute passed. Had she run out and left it open?

But she hadn't. When he reached the front room, she was standing on the threshold, her face distraught.

"What's wrong?"

"I can't leave."

He shook his head. "I don't understand. Why not?"

She shivered and dropped her eyes. "I don't know. I just...can't."

They were sitting in his kitchenette drinking coffee. "You're not at all what I expected."

Jamie had recovered most of her composure while he brewed the coffee, but he noticed that she still watched him warily. "What were you expecting?"

"I don't know, exactly. I mean, I know the parts you play in movies aren't really you, but you don't give interviews or anything, so I never had any idea what you're really like. I mean, you're incredibly shy in *Chopped Liver* when that guy propositions you, but I believed in the character, and I'm having trouble reconciling it with the way you're acting now."

Daniels dropped her eyes and folded her hands in front of her. "I'm just not ready to grow up right now."

Alan blinked. It was a direct line from the film, delivered with absolute loyalty to the original. He studied her face, realized she was much younger than he had thought. Too young, in fact. In an eye blink, she's shed ten years. Even her clothing was different.

"What the Fuck?"

She winced, turned away. "Do you have to swear like that?"

Alan shook his head. Another line from the movie. This was getting freaky. Was this all an hallucination? Was he sitting here talking to himself? If so, it was the greatest daydream of his life, because he was already coming back to life under the table, erect again even though he was still sore from his last ejaculation.

She was crying softly now and he rose, moved to her side, let her press the side of her head against his hip. Daniels sobbed softly and he shifted position slightly, so that her mouth was only inches away from his tented jeans.

"Would you just...hold me for a while?"

"Sure, Jamie. Anything you want." And he did hold her for a while, and then he carried her into the bedroom and discovered two things. First, that her figure was every bit as good as he'd always imagined, and second, that she was still a virgin. Though not for long.

She was in the shower when he woke up in the morning, convinced that he'd died and gone to heaven. When she stuck her toweled head around the corner and told him she was going to bring him breakfast in bed, he leaned back with his arms above his head and wondered if he was completely insane or if something truly miraculous had just altered his life forever.

There was sizzling in the kitchen, reminding him of the scene from *Rogue Moon* where Jamie seduced Hawks, as played by Ethan Hawke, performing an extremely sexy striptease that wasn't at all spoiled by the fact that it ended before the essentials were gone. Her aggressive character was everything that the diffident cheerleader was not, and Alan quite frankly couldn't decide which personality was more appealing.

"What can I get for you this morning?"

He blinked, disoriented. It was a line from *Rogue Moon*. Had he replayed it in his head? No, Daniels was standing in the doorway, staring directly at him. She seemed different today, not just attitude but physically more mature, her breasts stretching the material of the bathrobe she was wearing. And somehow she seemed to have redone her makeup.

He'd never seen her bathrobe before either, except in the movies. It was the one she'd worn for the striptease scene.

"What's on the menu?" His voice was uneven as he repeated Hawke's line.

"Let me show you the special of the day."

This time the film didn't stop when she reached back to unsnap her bra. In fact, it continued until he lay exhausted in a tangle of damp sheets, his swollen member so sore that he resolved to refrain from sex for at least a week.

He never had been very good with resolutions.

They were watching television together later that morning, still in his apartment. Jamie had made another effort to leave an hour earlier, but insisted that some invisible force prevented her from doing so. Alan walked out into the corridor and back, confirmed that if such a barrier actually existed, it did not apply to him, then returned and shut the door.

"I think I've gone crazy," he admitted openly. "But if so, I never want to be cured."

The news came on and Daniels went out to make them some lunch. Alan was wiped out, exhausted by his recent rapid-fire sexual adventures, and he sat stolidly, only half listening to the newscasters.

Until they mentioned her name.

"Jamie Daniels was reported missing from her Santa Barbara home this morning. Her publicist told reporters that Miss Daniels missed an appointment with her agent, and her housekeeper confirmed that the house was locked and empty this morning when she arrived. Miss Daniels' bed had not been slept in, but there were no overt indications of foul play."

Alan used the remote to mute the sound. Was it real then? Was it actually Jamie Daniels he had made love to last night, and who had made love to him in return this morning? But how had she gotten from Santa Barbara, California, to Managansett, Rhode Island?

Just what was going on here?

She'd cooked chili for lunch, although Alan had no idea where she'd found the ingredients. He ate most of his meals at the diner across the street from the apartment building, and most of his groceries consisted of coffee, crackers, cookies, and microwave rice dishes.

Everything went well until she offered him more coffee. He'd been preoccupied throughout the meal, running through the implications of this impossible situation, almost forgetting that she was there.

"More?" She was holding the steaming pot unsteadily.

"Sure," he answered absently, not really hearing, making no effort to push his cup closer. Jamie leaned awkwardly across the table, angling the pot to avoid the vase full of fresh flowers in the center of the table.

Fresh flowers? Alan frowned, memory stirred, but before he could make the connection, Jamie lost her grip, the pot tipped, and scalding hot water poured into his lap.

"Goddamnit!" He jumped to his feet, the chair toppling back with a clatter. Jamie cried out as well, and the half empty pot dropped from her hand, shattering on the tiled floor. More coffee splashed across Alan's bare feet and he danced back, praying that he wouldn't step on any of the broken pieces of glass.

"I'm so sorry." She sounded frightened as well, terrified in fact. Alan knew why; he remembered the scene clearly now, the audience's first hint that there was something seriously wrong between Rose and her abusive husband.

"God that hurts." He took a tentative step and the movement brought a fresh wave of pain so intense that he closed one hand into a fist and slammed it into the wall.

"It was my fault." Her voice was subdued, so self abasing that he felt a wave of anger. How could she stand herself this way, so spiritless, so clumsy. Clumsy? Alan shook his head, wondering where these thoughts were coming from.

"Damned right it was your fault," he admitted. "How many times have I told you to stop daydreaming and pay more attention to what's going on around you? Half the time you're reading those damned books of yours, and the other half you're imagining yourself living in them." Alan paused, astonished at the words coming out of his mouth, words that made no sense, words that were nevertheless familiar.

From the movie.

Jamie had retrieved a mop and was working on the mess, her entire body broadcasting submission. Alan knew it was unfair but at that moment, everything he'd found attractive about her in the past had the opposite effect. He was disgusted by her vulnerability, disappointed by the shape of her body, cloaked as it was in an ill-fitting, baggy sweatsuit, and infuriated by the way she turned her back on him while she mopped.

He slapped her across the bottom, hard enough to overbalance her. Jamie's head struck the side of the table as she fell to the floor, one hand coming down on the broken glass. A thin trickle of blood mixed with the coffee.

Alan was appalled with himself. He'd never struck a woman before, never even felt the temptation. But it had undeniably felt good, good enough that his scalded member was stirring once again. He kicked her then, hard enough to leave a good sized bruise, knocking her flat. She made no attempt to avoid him, just drew her arms and legs close to her body.

There was quite a bit more blood before he came to himself, saw what he'd done to her beautiful face, and staggered away, retching harshly. The front of his pants were stiff with dried coffee and semen.

"What the Christ is happening to me?" Alan lay on his bed, shaken, freshly showered but still feeling unclean. Had he really done that to Jamie out in the kitchen, had he actually blackened her eye, cut her lip, bloodied her nose? Was any of this real? Was he going to wake up soon to an empty apartment and an impossibly demanding boner?

"Are you feeling better?"

He looked up, saw Jamie standing slouched in the doorway, dress slit up to her waist, one long leg posed provocatively. Her face was gorgeous, untouched, self confident, the face she'd worn in *Deadly Designs*, her most recent film, the story of a tormented woman who killed the brother with whom she'd been incestuously involved, and who nearly killed Chris Hemsley's character when they became sexually intimate two years later.

"Are you all right?"

"I'm just fine, honey." She'd acquired a slight southern accent during the past few minutes, while she'd been shedding several serious injuries. "But I could be better."

"Yeah, I'm sure you could." He let his head fall back, too tired and confused to understand what was going on.

"Do you believe in perfect love, honey?" It was an echo of that long ago conversation with Lori, and he chuckled.

"No, do you?"

"Mmm, no. But I believe in perfect lust. I think you can

want someone so much, so powerfully, that it's a positive force that builds within you, and that force reaches out and touches the other person. Sex is power, you know, and sometimes it's magic."

She was coming closer to the bed, but Alan turned away, uninterested. It was another movie scene, clearly, but he couldn't remember exactly how it went. Jamie and Hemsley had three bedroom scenes together, after the third of which he was forced to kill her to save his own life. But he remembered that one distinctly, so he wouldn't be required to do anything violent right now. Which was just as well, because he felt so physically exhausted and emotionally drained, he doubted he could successfully swat a mosquito.

"Lust is like a chain," she was beside the bed now. He sensed rather than saw her there. "It makes the other person your slave. I want my freedom."

"You can have it as far as I'm concerned. Right now the idea of having sex with you is about as appealing as having my dick cut off."

"That could be arranged."

And that's when he realized that he wasn't playing Chris Hemsley's role. He was the brother Jamie killed to escape from their incestuous relationship, the brother she castrated and left to bleed to death in the bed they had frequently shared.

He opened his eyes then, saw what she held in an upraised hand, and realized he'd never see the closing credits.

REFLECTIONS

I was only a kid when all of this happened so my memories of Edwin Wallace are almost second hand. Edwin was a fervent man, a true believer; he spoke with God, and if they weren't exactly equals, well, Edwin figured he was at least close enough to be on a first name basis.

I've tried to remember when it was that I first became aware of Edwin's existence, but he was too much an integral part of life in Managansett to be experienced or described in any linear sense. You might as well ask me when I first noticed the moon overhead or the tree on the corner of our yard, the one that shaded out Ted Maxwell's garden until he pruned it one day without so much as a word to my father, which brought an end to our joint cookouts and my friendship with Billy Maxwell. My mother and Mrs. Maxwell stayed on good terms despite the feuding of their men folk, but they didn't visit each other anymore and after the first flush of outrage passed, I felt more a sense of loss than anything else.

We all feel righteous anger from time to time, I suppose, but we function better as human beings once we temper it with reason. Edwin Wallace, alas, was impervious to this moderating force.

Like I said, I can't tell you the first time I realized that he wasn't cast from the same mold as the rest of us, but I can give you an example. It was 1963 and I was ten, old enough to understand what was being reported in the newspapers and on the television news, young enough that it seemed too distant and abstract to concern me. At least that was the case until the local library purchased a copy of Henry Miller's *Tropic of Cancer*.

Grace Mitchell was head librarian at the time. My mother had taught me to read before I started first grade and I'd exhausted the tiny school library very quickly. In retrospect, the children's room at the Managansett Public Library was probably one of the best in the state, but I was already reading on an adult level by third grade and it had little to offer me. Mrs. Mitchell rarely smiled and wore her hair pulled back so severely that it looked like the skin of her face was being drawn taut, and I was more than a little frightened of her. She and the library seemed indivisible, and on the rare occasions during which I saw her outside its walls, I always felt a hint of disorientation.

One Saturday morning, I was so desperate that I decided I could probably stand to read *The Wind in the Willows* or one of the other decent children's books at least one more time, so I bicycled down to the library, hid my bike behind a hedge, and went inside. Susie Pruitt was sitting at the front desk and I waved at her; she was a high school senior, mildly pretty, and I had a bit of a crush on her at the time. She waved back vaguely and went back to the magazine she'd been reading. I glanced through the doorway into adult fiction, which was forbidden territory, sighed and started downstairs into the children's department.

I had the room to myself. It was a Saturday and it was nice out. Most of the boys my age were gathering to play baseball in the field behind the elementary school, and the girls were all off on some mysterious business of their own. I wasn't the only kid in Fairdale who enjoyed reading, but I was the only one who read compulsively. Anyway, I was looking for Kenneth Grahame, running my finger along the spines of the neatly arranged books, when I found something that didn't belong there. Someone had shelved *Hercules My Shipmate* by Robert Graves in the wrong section.

My first instinct was to go back upstairs and report the error to Susie Pruitt. I even took a couple of steps in that direction. But then I thought about it, and instead I pulled the book from the shelf and carried it over to one of the tables. I'll just read a few pages, I told myself, and then I'll take it to Susie. It was an act of rebellion at first and I looked up nervously after every paragraph. At some point the story caught hold of me, though, and I turned page after page, immersing myself ever deeper in the story and the prose. I thought it was the best thing I'd ever read, and at that point, it probably was.

I'm not sure how long Mrs. Mitchell had been standing behind me before I became aware of her presence. She had this amazing ability to almost glide through the library, without giving off even a whisper of sound. I wasn't surprised that I hadn't heard her, but I'd seated myself with a good view of the stairway, the only way she could have entered, and to this day I'm amazed that I didn't see her at least in my peripheral vision.

Something warned me though. My head shot up, I slammed the book shut, and swiveled violently in my chair. She was close enough to touch, and had obviously been looking down over my shoulder. She wasn't smiling, but that wasn't surprising. I had never seen her smile. I don't think there was enough slack in the skin of her face to allow such a violent contortion.

"Isn't that book a little difficult for you, boy?" Her voice was a raspy whisper, completely devoid of emotion, but I fancied it masked hidden menace.

I had to try twice before I could find my voice. "Just a little, ma'am. I don't know some of the words, but I can figure them out most of the time."

She held my eyes with hers for several seconds and it felt as though she was peering into my brain. Her face never changed, but after a moment, she walked over to one of the shelves and extracted a heavy book, brought it to me and set it down beside the Graves. It was an unabridged dictionary. "Look them up," she said quietly, and then she slipped away so quickly that the big red dictionary was the only proof that I hadn't imagined the whole thing.

She called my mother later that same day and suggested that I be given an adult library card.

Miss Mitchell ran her library with an iron hand, and adults deferred to her almost as readily as did children. When the controversy about Henry Miller's sexually explicit *Tropic of Cancer* erupted in Providence, it led to predictable curiosity even in remote Managansett. So Miss Mitchell announced that the library had acquired a copy, although it would not be kept on the open shelves. Most people in town couldn't have cared less either way, and the local impact might have been limited to a few off color jokes if Edwin Wallace hadn't caught wind of it.

He was angry. No, that's not an adequate description. He was outraged, personally offended, and righteously indignant. Public money, his money, had been used to purchase pornography. Henry Miller was a known Communist, he announced, and his books were part of a clever plot to undermine the morals of Americans. Not only had Miss Mitchell advanced the cause of the enemy, consciously or otherwise, but she had paid good US tax dollars to a Communist agent. Edwin went before the town council and the PTA, he wrote letters to the newspapers and he picketed the library, he accosted Miss Mitchell on the street and he tried to convince Chief Owens to arrest her as a traitor.

I'd like to say that the citizens of Managansett rallied to Miss Mitchell's defense, but unfortunately that's not the case. They didn't rally behind Edwin either. For the most part, they were embarrassed or amused or uninterested, and a few were annoyed at Edwin for making such a fuss and a few more were annoyed at Miss Mitchell for "setting him off".

Unwisely, Miss Mitchell eventually made a concession, hoping to disarm him. She wrote a letter to the local weekly in which she explained that Edwin Wallace was mistaken, that no tax dollars had been spent on the Miller novel. She had purchased it out of her own funds and donated it, as she had done several times in the past when she wanted to carry something that would not otherwise fit within the small allowance the town allocated for new purchases. Rather than derail the opposition, she only stimulated him to greater efforts. By acknowledging his charges, she had given them credulity, and he redoubled his efforts, writing to the governor, distributing leaflets door to door, and haranguing people on the telephone.

There was enough polarization in town to make the book the subject of controversy, but only briefly. After a few days, people turned back to more pressing issues and Edwin decided to act before he lost his audience. He called the state's largest newspaper and announced that he was going to take the Miller book out on his own library card – which he'd only acquired the previous day – and then burn it on the front steps.

Edwin showed up with a small following of reporters and cameras. It was August and there wasn't much real news. It seemed like half the town had shown up to watch, and I'd had to squeeze and inch my way through the crowd to find a spot where I could watch. Miss Mitchell indulged a previously unsuspected flare for the dramatic by meeting him halfway up the stairs, which was exactly what Edwin thought he wanted. The photographs in the next day's paper showed him staring up into Miss Mitchell's calm face, much like an indignant child importuning its mother.

Brandishing his library card like a dagger, his face working furiously, Edwin demanded that the offensive book be delivered into his hands.

"I can't do that, Mr. Wallace," she replied calmly.

"I am a citizen of this town, a taxpayer, and I have a valid library card. You have no right to deny me!" His voice crackled with fury.

"I'm not denying you anything, Mr. Wallace, but the book you want – I assume it's *Tropic of Cancer* – is currently out. I'd be happy to put your name on the waiting list if you'd like."

Apparently the possibility that someone might actually have borrowed the book had never occurred to Edwin. He stammered and glanced around nervously, checking to see if he was losing his audience.

"Who has it now? Is it some innocent child?"

"The book is on the restricted list, Mr. Wallace, as you well know. Only adults may borrow it. And I'm not allowed to divulge the names of people who borrow books. Do you want me to put your name on the waiting list or not?"

Edwin hesitated, and by now he probably knew he was in trouble. It would be anticlimactic, but he decided to put the best possible face on it. "All right, then. But this is only a delay, not a defeat. This piece of smut shall end up in the gutter where it belongs." He glanced up toward the façade of the library and escalated his threat. "As shall any other obscene, immoral, or un-American trash which might have found its way into this building."

Her expression hadn't changed throughout his tirade, but now an eyebrow lifted and her lips twitched into what might have been the suggestion of a smile. "I should warn you that the waiting list is rather long at the moment. The controversy has made Miller's book quite popular. But rest assured that I will call you personally as soon as we reach your name," she paused for a few heartbeats, "in about two years."

Most of Wallace's battles ended in defeat, although he never acknowledged them as such, always claiming that he'd stimulated public awareness of a problem, or had put the enemies of God and justice on notice, or some similar platitude. In some ways he had become the village idiot, a comical figure no one took seriously. But there was a darker side that few acknowledged. Sometimes he didn't stand alone, and most of the time he had secret supporters. Even those who opposed him occasionally backed away from a controversial stance, just to avoid the hassle of dealing with him and his small band of followers.

A year passed and Edwin finally got his chance at the Miller book. True to his word, he burned it in the street in front of the library. Unfortunately, public interest had waned by then. There were no reporters and almost no audience other than a half dozen of his allies. Miss Mitchell suspended his card when he didn't return the book on time or pay for it, and quietly donated another copy to the library. He must have known that she'd done so, but he never publicly acknowledged the existence of the replacement, and continually proclaimed his victory over the "perverted pornographers" who were trying to undermine American values.

Then came Halloween.

That was the first year during which we'd heard scare stories about sabotaged candy, ground glass in the cookies, pins or razor blades in the fruit. Everyone knew someone who knew someone who had firsthand knowledge, even though nothing had ever been reported in the newspapers or on television. Parents in Managansett were concerned and sought an alternative to Trick or Treating. The local fire station had been the site of a Fourth of July celebration for the past several years, so when the town council and the local PTA agreed to pay for refreshments, we kids were told that we wouldn't be going from door to door this year. Instead, we'd be wearing our costumes to a big party at the fire station.

Needless to say, we weren't overjoyed by the news. Part of the joy of Halloween was being out after dark without adult supervision. Edwin Wallace wasn't overjoyed either. He had inveighed against Halloween every previous year, characterizing it as a "glorification of Satanism" or "an excuse for delinquent children to rampage through the neighborhood", depending on his mood. The announcement of a Halloween party on publicly owned property prompted the usual mix of rage and indignation, and he had enough supporters, tacit and otherwise, to cause considerable trouble this time. In an effort to defuse the situation, the town manager suggested that Wallace be appointed to the committee running the party, "to see that there is no inappropriate content", and to everyone's surprise, Edwin accepted.

I heard a lot about the committee meetings because my father was involved as well. Dad never understood why Edwin didn't resign; every suggestion he made, every objection he raised, was overruled. There would be no ban on costumes depicting ghosts, witches, and the like, and the decorations would be traditional mock spooky stuff. There would be no prayer either at the beginning or the end of the party, and the entertainment would consist of a professional magician, not choir singing or a rented Disney film. Edwin grumped and orated and sulked and argued but he didn't resign, and although it was a mystery to Dad, I knew instinctively even as a child the reason why. For the first time, the people of Managansett had taken some official notice of him, put him in a position of authority, however nebulous.

The day came at last. All of the overhead doors had been raised and the two utility trucks and the emergency van were parked in the adjacent field. The interior of the station was awash with black and orange crepe streamers, the most elaborate arrangements swirling around the two fire poles. There were cakes and ice cream and cookies and soda pop and fruit punch and popcorn and cotton candy. A row of carved pumpkins marched down each side wall and an oversized scarecrow dominated the rear, half drooped over the small stage where the magician had arranged various props, although he was nowhere in evidence prior to the actual performance.

Several parents had agreed to serve as chaperones, but most of them had drifted into the Fire Chief's office, where a smaller punch bowl had been doctored to provide a little more appeal to adult tastes, and only two or three actually remained to watch forty to fifty of us kids. There were board games set up on card tables, and a badminton court and horseshoe plot just outside. I played badminton for a while, but I was watching for Muriel Bates, a freckle faced young girl one year younger than I. Although I hadn't been much interested in girls, Muriel was an avid reader and I found her company pleasant in a way that wasn't true when I was with my buddies.

The magic show started just after the sun finally went down, snuffed out behind a fringe of blue spruce that separated Managansett proper from the necklace of farms to the north. I don't remember too much about the magician, who wore a voluminous cloak with a wide collar and a broad billed hat that hid most of his face. He was tall, though, and his voice was pitched very low, probably so that he sounded more mysterious. Edwin stood in a corner with his arms crossed, scowling constantly, watching for any sign of satanic influence. There were the usual tricks, objects pulled from his pockets that were too large to fit, an empty box that suddenly held a rabbit, a rope that somehow reattached itself after being cut with a pair of heavy scissors, things like that. We had seen it all before on television, but it seemed much more mysterious in person, and even the rowdier boys quieted down to watch. I had managed to sit beside Muriel and we were both pretending that it had happened by accident.

After thirty minutes or so, the magician announced his final trick. "And now, boys and girls, it's time for the ultimate test. Who among you will have the courage to look into the Mirror of Souls." So saying, he whisked the cover from a tall, shapeless object at the rear of the stage, revealing a large, oval mirror set in an ornately carved frame. Despite the inadequate artificial lighting, the glass shone so brightly that it was almost as if it had an internal power source of its own. The frame consisted of elaborate carvings, animals I thought at first, although I couldn't quite identify any of them, and when I looked closely, they seemed to be oddly distorted, their limbs disarranged in some subtle fashion, and their faces an odd mix of animal and human features.

As it happened, I glanced toward Edwin at that moment, perhaps just to move my eyes away from the mirror. He had dropped his arms to his sides and was leaning forward, staring toward the stage, and the expression on his face was strangely intense. Much to my surprise, he actually seemed to be smiling. Then the magician was talking again and I looked back in that direction, forgetting Edwin completely.

"The mirror knows all your secrets," he told us. "It reflects the expression of your mind, not your face. If you look into its depths, really look into it, you will see whatever it is that you find the most horrid and frightening." He went on in that vein for a while but I don't remember much of what he said. His voice and cadence became soothing and monotonous and I think he was trying to achieve some kind of low grade hypnosis or suggestibility. At last he called for volunteers, and at first no one moved, but then Jamie Carr, a slow witted bully, was nudged by his friends and he came forward and climbed onto the stage and stared into the mirror.

He stood there for several seconds, and I saw his head jerk a little when he first looked. Then he turned around and smiled and waved to his friends, but I thought his face was paler than before and he almost ran back to his place. Danny Shields went next, and then his little brother, who was crying when he came back, and Prissy Connors and Belinda Mathers and Jimmy Perez and a whole lot more. I started to get up a couple of times, but something seemed to be holding me back, and as it happened I was the very last one to look. But I'll tell you about that later.

Some of the kids seemed unaffected, but they were so obviously unaffected that you knew they were hiding something. Others cried out and ran from the stage, and a couple just cried quietly as they walked away. Our adult chaperones had finished the spiked punch and weren't paying much attention or they might have intervened. About half of the kids present had gone up to look before Edwin finally bestirred himself and strode up to the stage.

"This is all nonsense! There's nothing magical about the mirror! It's just some kind of trick and he's getting you kids all worked up over nothing! "

The magician's voice was as calm and even as ever. "Why don't you look for yourself then?"

Edwin hesitated, staring up at the magician. He had clearly been challenged and the magician's confident tone made him wary. "I'm not a child. I can't be fooled the way they are." His voice sounded just faintly uncertain.

"I'm sure you can't. So why not look into the mirror and reassure the children that there's nothing to be afraid of, that there's nothing evil or loathsome or frightening waiting for them there?"

It sounded so reasonable that even Edwin couldn't object. He climbed the steps slowly, clearly still afraid of being made to look foolish. When he reached the stage, he turned and looked out at all of us. "You're all just being fooled, like you always are. You have to keep a clear head to know the difference between real and make believe."

He turned and walked toward the mirror, but his steps were shorter than usual, as though he didn't want to reach his destination. It was a very small stage though, and almost immediately he stood directly in front of the mirror. I saw his fists clench at his side, and then he leaned slightly forward and peered into the glass.

Time seemed to stand still for the next second or two, and then Edwin turned to face us and his expression was one of complete triumph. "I see myself and nothing else! I told you there's no such thing as magic!" He glanced confidently at the magician, who nodded, and then he was descending from the stage, finally victorious.

Most of the rest of us, including myself at the very last, went up and looked at the mirror before the party ended, but Edwin had already stolen most of the magic from the moment.

I don't doubt that he told us the truth. I'm absolutely certain that when he looked into the magician's mirror, he found only his own reflection. He was too bad an actor to have pretended otherwise convincingly. But I also know what I saw when I looked, an image that still occasionally troubles my dreams more than twenty years later, and which I will not describe here. And Belinda Mathers, who was diagnosed with intestinal cancer the following year saw something like a nest of snakes and Jay Underbrook, who fell into the reservoir and whose body wasn't recovered for almost a week, saw a rotting corpse and some kids would never admit what they saw. The mirror was magical, all right, and just like the magician said, it showed us whatever we despised and hated but could not escape.

And Edwin Wallace saw himself.

MAKING FRIENDS

Most of us made fun of Dewey Ward back in grade school, with the thoughtless cruelty that some of us outgrow and some of us subdue and some of us embrace even in our adult lives. He was an easy target, a bookworm who kept to himself, with a mother who'd been bitten by the Bible so bad that she'd become a kind of religious Typhoid Mary and a father who'd been in so many bar fights that he finally had to do most of his drinking at home. Dewey was an awkward looking kid, skinny arms and legs, a neck just a little too long, small head, pinched features, raggedy hair that stuck out at all angles. His mother kept his clothes mended, but they were old clothes, and for a while everyone called him "Patches" after that silly teenage death song.

I was guilty of persecuting Dewey a few times myself. It wasn't that I had anything against him, but I'd be hanging around with some of my friends and Dewey would walk by and they'd start in on him and I'd join in just to be part of the group. He never acknowledged the insults, never cried or argued with us or reported us to the teachers. Most of the time he wouldn't even look in our direction, and sometimes I swear he'd tuned us out completely, wasn't even aware of our existence. We'd make fun of his looks or call him a fag, sometimes competing with each other to come up with the most outrageous sexual reference. This went on all through grade school, but it wasn't until the eighth grade that I realized that no one ever actually touched Dewey.

Managansett Elementary was a pretty tough place back in those days. Teachers held themselves aloof from students and whenever someone complained that they were being picked on, they were lectured about the importance of "standing up for yourself" and left to beat off the predators on their own. Most of the parents in town probably felt the same way. I know my Dad did. The first time I came home with a black eye he told me that the other kid had better be worse off, and the second time around I could honestly give him the answer he wanted. Although I don't think I was a bully, I was bigger than most kids my age, and when push came to shove, I was probably the one doing the pushing and shoving.

I had my first epiphany about Dewey during a crisp fall day just after school got out. I was sitting on a dumpster near the loading dock, my attention split between a handful of girls playing badminton on the baseball diamond and Jimmy Nicholson, who was methodically pummeling little Tommy Noones, for about the fifth time that month. Most bullies don't really want to fight; they just want their victims to acknowledge their own inferiority. Jimmy was different. You couldn't appease him. Jimmy wanted to hurt other kids, usually younger ones, boys or girls, popular or not. He was an equal opportunity abuser blessed with the ability to charm adults into believing the most outrageous lies. Most of the teachers considered him a model student.

But this isn't about Jimmy, who grew up to become an abusive husband and a powerful but cordially detested business executive. It's about Dewey Ward, who walked right past Jimmy with an armful of books clutched against his side. Jimmy glanced in his direction and said something, but I was too far away to hear it. Dewey ignored him and kept on walking and Jimmy jumped to his feet, which gave the unfortunate Tommy the chance to run for his life. I'm not sure what got into Jimmy that day, but he started off after Dewey with his big hands closed into fists and I sat up, instinctively realizing that this was something out of the ordinary. It wasn't until later that I realized what it was that caught my attention so fully.

In all the years that we'd been tormenting Dewey, I'd never seen anyone lay a hand on him.

It came to me in a rush as I watched the distance close between them. Dewey had never been in a fight, had never been dumped in the small pool behind the school or locked in his locker. No one ever swatted his pale backside with a towel after gym class or pushed him out of the way at a drinking fountain. I'd never seen him with a black eye or torn clothing, and I'd never heard anyone boast about harassing him physically.

Jimmy Nicholson's charge struck me as incongruous even before I made that connection. He closed the distance between them quickly and reached out, his right hand landing squarely on Dewey's shoulder, then spun the smaller boy around to face him. I was sitting forward now, not close enough to see the expression on Dewey's face but somehow sensing that I was about to witness something extraordinary. But I didn't. And that in itself was extraordinary.

Nicholson's hand fell away and he took a half step backward, then sat down right on the grass in a sort of controlled collapse. Dewey turned away in that same moment and continued to walk as though nothing had happened.

I climbed down from dumpster and started toward Nicholson, not quite running. Like I said, I never liked Nicholson and barely knew him, but I was curious. Something had just happened; I was sure of it. I just wasn't sure what it was, and I wanted badly to know.

He was sitting with his legs crossed, his arms at his sides, his expression completely neutral. I had to call his name twice before he reacted, glancing up at me, then climbing to his feet, brushing off his pants with both hands. "Hey, Kerrigan, how're you doing?" He sounded just the slightest bit distracted, or maybe that was just my imagination.

"Are you all right, Nicholson?"

"Yeah, sure. Why shouldn't I be?" A bit of his usual belligerence returned to his voice.

"I saw you fall and thought maybe Dewey hit you or something."

"Who? Patches? He couldn't hit me with a machinegun, the little pansy. Besides, I haven't seen him all day."

He sounded sincere but there was something funny in his eyes. "He was just here a minute ago. I saw you grab his arm just before you fell."

"What're you trying to pull, Kerrigan? I didn't fall; I just sat down. And I haven't seen that asshole Patches all day."

My mouth fell open but I couldn't think of anything to say, and then he had brushed past me and was gone. It took me a while to shake it off, and I never picked on Dewey Ward again.

I kind of lost track of Dewey the next year. Managansett High was still a pending bond issue at the time and we were all bussed to a consolidated regional high school in North Smithfield. The classes were bigger and there were more of them, and even better there were three times as many girls to date. I probably ran into Dewey in the corridors or at assemblies from time to time, but I never spoke to him or heard anything unusual.

Up until our senior year, that is.

My grades were good enough to get me into college, but I was never a great student. Today I'd probably have been diagnosed as having a mild attention deficit disorder, but in those days the phrase was "doesn't apply himself" and I heard it a lot. I was a bit of a jock, though not good enough to be scouted, but I did it because the girls went for it. I really didn't care whether we won or lost so long as I looked good on the field. I took guitar lessons for a while and talked about playing in a rock band, but lost interest just jut when I was starting to play recognizable tunes. Even while dating, I was a dilettante; I probably went out with forty different girls during my four years of high school, and flirted with twice as many more. The only time I went steady, I cheated after three weeks. I lost my virginity to Dolly Garfield during my sophomore year, and helped Michelle Weldon to lose hers a year later. I am pleased to say I wasn't one of those guys who kisses and tells, and when Michelle dropped out of school six months later to marry Hugh Lane, he probably thought she was still a virgin.

The last person I expected to see at the Senior Dance was Dewey Ward. As far as I know he had never previously come to any social event during his entire school career, not to mixers, sports events, holiday parties, the big annual summer's end barbecue, or even any of the after school clubs. I had been driving my own car to school for the past two years, so I didn't even know if he still rode in on the bus every day or if he had a set of wheels of his own. Anyway, I was there with Dawn Fairfax, our third and ultimately final date, pretending to listen to her chatter about how great a job the decorations committee had done or provide a running commentary on the poor style choices of any other girl who was out of earshot.

More than a little bored, I was looking toward the door, hoping to see one of my buddies show up so that we could talk sports or something, when in comes this tall, thin guy I didn't recognize, and with him this absolutely stunning girl. For several seconds I thought they must have come to the wrong place, because I knew damned well that the girl wasn't a student here. She was too distinctive to be missed. I tracked them with my eyes, but another couple stepped in front of them and all I could see was the guy for a while, so I checked him out. It must've been another minute or two before I realized it was Dewey.

Superficially, he was completely different. He was taller, of course, which only emphasized his prominent neck, the awkwardly long arms and legs, the pasty, pockmarked complexion. His clothes were no longer covered with patches, his hair was combed, and at least for the moment he wasn't carrying a stack of books, but the quick darting motion of his head – which reminded me of my aunt's chickens, the prominent crooked nose, and the close set eyes were all unmistakable.

I was curious about Dewey, but I was fascinated by his date, and the fact that she'd showed up with the least desirable guy in the entire school didn't bother me one bit. There was a mystery here, and I planned to solve it before the dance was over. If I was inattentive to Dawn for much of the rest of the evening, it was partially because of Dewey and his companion, but truthfully it was a date of convenience and I think both of us already knew that we didn't particularly like each other.

The crowd grew and I lost track of them for a while, and would have gone hunting if Casey Douglas and his date hadn't showed up just then and invited themselves to sit at our table. Normally Case and I get along real well, but I was preoccupied and fretful and when the girls excused themselves to powder their noses, he told me rather pointedly that he was going to make the rounds and walked off without inviting me to come along. That suited me just fine, and I stood up and walked off in the direction where I'd last seen Dewey.

It took me a few minutes to find them. They were sitting alone at a table in a dark corner, close together but not intimately so. I found that fact encouraging. I've never been the shy type or particularly at a loss for words, but I suddenly felt very awkward about approaching them and had to run through several rehearsals in my mind before I gathered enough courage to act.

It was like walking through molasses to take those last few steps, but I was determined.

"Hey there, Dewey. Haven't seen you in a while. How've you been?" He glanced up at me incuriously with those unsettlingly small, dark, and deeply set eyes. I felt suddenly naked and unconsciously reached down to make sure my fly was closed. It took an act of will to look away from him toward the girl, who was even more spectacular at close range with her thick mane of dark red hair and just a suggestion of freckles under each eye. "Hi, I'm Paul Kerrigan."

She met my eyes evenly and said "windy night", and I nodded and almost agreed with her before realizing that it was dead calm outside and that she'd actually said "Wendy Knight".

"I don't think I've seen you around the school before."

"No, you haven't." She smiled, but not warmly, and for just a split second she reminded me of Dewey. Not physically, of course, but something in her attitude, her presence, was reminiscent of the effect he had on me.

"Well, have a good time. I hope to see you again." But I never did, or at least not for a very long time. Nor did anyone else, except perhaps Dewey Ward. I'm pretty certain of that because I went to great efforts to track her down during the next few weeks. I never found a single person who knew her, and in fact no one else remembered seeing either Wendy or Dewey at the dance. I staked out the Ward home intermittently, and followed Dewey once or twice when he left. But Wendy Knight was gone as though she had never existed, and then my Dad died of a stroke and I was off to a two year college and I pretty much put Dewey Ward and his mysterious girlfriend out of my mind.

Three years later I was working for the *Managansett Call*, a little weekly community newspaper. One of the reasons I consistently got good grades in school without applying myself was that I wrote tolerably well, and sometimes shadow earned me grades that substance could not. I had a two year business degree and originally worked part-time keeping their books up to date, but I'd filled in temporarily when Bill Knapp, who wrote most of the content, died unexpectedly, and the temporary became permanent once it was clear that unlike Bill, I could spell and compose coherently.

I was reading through the sticky notes that lay like fallen leaves all over my desk when I noticed one with a familiar name on it. Ellen Ward, aged forty-five, had died the previous evening in her home after a protracted illness, some form of cancer. She was survived by her son, Dewey. Her husband had drunk himself to death while I was off at college. I stared at the note for a long time, wondering what had become of Dewey, and for some reason an image of Wendy Knight came to me, clear as day, and I even felt a momentary arousal.

So I decided to take a drive.

I went past the Ward house twice before I found it. They lived in an aging and rather dilapidated old farmhouse right up on the northern edge of town, and the area had become so overgrown in recent years that you couldn't see half of the houses from the road unless you already knew what you're looking for. I parked on the street and walked along the short, badly maintained driveway to the dark, badly maintained house. One step on the front porch was broken and the wood was almost bare of paint and full of splinters.

The doorbell didn't seem to be working so I knocked.

There was a brief pause and then the door was opened by an older woman whom I instinctively liked. She gave me the warmest possible smile. "Yes? May I help you?"

"Excuse me, I might be in the wrong place. I'm looking for the Ward house."

"Then you're not in the wrong place, young man. How can we help you?"

I introduced myself and told her I was from the *Call*. "We just wanted a few details for the obituary, if that's all right. We like to make them a little less impersonal than they do in the big papers."

"Well come right inside and I'll call Dewey. Can I offer you something to drink, Mr. Kerrigan? Coffee, tea, a soft drink?" Her voice was rich and her manner so open and friendly that I immediately liked her.

"No, I'm fine thanks." Unlike the exterior, the interior of the house was spotlessly clean and orderly, or at least as much of the hall, den, and dining room as I could see.

She gestured toward the den and I headed that way while she went to the staircase, inclined her head and shouted for Dewey. There was an incomprehensible reply from above and then the sound of footsteps coming down.

"Yes, Aunt Rose. What is it?"

I felt a sudden chill, and all the weirdness of Dewey Ward came back over me in a rush.

Dewey looked very much like he had the night of the dance. His clothing was less formal but neat and clean, his hair was cut, and he met my eyes evenly. He was physically as awkward looking as ever, but he had clearly become much more self confident. We shook hands while I explained the purpose of my visit, and he invited me to sit down.

"Mr. Kerrigan said he didn't want anything, dear, but can I get you some coffee?"

"Not right now, thanks."

"Well, just call if you need anything." And she was gone as though she'd melted into the carpet.

I asked the few questions I'd come up with to justify my visit, a visit whose real purpose I didn't understand myself. Perhaps I was just trying to scratch an old itch. Dewey told me his mother had led an unhappy life but found solace in religion for her unhappy marriage, continuing financial difficulties, and ultimately a protracted and fatal illness.

I closed my notebook to indicate the interview was over but made no effort to rise. "So what have you been up to Dewey? I lost track of everyone after high school. You and I are almost the only ones left in Managansett."

"It suits me here." He wasn't going to volunteer anything.

"Do you work here in town somewhere?"

He smiled thinly. "No, I'm unemployed. Fortunately I have some friends now and we look after each other." I took that as a reproof for our high school days, a deserved one, but didn't let it show.

"Do you have any family left? Other than your aunt, I mean?"

He seemed genuinely amused this time. "She's not really my aunt. That was Mrs. Knight. She seems like family sometimes, a second mother in fact. But she's just a friend."

"Knight? Didn't you used to go out with a girl named Knight back in high school?" I was sure he could see right through my pretended uncertainty. "Are they related?"

"Distantly, I suppose. But we're really all just friends."

And that was pretty much the end of our conversation.

The interview left me with an uneasy feeling, but as before, it soon got swept away by other events. My Mom went to California when my brother's wife died giving birth to my niece, and another temporary arrangement soon became permanent. I gave up my apartment and moved back into the family place, managed to date the same woman for almost six months, then broke my leg trying to cross an ice coated parking lot in too much of a hurry. Somewhere in there I heard that Dewey Ward bought the Hudson place up on Reservoir Road and wondered where he'd gotten the money, but I disliked thinking about Dewey so I didn't wonder for very long.

Now comes the really weird part.

Another year passed and the *Call* got bought up by a regional chain that collects small town newspapers, standardizing their formats, consolidating production costs, and charging more for advertising. Four of our eight employees were suddenly unemployed, but I actually made out well, with the biggest raise I'd ever had, although I would also be working more hours. I even had a budget, a very small budget admittedly, from which I could pay occasional part time stringers for stories I might not otherwise have noticed.

My best stringer was a housewife named Myrtle Boyle, a newcomer to Managansett but nosey enough to make up for it. One afternoon she asked me a very provocative question. "Are you interested in covering a religious cult right here in our own backyard?"

"What are you talking about Myrtle?" She was good, but she often had to be coaxed into revealing what she knew.

"There a place over on Reservoir Road, big spread with a greenhouse and pool."

"The Hudson house. So what?" The small hairs were rising on the back of my neck, however. I remembered who was living there now.

"Well, near as I can tell there's at least eight people living there. The owner is a local boy, but no one had ever heard of the other people until they moved in with him. Four of them work at Eblis Manufacturing here in town. They carpool to work every day and no one ever sees them anywhere else. There are two others, a man and a woman, who do most of the shopping and errands, but they aren't particularly friendly either. I stopped by one day and met a very nice woman, Mrs. Knight, who seems to be their housekeeper, and she was pleasant enough, but I think the rest of them are part of a cult or something."

"It really doesn't sound like anything that the paper would be interested in. What they do in private is their own business, Myrtle."

She sniffed and dropped the subject, clearly disappointed that I showed so little interest. What she didn't know was that I was very interested indeed.

Very quietly I confirmed what Myrtle had told me. Four of Dewey Ward's housemates worked at Eblis, three men and a woman. They were good at their jobs but not particularly popular with their co-workers, who characterized them as standoffish or even peculiar. I was unable to discover anything about their lives before they moved to Managansett, though admittedly I didn't try very hard. The three guys were all good looking but "probably gay". The woman was stunningly attractive and her name was Wendy Knight. I struck up a conversation with the gate guard one night and stood beside him when the parking lot emptied out. She was sitting in the back, but I caught enough of a look to confirm she was the same girl, woman now, who had gone to the dance with Dewey Ward. She didn't seem to have aged much.

I thought about it for a while and decided it was still none of my business, but I was restless and preoccupied and it wasn't hard to figure out why. I had to know what was going on.

So I called Dewey Ward, after getting the unlisted number from a friend who worked in personnel at Eblis. A woman answered, probably Mrs. Knight, and after a short pause, I heard Dewey's distinctive raspy voice. I told him that we were considering doing a series of articles on local people who made good and that he was an obvious candidate, which was a lie and which he almost certainly knew was a lie, and asked if I could drive up and talk to him. He told me that they were redecorating at the moment and the place was too much of a mess for guests, which was a lie and which I knew was a lie, but that he'd be happy to meet me for lunch someplace.

We agreed to meet at Wilson's Tap, an only slightly grungy bar and grill right on the border with Lincoln. It had only been open a few months, but its initial popularity had faded quickly. The food was palatable but unmemorable, the décor memorable but unpalatable. I showed up early and had a drink at the bar, and when Dewey walked in, alone, I felt a resurgence of the old high school revulsion and almost ducked down out of sight.

They had no trouble seating us. It was a Wednesday evening. There was an elderly couple in one corner, a pair of lovebirds in another, and us in the middle of the floor. All the remaining tables were empty.

After we'd placed our orders and passed beyond the usual small talk, I took out the notebook in which I would take notes for the article I had no intention of writing. "It was quite a surprise when you bought the Hudson house. You must have done well for yourself since high school."

"Not really. Several friends of mine were looking for a place to live so I borrowed a little from each of them and the rest from the bank."

"So they're all living with you?"

"Yes. There are nine of us altogether, and sometimes we have visitors as well."

"It must be crowded. I know that house. It's big, but it's not that big."

"We manage. I told you, we're in the middle of redecorating right now."

I asked more questions, which he evaded easily. Clearly he didn't want to talk about his friends, their living arrangements, or their finances except in the most general terms. Whenever I tried to push the issue, his face changed slightly and I felt the sudden desire to go away. It was uncanny, almost as though he could turn it on and off, and I realized that I'd never managed to outgrow my childhood feelings toward him. I spent more time eating and less time talking, impatient now just to have this over with and leave. And then disaster struck.

I'd been vaguely aware of a bad odor ever since I'd walked in, but it hadn't really registered. My parents had oil heat and my apartment had electric. We never had a gas stove or anything similar. There was a cracked fitting somewhere in the restaurant's basement, and eventually the fumes reached the kitchen. Fortunately, the wall between the kitchen and the dining area was unusually sturdy. Unfortunately, the floor was not. The force of the explosion knocked Dewey and I from our chairs and sent us sprawling, but at that point we'd suffered nothing more than bruises and slight cuts and abrasions.

That's when the floor collapsed.

We were on the landing, an elevated portion of the dining area. The landing dropped as a unit, and the main floor below splintered and collapsed like a pile of pickup sticks. We fell through into the basement, followed by most of the tables and chairs and other debris. The blast was so violent that there wasn't much of a fire afterward, but the roof collapsed after a minute or two, trapping us quite effectively.

I blacked out; I'm not sure for how long. When I opened my eyes, I was in considerable pain, but most of the blood on my face came from a not particularly serious scalp wound. My legs were, however, pinned under a piece of fallen timber, and my left ankle alternated between hurting very badly indeed, which frightened me a bit, and not hurting at all, which terrified me.

Dewey was in worse shape. He was sitting up against a mangled freezer chest with both hands gripping his left thigh. The light from the nearby fires was good enough that I could see that, despite his best efforts, blood was spurting into the air. He seemed stunned, staring at the injured leg with an expression of disbelief, and didn't respond when I called his name.

I craned my neck toward the one patch of open sky I could see and shouted as loudly as I could. "Help! We need a doctor down here! Someone get us a doctor."

Convinced that Dewey was going to die if I didn't do something, I strained with all my strength to pull my legs free. The burst of pain from my ankle was so intense that I fainted.

When I came to, I could hear voices shouting in the distance and a couple of muted sirens. I turned toward Dewey and saw that he was no longer alone. A tall man in a dark suit stood up as I watched and turned toward me, and I could see a thick white bandage around Dewey's thigh. "I'm Doctor Smith," he said. "Just lie still while I examine you." And then I must have fainted again.

Dewey survived, and so did I, but to this day we've never met or talked again. Frankly, he terrifies me. I faded in and out of consciousness during the rescue and only recall fragments. I remember Dr. Smith giving me a shot for the pain, and I think I remember him putting splints on my ankle. But I also remember two other things, and that's why I'm scared.

I don't know what it was about Dewey Ward that made him unlikable but also untouchable. Maybe he was just so different that our collective unconscious minds rejected him instinctively as not one of our kind, something of us but also alien to us. And maybe that awareness worked both ways, so that Dewey could reach into our minds and push us away without our noticing it.

Like I said, I don't know what barrier existed between Dewey and the rest of us, but I do know that Dr. Smith lied when he told the paramedics that he'd been eating at Wilson's when the explosion happened. They believed him even though he was completely unhurt because he was, after all, trapped in the wreckage with the two of us. I also know what I saw when they carried my stretcher out to the ambulance, but I've never told anyone because it would be dismissed as an hallucination brought on by shock or the drugs. I am absolutely certain that there was a human shaped depression scooped out of the soil only a few feet from where Dewey Ward had sat bleeding to death. A depression just about the size of Dr. Smith who, incidentally, now lives with Dewey and the others at the Hudson house and who seems to have had no past history at all.

When Dewey Ward says he's recently made a new friend, he's telling you the literal truth.

CONTEXT

There is someone else living in my home.

That bald assertion seems innocuous enough, but that's only because you lack a broad enough view of the context to understand its significance. Context is, you must realize, all important. This is a point I endeavor with notable lack of success to introduce into the unformed and uninformed minds of those placed in my charge, the reputed students who attend my classes. We seek to resolve differing perspectives and achieve something we would like to call *truth*, but which is actually *consensus*.

Now here's a contextual conundrum for you. A "student" according to my dictionary is an individual engaged in a program of study, an organized procedure to obtain knowledge and understanding. During the course of an average day, over one hundred of these "students" suffer varying increments of obvious boredom, often bordering on outright hostility, while I struggle in vain to impart some knowledge of the subject matter, some justification for the labels "student" and "teacher."

It wasn't supposed to be that way of course. I came to teaching with high ideals. The enthusiasm with which I approached each class that first year amused my colleagues, whose usually good natured jibes alternately puzzled and hurt the younger version of myself, a person who now seems so alien to me.

"Don't expect too much from them. They're only kids," they warned me. In the faculty lounge one afternoon, Caulfield, a biology teacher, dubbed me "Evan Siever, the eager beaver" in that irritating braying voice of his. Even the Vice Principal, Edna McGuire, suggested that I take a more realistic view of the situation. At the time, I foolishly ignored their advice, secure in my conviction that the deep and abiding respect which I held for literature could not help but affect others, if only I could present it in the proper context.

I first noticed that I was no longer alone two months after Susan moved out.

Susan is my wife, although the tense of the verb in the initial clause of this self referential sentence will change in due course, as she has advised me she wishes to formalize our separation permanently. She left after a spiraling series of petty confrontations arising from her inflexibility even when faced with overwhelming evidence that she espoused a false position. To be fair, she insisted that I was the intractable one, but the fact is that if she had taken the time to examine my carefully arrayed arguments, I feel certain he would have drawn the proper conclusions. In most ways Susan is an eminently reasonable woman and I feel that my single greatest personal failure was my inability to convey to her an understanding of her own shortcomings.

She was replaced in short order by the entity I know think of as my roommate.

I dismissed the initial incidents offhandedly, recognizing their significance only later when subsequent events provided a context. This is an old house, built just after the turn of the century, constructed in large part from packing crates in which pianos had been transported from Europe. Elderly Mr. Helmsdale, from whom Susan and I purchased the house shortly after our wedding, had been just old enough to remember his father's painstaking trips with horse and wagon down an unpaved road from Managansett to the head of Narragansett Bay and back, retrieving the materials from which he built this boxy but spacious house. Solidly constructed though it might be, the decades had placed various strains on the structure, and mysterious creakings and groanings were a natural consequence.

The fact that the sounds I heard seemed more purposeful, footsteps, the opening or closing of doors and drawers, distant laughter or whispering, could be trained as tricks of the imagination, the mind's attempt to ascribe order to disorder. As the frequency and intensity of these manifestations grew, I became increasingly convinced that something out of the ordinary was happening, initially wondering if some unsuspected malady of the inner ear was influencing my mind's interpretation of perfectly ordinary sounds. At first, you see, there was no physical evidence of a foreign presence.

We furnished the house over a period of two years, taking great pains to secure items which we felt would survive our transient preferences. Susan thought my choice of oil paintings indicated perhaps an unhealthy preoccupation with death. She was mistaken, of course. What she interpreted a necrolatry was in fact just the opposite; the totality of human existence is one of the abiding obsessions of my life, and death, as the termination of that existence, is a revealing reflection; shadows can be just as illuminating as spotlights contradictory thought that might seem. Students of literature, life, or any subject, must contrast as well as compare to achieve revelation.

I was sitting in my den the night I first had proof that another entity dwelt within the walls of my home. The den is a room of which I am inordinately proud. Susan and I had an unspoken agreement about territory; the choice of furnishings and their arrangement was theoretically a joint venture, but in practice, although I was in charge of the garage and basement, she possessed the final say everywhere else.

Except my den.

I think this was the room that convinced me to purchase the house in the first place. During the early years of our marriage, Susan was unalterably deferential to me in such matters, a situation that was both flattering and frustrating. It was while reflecting upon this state of affairs that I first began to understand Whitman's point that we all encompass contradiction within ourselves. The Helmsdale home was a bargain even though the asking price was at the very upper limit of what I thought we could afford and the numerous oversized rooms provided far more space than I thought we needed. But the den took my breath away.

A fireplace had been built into one wall, with a tiered series of steps cascading down to the main floor, symmetrical brick wings extending to either side. It was too large for the room, clashed with the newly installed paneling, was both incredibly ugly and unbelievingly appealing.

Our initial offer was accepted and we moved in. Susan quietly reproached me about the amount of money I allocated to the den, the genuine Persian rug, the original oil painting, the antique oak desk. Perhaps I did place too much strain on our groaning budget, but even Susan later agreed that the room possessed a spirit of its own.

She must have continued to harbor some resentment, however, because even during the good years of our marriage, she rarely spent any time there, even though I used to build boisterous blazes in the immense maw of the fireplace.

I have not done so for several years now; it seems in some way inappropriate.

I was sitting in the den, nursing a brandy, when my unseen roommate provided the first concrete evidence of his existence. And his gender.

It had been a particularly frustrating day. Carlyle, newly appointed Principal at Managansett High School, had once again succumbed to parental pressure. He characterized our discussion as a conference rather than a reprimand, but its true purpose was abundantly clear.

"You have to ease up, Evan." As my nominal superior, Carlyle was entitled to the familiarity.

"With all respect, Mr. Carlyle, you don't understand the situation." Even though I knew I was wasting my breath, I felt compelled to make some effort to influence the man. "If I am to have any chance at all of instilling some minimal knowledge of literature in these...children, some discipline is essential."

I knew from his faint expression of distaste that Carlyle was unwilling to even consider my opposing viewpoint. Tension locked its fingers in my gut and threatened to tear me apart. "You have to be more flexible, Evan. Today's teenagers aren't willing to accept doctrinaire pronouncements from their elders, and frankly the tide of educational theory in the country supports their skepticism. Everything should be subject to question. If we teach the truth, whatever that might be, then surely it can withstand a little criticism."

I tried not to sigh but the sound slipped out before I could assert control. "I've come to learn over the course of years that 'truth' is just another label. Christianity and Islam both claim to be true although they contradict each other, as do communism and capitalism, liberals and conservatives, censors and pornographers. We're not teaching truth; we're creating a commonality of experience so that our culture can continue."

As I spoke I saw the tension lines change on Carlyle's face, the slight clenching of one hand just short of making a fist, unconscious but clear indicators that, as expected, I was not helping my case.

"I'm not prepared to debate philosophy with you, Siever," he said at last, voice level, eyes moving to meet my own, then skipping away. Carlyle was a weak man in a strong position and the contradictions inherent in that had yet to be resolved. "The point is that you need to loosen up. If one of your students disagrees with something you say, you have a perfect right to support your case. But that does not," and he emphasized the last word by slamming his palm down on the desk, "that does not entitle you to indulge in humiliating sarcasm."

Now I knew from whence the complaint had come. That insufferably smug little bitch Julie in second period had gone crying to her mother after our confrontation about acceptable extra credit reading. Her term paper was on my desk at home and I made a mental note to grade it that night, while the affront was still fresh in my mind.

I had in fact just finished doing so and had lapsed into seeking patterns in the placement of bricks in the fireplace when the sound came. It was too clear to be an illusion, too distinct to be anything other than what it was.

Someone had closed the medicine cabinet door in the bathroom.

There was no question about it; one of the hinges was slightly out of alignment, which caused a twisted squeal just before contact was made.

Obviously my first thought was that I had a burglar, although why a burglar should be searching through a bathroom medicine cabinet mystified me. Looking for drug perhaps? I armed myself with a fireplace poker before venturing down the darkened hall that separated the den from the ground floor bath. My heart raced with fear and excitement as I proceeded, and even while I dreaded the possibility of placing myself in danger, I thrilled at the thought of a physical confrontation. The idea of defending my home from an invader stirred some atavistic core of violence I had not previously suspected and I was in fact disappointed when the bathroom proved to be empty. As did the rest of my house.

But the sink was speckled with tiny black hairs just like those I washed away after shaving each morning and before leaving for work. Just as I had most certainly done that very morning as well.

During my college years, I was convinced of the perfectibility of the human spirit. That phrase was a cliché even then, of course, so we used different words to express the same concept. But we all knew what we meant. There's a war waged within each of us between opposing forces that many call good and evil, though I for one believe these terms to be inaccurate in describing this duality. If there are truly deities contending for control of the universe, surely the matters that concern them are too abstract for our simple minds to comprehend.

My disingenuous compassion for the downtrodden persisted into the early years of my marriage. When Susan and I were mugged by four Hispanic teenagers during our visit to New York City in the 1990s, I achieved a more perfect understanding. Somehow minorities had acquired a kind of "noble savage" status in my mind and I habitually dismissed their criminal acts as a reaction to oppression by the white majority. As I stood there helplessly while one of the cocky bastards searched Susan' purse, I felt an almost irresistible urge to protest.

'No!" I wanted to say. "You don't understand. We're on your side; we understand the situation and we're doing everything we can to help. We're not your enemy." But then revelation burst through my mind like a cleansing fire and I realized that our assailants were just as corrupt as their white counterparts who lounged indolently in their country clubs and stole our money through more clandestine and "legal" methods. Race and nationality were irrelevant; the only important attribute was power, who happened to have it at the moment and who did not.

This insight was worth every dollar they took from us that day, as it resolved for me an internal conflict that I had not even realized was fulminating in the depths of my character.

Susan had particularly disliked the painting I had placed directly above the fireplace. It's an unsigned watercolor, reliably authenticated as having been in the possession of the Eastern Orthodox Church in Constantinople until early in the 20th Century. From left to right, the mystical bridge Chinvat offers passage across the river of life and death. To one side, Asha-Vahista, the god of supreme virtue, gestures with one hand, causing the bridge to broaden, while the other hand directs a spear of fire toward his adversary, Indra. The latter god holds a shield to protect himself while squeezing one fist to cause Chinvat to shrink at his end. Several of the souls of the dead are depicted falling where the bridge has shriveled beneath their feet. Where Susan considered it morbid, I find it to be an excellent metaphor for human existence, the narrow path we tread seeking balance between conflicting forces. Self interest and philanthropy, love and hate, compassion and revulsion, pride and humility. In each case we struggle to find an acceptable middle ground while influences which we cannot even begin to comprehend seek to pull us one way or the other.

Initially, I dismissed the whisker incident as a lapse of memory. Despite my invariable policy of cleaning the bathroom before leaving each morning, I convinced myself I had somehow forgotten to do so. Perhaps my brooding about Susan's departure had interfered with my normally crisp, clear thought processes.

Two nights later there was an even more disturbing incident.

I was grading tests in my den when I heard what sounded suspiciously like the opening of the refrigerator door. Motionless, I listened intently and a few seconds later came the unmistakable impact of the door against its cushioned frame.

Oddly enough, it never occurred to me to arm myself on this occasion, so it was just as well that when I entered the kitchen I found it empty of intruders. All the lights were off except the dome light over the sink, but I turned on the overheads as soon as I entered the room. The dishes I had washed after supper were now dry on the drain board, two empty beer cans were sitting on a shelf awaiting my morning trip to the garbage can in the garage, and the table was completely bare. Everything was exactly as I had left it, with one exception.

I had only consumed one beer that evening.

I let my fingers touch the two cans tentatively. One was cool, room temperature; the other cold, beads of moisture clearly visible.

Naturally I performed a thorough search of the entire house but my mysterious visitor had left no other evidence of his intrusion.

Nor was that the only manifestation of my roommate's presence that evening. An hour later, while I was still struggling to retain my composure, the toilet in the second floor bath flushed noisily. Overcoming a momentary paralysis, I raced up the stairs and into the master bedroom, stabbing at the light switch with one hand as I turned toward the bathroom door.

I had taken to sleeping in the den following Susan's departure; the master bedroom seemed inordinately large, contained memories of arguments and reconciliations too painful to face, and the sofa bed in the den was comfortable and convenient, free of the freight of earlier frustration.

The toilet upstairs has always been a problem. The chain which lifts the plug and drains the tank becomes tangled and does not fall back into place properly, causing the water to run endlessly unless the handle is jiggled repeatedly to loosen it. I could still hear the rushing water as I approached, and that detail made this unwelcome phenomenon even more disconcerting.

Just as I extended my hand toward the doorknob, the toilet handle quite distinctively jiggled.

Suddenly I no longer wanted to open the door, lost all desire to unmask the strange presence who shared my quarters. But even as I grew increasingly terrified of more certain knowledge, so also was I possessed by a desperate fear not to know. Of such contradictions are we all constructed.

I compromised, of course. Our lives are a series of such accommodations; the context of our personalities is determined by the patterns which we choose and which ultimately become us. I was convinced that I could not possibly summon the courage to open that door, but I was nevertheless unwilling to allow my elusive guest to escape.

There was no way to lock the door from the outside, but I could erect a barricade. The adjoining closet was filled with the detritus of my marriage, some of Susan's things she had left behind as well as some of mine for which I had no present use. There were spare blankets, pillows, boxes of old paper and photographs. From these I constructed a pyramid which leaned against the bathroom door, topped with a tray full of abandoned cosmetics from the dresser in the corner. If the door was opened more than an inch, these would be overturned and their impact on the hardwood floor would provide warning that my quarry was on the move.

Just after I finished, the shower went on.

Tension became a sudden acid flame burning in my stomach and I sat down on the bed, affected so intensely that I was dizzy. My uneasiness grew steadily as the seconds passed and more evidence of an alien occupancy presented itself. I heard the shower curtain shift, its rings sliding along the aluminum runner. The susurration of the water changed, as though a body had interrupted its flow. I lay back, eyes closed, willing the weakness to leave me, summoning the strength to deal with this unexpected turn of events.

Inexplicably, I fell asleep.

It could only have been for a few seconds, or minutes at most. There was no sense of an extended passage of time and my watch suggested my nap had been brief. The shower had been turned off, although I could still quite distinctly hear the drip of water from the showerhead. Too distinctly, in fact. I struggled erect, blinking the confusion from my eyes.

The bathroom door stood open, revealing darkness within except for the dim nightlight that glowed over the sink. The walls dripped with moisture, the residue of the shower's steam.

On the bedroom floor, my barricade was intact, exactly as I had created it. The tray of cosmetics was still balanced precariously at its apex.

But the bathroom door had been opened completely and now rested against the bathroom wall... as though it had been opened right through my impediment without disturbing it.

I am told that most marriages break up over money or because one of the partners in the relationship has indulged in an affair. Neither of these tolled the death knell between Susan and I; we differed primarily over more abstract issues.

"You've become narrow minded and polarized over the years, Evan," she accused me. "Even when we agree, your reasoning is too focused. You assume that every issue can be reduced to black and white. There are no nuances in your arguments. Everything is absolute. Except that you're not even consistent from one year to the next."

"We all change our opinions as we mature and experience things, Susan. You don't claim to believe the exact things now that your did when we were in our twenties."

"Of course not. Experience has taught me that a lot of things are much more complicated that I used to believe. I feel ambivalence more and more often. But you believe that every issue has a single dimension, that there is a discernible right and wrong answer to every question, and that you can tell them apart."

It was an argument that rose between us with increasing frequency. There was an element of truth in her charge, of course. I WAS refining my thought processes. In order to create the proper context in which valid conclusions can be formed and courses of action determined, it was necessary to clear away the clutter of contradictory and distracting emotions and prejudices.

The difficulty I faced now was to distinguish between genuine phenomena and the fancies of a nervous imagination. Once I was in possession of enough facts, I could draw the proper conclusions.

The incidents grow more frequent now. From time to time, I catch a glimpse of movement out of the corner of my eye, as though someone had just passed from one room to another, a figure whose stature is equal to my own and who seems somehow familiar, an old acquaintance emerging from the morass of years. Fragments of conversations drift through the house, a male voice, the words falling just short of audibility. Almost every day now I find evidence of this dual occupancy; food disappears from my pantry, books that I have shut away in the attic return to the living room shelves – *The Wretched of the World, The Dialectic of Sex, The Politics of Experience*, and *Soul on Ice*. If I believed in ghosts, I'd suspect that the spirit of that vanished, gullible, youthful version of myself had returned somehow to quietly accuse me of straying the path of virtue that I once fancied lay beneath my feet.

This past week has been the most unsettling. One of my neighbors thanked me for the loan of my lawn mower, a gesture of which I have absolutely no recollection; I can't stand the man, as a matter of fact. And when I tried to pay the paper carrier this week, he insisted that I had taken care of it the previous day. I find groceries in the cupboards that I know I have not purchased, things in some cases which I have not eaten in years. Worst of all, the most heinous transgression of all, is the trespass into my personal retreat, the den.

I found ashes in the fireplace this morning, the remnants of a large fire which I never lit. And the log rack to one side has been filled with fresh wood.

For the first time in my life, I feel out of context.

As each day passes, I grow more and more frightened of mirrors. Susan would probably say that I dreaded the sight of gray hair or other indications that I was growing old. But she'd be wrong.

I don't believe that I fear death. Certainly I don't contemplate the idea with pleasure either. Whether the final act of every human being's life leads to eternal nothingness or the sentence of Heaven or Hell is something we will never know in this life. Even the faithful, though they may not admit it, fear the terra incognita that lies beyond the river Styx.

No, I don't particularly fear death and its physical previews don't dissuade me from looking into mirrors. What really concerns me is another matter entirely.

What terrifies me to the point of paralysis is that I might glance into a mirror someday and discover that it is I who trespass here and that rather than stand staring into those mysterious depths...

...I might be staring out.

COMPLEXITY

Jake watched through the beveled window in the front door until the mailman drove up, then hastily went outside to wait for him.

"I'll take those," he said hastily, trying not to look at the mailbox. He had closed it the day before, but it was looming open again, the interior wrapped in shadows. The mailman probably wasn't a conscious tool, but he was potentially their most effective way of bypassing his defenses.

"Here you go, Mr. Sanford." Two bills, three circulars, a magazine. He would have to open each carefully, just to be safe, but they looked all right.

"Thanks." He waited until the mailman had passed behind the hedge on his way next door, then reached around behind the steps to where he'd left the shovel. It was still there. No one had crept up during the night to steal it. Jake set his mail down on the steps and took the shovel in both hands, raising it until the business end hovered just below the fallen mailbox door. One quick twist of the wrists and he popped the plastic door back into place with a small thud. It looked secure, but they could open it again whenever they wanted to, of course.

He stowed the shovel, retrieved the mail, and went inside, locking the door and throwing the deadbolt. The front hall was completely bare. He had gotten rid of the coat rack, the grandfather clock, and the umbrella stand. The Salvation Army had given him a receipt, but he had thrown it away, severing that connection. Some of the things he had sacrificed had probably been all right, but it was safer to do without than risk infiltration.

The living room was largely empty as well, no couch, no paintings on the wall, and definitely no television. He spent most of his time here now, having closed the doors to the other rooms and nailed several shut. The bathroom was particularly problematic because it offered direct access to the outside via water pipes and drains, but unless he could think of some viable alternative, it would remain necessary to take that risk. He had yet to be attacked there. Maybe they thought it was too easy. Like shooting a pissing duck.

He slept on the mattress he'd dragged down from the upstairs bedroom. It was pushed into one corner of the room, neatly made up with sheets, one blanket, and a pillow (but no pillow case). There was a card table in another corner, covered with canned and packaged food, nothing fresh. He always ordered the same things and he used a magic marker to cover over all of the small print on the containers. It had taken a while to find someone who would take the refrigerator away; it had stood on his front lawn for almost a month. There was no trash here; he took all waste outside immediately. Cobwebs were particularly dangerous and must be avoided at all costs. He had kept the vacuum cleaner and used it twice a day, and he dusted everything, even the ceiling, much more frequently. There were two folding chairs; one for when he wanted to sit, the other to stand on when he needed to change one of the overhead lights. There was one other lamp, on the floor beside his bed. He had thrown away the lampshade.

Jake had considered taking down the curtains but the Venetian blinds were missing some slats and he didn't dare risk letting them spy on him. Not that there was much they missed despite his precautions. There was no doubt in his mind that he was at their mercy, that they were playing with him and could deliver the final blow at any time they wished. He wasn't sure why they restrained themselves. Perhaps they were increasing the pressure gradually so that they could determine the precise point at which he would break, throw himself upon their non-existent mercy, or finally turn in a desperate, doomed effort to resist. Or perhaps they were trapped by their own complexity and were barred from simple solutions.

Jake went through the mail, setting aside everything except the bills. He found his checkbook sitting on top of the microwave, which sat on the floor in yet another corner, and paid the bills and stamped the envelopes. He carried the waste out to the trashcan at the side of the house, giving a wide berth to the mailbox (which had remained closed this time), then returned hastily to the house after hearing something rustling in the hedges. He would hand the stamped envelopes to the mailman when he delivered the next day.

Next he conducted an inventory of his supplies, made a short list, and called it in to the grocery story. "Delivery tomorrow morning is fine," he told them. He used his cell phone. He had ripped the other out of the wall and thrown it into the trash, denying them another entryway into the house. Jake knew that his precautions were inadequate at best, but he had to try, didn't he? He couldn't just acknowledge their power over him without at least token resistance.

That thought reminded Jake that he hadn't conducted his daily clothing inspection. The fourth and final corner of the living room was the most cluttered, if you could call such rigid orderliness clutter. His shirts, all solid colors, neatly folded, stood in two piles, his pants in a third. Underwear, socks, shoes, handkerchiefs, and belts were arranged in parallel rows. None of the categories physically touched another, to prevent cross contamination if they should be infiltrated, and his sweaters – which would not be needed for another month or two – were even further segregated, a full meter away from the rest. Jake examined each element of his array in turn, satisfying himself that there was no visible evidence of outside influence. He'd found an ant on one occasion, and killed it immediately. He didn't think they could use the ant directly, but they could probably follow it back inside if it ever returned.

Satisfied, he returned to his sitting chair, and sat in it. Centrally located, it allowed him to survey the entire periphery of his domain without having to change position significantly. He always tried to keep his movements slow, deliberate, and silent, so that they would have fewer cues by which to pinpoint his location. He was three quarters of the way through a survey when a sudden buzzing sound made him jump.

The cell phone!

Jake had set it on the floor – his pockets were always completely empty. He had even sewn most of them shut so that he couldn't absentmindedly insert something. Now he picked it up tentatively and, steeling himself, accepted the incoming call.

"Yes? What is it?"

"Jake? Is that you?"

"This is Jake. Who am I talking to? What do you want?"

"It's Darleen, Darleen Thompson. Am I calling at a bad time?"

Yes, he thought. "Hello, Darleen. How can I help you?" Darleen seemed all right. He didn't think they were using her, although you never knew. Sometimes people became their instruments without realizing that they'd been reduced to puppets.

"I just wanted to touch base with you. We haven't talked in ages, and I'm going to flying into Providence for a few days next month. I thought we might get together, go out for dinner or something."

Jake was wary of anything designed to lure him out of his stronghold. "I don't know, Darleen. I've been pretty busy lately. Work, you know."

"Are you still working as a programmer at Eblis?"

"No," he replied. "I've moved on to something else. I'm sort of self employed, freelance, and you know how it is when there's no one else to hand the work off to."

"So do you think you might give yourself an evening off? For supper, I mean. For old time's sake."

"Well, I'd like to, Darleen, but I'm going to be really busy for the next six or eight weeks, working nights. I might even be on the road, you never know. There's a whole lot of things that I have to get done right away in order to build my reputation, establish myself with the clients, you know?" He realized he was babbling, trying to overwhelm her with detail so that she couldn't come up with a counter argument, and then he realized that he was playing right into their hands, giving them what they wanted. "Thanks anyway. Maybe some other time." That was more like it. Simple, final. He probably shouldn't have suggested another time, though. It provided an opportunity for another attempt. There was no question about it. Darleen was being used, possibly even consciously.

She may have intended to say more, but he pre-empted her. "I have to go. I'll call you when things aren't so crazy." He broke the connection.

He felt a sudden urge to put the cell phone in the trash outside, but it wasn't a practical solution. There was no other way to order groceries and other things he needed to survive. It was a small concession. He hated to give way even that much, but he had known all along that there was never a chance that he might prevail completely. A holding action, he told himself. That's all that's left to me. But at least I'll go down fighting.

There was another buzz. Jake turned to the cell phone, but it was silent. Puzzled, he stared dumbly at it. The buzz hadn't sounded right. Then a series of thumps revealed the truth. It had been the door bell, and whoever was outside had just knocked on the door. Could the grocery store have made a mistake, delivered a day too early?

Jake rose to his feet, checked the immediate area, then the path he would have to follow to reach the door. It was probably safe, but even a small unnecessary risk might be fatal. If he just remained where he was, the outsider would probably go away. Even if this was just another of their ploys, they'd desist once it was clear that he wasn't taking the bait.

But if he remained unresponsive, that in itself might attract attention. Other people might begin to ask questions, and questions would play right into their hands.

He walked to the door, trying to remain calm.

Though the peephole he could see that it was Abner Whitfield, his next door neighbor. "What's that old busybody want now?" Jake wondered. "Maybe he'll go away."

Another fusillade of knocks, louder now. Jake sighed. Should he be brusque to the point of rudeness, hoping to drive the man away permanently, or pleasant, agreeable, and compliant? Either strategy had its drawbacks. He would have to improvise.

He dithered a few seconds longer, then opened the door.

"Oh, there you are. I was wondering if I'd have to leave a note. Say, do you know your phone is out of order?"

"You know the phone company. It takes them forever to fix anything. What can I do for you?" He had parried that easily enough. If Abner had pursued the matter, raised the level of complexity, it might have been disastrous. There were so many ramifications inherent in even the simplest statement. He might have asked if they had scheduled a repair date, or offered to let Jake use his own phone, or responded in some fashion that Jake could not even imagine.

"Well, I wanted to talk to you about your tree. You know, the one that hangs over my fence." His eyes kept slipping away from Jake's face, trying to see what lay behind him, or perhaps he was expecting to be invited in.

"What about the tree?" All of his senses were on alert. This was an attack from an unexpected angle and he had no ripostes prepared.

"I wondered if you were going to do anything about removing it."

"Why would I want to remove the tree?" He wouldn't mind at all, actually. It was an elderly Japanese Maple whose branches intersected with those of the adjacent spruce. The last time he'd been outdoors on that side of the house, he'd seen squirrels leaping from one tree to the next, and the interlaced highway had caught him off guard. He'd stood frozen, tracing the intricacies of one branch, following it to where it intersected the next, finding hints of patterns so enticing that he had been transfixed. It couldn't be part of their plan, of course, because the tree and the squirrels were true living things, but they were insidious, and he was not about to underestimate their capacity for affecting their environment.

"Well, maybe because about half of it split off and fell into my yard during that storm we had last week." Abner sounded sarcastic and Jake flinched. Sarcasm suggested a conflict between specific meaning and intended effect, and that relationship was necessarily complex. "If you don't want to take care of it yourself, I can find someone, but you'll have to pay for it."

A three way business arrangement. Jake had to clench his fists so that his nails drove into his flesh to keep from betraying his panic. The complications implied by such an arrangement surged against his defenses. Would they accept a check? When would it have to be done? Which tree service would be chosen? What if they wanted to know how much to cut away and how much to save? He felt faint.

"Are you all right?" Abner was looking at him strangely. "You're awfully pale. Maybe you should sit down."

"I haven't been feeling well." Jake grasped at the straw, a simple answer to a complicated question, then hastened on. "Nothing serious." A doctor would have questions, forms to be filled in, symptoms to inquire about. That wouldn't do at all. "I just need some rest."

Abner looked concerned, or was that suspicion? Jake couldn't read expressions very well anymore. There were so many parts to human faces, and they could alter themselves into countless patterns. "Look, I can arrange to get it done and just send you the bill if you want."

"That would be fine with me. And I appreciate your patience." That was good. Jake was certain that he sounded normal, unsuspicious. He was dealing with this quite nicely, if he did say so himself.

"Yeah, well, take care of yourself." Jake watched Abner make his way to the end of the front walk. He paused there, glanced back as though he might return, but then shook his head and disappeared behind the hedge. Jake took a deep breath and waited for the muscles in the back of his neck to relax.

Realization of the true state of affairs had come to him gradually. Prior to that revelation, he had been happy, more or less. He took pride in his work, weaving lines of code into routines, routines into modules, modules into finished programs, and programs into complex systems. The unrealized potentials of the network intrigued him. Why couldn't the inventory system speak to the purchasing department's procurement software? If you were going to go to the trouble of creating a personnel database, why not integrate it with the payroll and security programs? He was handed simple mandates by his supervisors and always provided everything they asked for and more. Jake had thought he was doing a good thing, helping make the world a better place.

That was before he realized that he was not the real creator. The interface between the advertising and sales departments had been suggested by a data array that had "just happened" to be identical in both modules. The improvements in the telephone sales interface had been adapted from the inventory control transaction recording screen. Even the shareware game he'd developed at home had been a spiffed up version of a training exercise program he'd previously modified for the distribution department.

At first, it hadn't struck him as particularly important. He was considering applying for a job in Providence because Eblis was clearly on the verge of staff reductions and he was writing his resume on company time in his tiny office. Although he had typed up a healthy list of accomplishments, a closer look had disconcerted him. None of this was really original work. Oh, he had made some of the programming more elegant, possibly even saved some processing time, but these were modifications he had copied from other programs. None of it was really his work. And the resulting code was so complex that if he left, his replacement would probably scrap large sections and rewrite it rather than attempt to ferret out Jake's chain of reasoning. His greatest achievement was to have made things more complex than ever.

That had bothered him and he had started thinking about other aspects of his life as well. He rarely carried his cell phone because he could never figure out how to use most of its features – the camera, the varying ringtones, call waiting, caller ID – and it was embarrassing to explain if someone asked about them. His new television had a row of controls in a flip down box, most of which he had never touched. One morning he was sent off to a conference in Providence and he borrowed one of the company cars, but he couldn't figure out how to turn on the windshield washer or the parking lights.

How did life get to be so complex? He thought back to his childhood. Televisions used to have a power switch and a channel selector, and maybe a contrast knob. Radios had AM or FM or both, but what was the difference between FM1 and FM2? DVDs made it possible to watch movies, but should he buy a conventional player, or Blu-ray or some other format? What was the difference between DEFROST and AUTO DEFROST on his microwave? Even the fan on his office desk offered Oscillating or Non-Oscillating, Filtered or Unfiltered, in addition to On and Off and four separate speeds.

It was as though there was some underlying force or consciousness directing things. Jake didn't know much about natural history but he knew that living organisms had started out as simple, single cells, then became multi-cellular, living in the sea and subsequently moving to the land, growing more specialized, more intelligent, more complex. It was almost as though the inorganic world was going through some similar genesis now. Where organic life had been started by a chance accretion of chemicals, sparked perhaps by a stroke of lightning (or the hand of God), could it be possible that the inorganic world was, or had already been pushed across the same gap by the advent of human technology?

He had laughed it off at the time, but apparently not soon enough to avoid attracting their attention. Jake wasn't entirely sure who they were, but he was pretty sure he knew what they were. Little things started to go wrong at first. He was paid through direct deposit and somehow the account number got suspended. It took three visits to the bank before that was cleared up. Then he was stopped because his license plate number had somehow been erased from the DMV database. His phone bill had arrived one month demanding $1147.84. The charges from a local florist shop had inexplicably been debited against his account. The fuel injection system on his car malfunctioned, the cable box for his television had refused to unscramble incoming signals, and his programmable clock radio had started resetting at random. He was late for work three times before he threw it out.

Jake's suspicions began to grow. The more he thought about the malfunctions – it was only later he recognized them as attacks – the more frequently they occurred. The more frequently they occurred, the more he thought about them. It was as though some cunning but unsophisticated intelligence was pitted against his.

He decided to test his theory. One afternoon, he accessed the inventory processing module and altered a few lines of code. The effect would be to delay the transfer of some finished goods into inventory long enough that there would be negative – hence impossible – figures in the on hand balance field. For the next week, he monitored the reports much more closely than usual, and not once did any item actually show up as negative.

It took almost a week for him to discover the explanation. The error handling routine had an embedded patch that kicked in whenever a negative would have resulted. It adjusted the balance to zero and tagged the item for priority processing in the following batch, which naturally contained the belated transfers. It was very neat and a very nice refinement, but Jake had written the error handling routine himself and he had no recollection of including any such safeguard.

He tried two more carefully controlled experiments. A glitch in the shipping and billing interface was corrected by part of the order entry module. A redundant checksum in the personnel management software adjusted a payroll error before the checks were issued. In neither case could Jake remember writing the relevant code.

And by then his interest had been noticed.

In April, the month end reports didn't foot properly. In fact, they showed dramatic profits even though the drop off in sales had deepened. Nicholson called him in and expressed his displeasure succinctly and loudly. Jake spent two days locating the problem, which was well concealed in the backup routine, and by then the production scheduler was screaming because production runs were being routed to machines that were already at full capacity. Jake fixed that one too, but when the daily production data was found to be corrupted in multiple places, Nicholson exploded, Jake defended himself by claiming that it was sabotage, and Nicholson fired him.

Fortunately, Jake was a man of few desires. Until Eblis had switched to direct deposit, he had been in the habit of accumulating as many as a dozen paychecks before taking them to the bank. He lived so frugally that he figured his bank account would last longer than he did. Which was just as well, because he had a feeling that they weren't going to let him get into another position where he could threaten to expose them.

Jake began thinking about the situation and realized how easily it could all have happened. A checkered shirt is, in itself, perfectly innocuous, he reasoned. But arrange checkered shirts with striped ones, and you have binary code. Add enough shirts and you have a statement, then a routine, and on from there.

He had purged his house of almost everything that they could use. Some he gave to the Salvation Army, some he put in trash bags, some he simply left on the curb. It all disappeared eventually. But they were omnipresent and perhaps omniscient and Jake knew that he survived only on suffrage.

Three days after Abner's visit, the doorbell rang again. Jake hadn't slept well the night before. The nearby highway was under construction and the interlaced sounds of a pile driver and an electrical generator had been audible, suggesting yet another strand of binary data. Audible DNA.

Someone was knocking on the door. Jake roused himself; he felt increasingly disengaged from the world around him. He stood awkwardly, his knees aching, and stumbled forward, remembering only at the last minute to check his route as he advanced. There was someone standing outside, a large man with thick, black, unruly hair.

Jake opened the door. "Can I help you?"

"I'm looking for 44 Parity Lane. Is this the place?"

Jake had to stop and think. "Yes, it is."

"You need to put a number out somewhere so's people can find you. Are you Mr. Sanford?"

Jake admitted to that as well.

"I got a call that you need a tree taken down."

"Yes, it's out there." He gestured in the right direction. "My neighbor, Mr. Whitfield, is handling all the details."

"Yeah, well he's not home and anyway I need to get you to sign this before we get started since it's your property and everything." He thrust out a clipboard; a pen dangled at the end of a short metal chain.

Jake glanced down at the paper. There were only two pages, but it seemed like much more. The print was small, some paragraphs numbered, others bulleted. Blank lines intersected the code – no, the words – in various places. He tried to read it, but it didn't make sense. The coding was too subtle; it had to be a trap.

"Where do I have to sign?" His mouth was dry and his voice barely rose above a whisper.

"At the bottom of each page. Hey, mister, are you all right?"

Jake was sweating profusely. "It's awfully hot, isn't it? I'm probably a little dehydrated. Let me sign this for you so you can go." But he didn't reach for the clipboard. In fact, he retreated a step.

"Maybe you should have a drink first. Gatorade or something. It's got some kind of chemicals in it that your body needs." Jake thought about chemistry, molecules and atoms, all parts of the programming of life, organic and otherwise, and he felt sudden terror.

He turned, intent upon bolting back to the sitting chair even if that meant leaving the door open, but he tumbled over his own feet, lost his balance, saw the carpet runner on the stairway rushing toward his eyes, and then felt nothing at all.

Jake was lying on his back. He understood that before anything else, before he even remembered how to open his eyes. And there was movement, forward a lot and side to side a little. Sounds too, but he couldn't process these yet. He opened his eyes cautiously, saw a pale blankness passing overhead. It was refreshingly simple, but then a light fixture went past, and then another, both identical, suggesting a pattern. Jake turned his head away, saw that he was lying on a gurney and that he was being pushed along a corridor. He tried to raise a hand and found that he couldn't. In fact, he couldn't move any of his limbs, although he thought he could still feel them.

There was a loud thump and the light became brighter, more intense, more artificial. Faces passed through his field of vision, and voices spoke meaningless strings of syllables. Jake closed his eyes and tried not to listen, but then someone was calling his name, over and over, and that was a pattern too and he wondered if responding might interrupt the code, create a programming flaw.

"Where am I?" he asked unnecessarily, but it seemed the right thing to say.

"This is University Hospital and I'm Dr. Clark. You've had an accident, Mr. Sanford. It's not life threatening but we need to get you into surgery as soon as possible to prevent any permanent damage. You've struck your head and there are bone fragments that we need to remove. We're already doing the preliminary blood workup and you'll be in the OR in about thirty minutes."

Dr. Clark smiled, perhaps trying to be reassuring. "We don't want you to lose consciousness until we're ready with the anesthesia." White coated men and women were suddenly all around him and Jake saw them doing something to his left arm. His face must have changed because Dr. Clark was quick to reassure him. "Don't worry about that. We're just attaching some monitoring equipment and a saline drip. You're perfectly safe. You can trust these machines to look after you better than any nurse." He chuckled lightly. "It's almost as if they had minds of their own."

Dr. Clark disappeared from his field of view. At first Jake felt fine, but then there was pain, intense pain, and he tried to cry out but something was wrong with his throat. He couldn't make a sound and it took all of his concentration just to flutter his eyelids. Help me! The words were in his mind, but he couldn't set them free.

And then a nurse was hovering over him and her eyes went wide and she turned and shouted for someone to come. "Get the crash cart! Something's wrong with the monitors and this patient is going into cardiac arrest!" They were the last words that Jake ever heard.

That's life.

MISADVENTURES IN THE SKIN TRADE

Someone stole my skin the other day. I know how that must sound, but it's the simple truth. They were clever though, replacing it with a substitute that was so close it fooled me for a while. But not for long. I mean, how much more intimately can you know anything than your very own skin? It's not like clothing, for Christ's sake!

Sorry. I didn't mean to lose control there, but you have to admit, it's an unsettling thing to discover, that your body is covered with something foreign, a synthetic of some kind, perhaps, or in this case a stranger's skin. How's that for a disgusting thought? Would you want something like that wrapped tightly around your flesh? No, I didn't think so. So maybe you can understand how I feel about it.

I have to concede I was fooled for a while, even though I noticed some inconsistencies first thing that morning. It's not the kind of conclusion you accept readily, though, and I made excuses. Perhaps I had just never noticed the small blemish on the right thigh, and that fresh scratch on my side...I could have done that with a fingernail in my sleep.

There were other clues that I chose not to recognize. When Marie walked out, years ago now, she complained that I thought more of my own body than I did of hers. It did no good to point out that unless she began to take adequate care of herself, she would never regain the firm muscle tone, proper ratio of weight to height, or that wonderfully clear complexion which had attracted me to her in the first place. I myself had not varied more than a few pounds from my base weight in over a decade, and I examined my body constantly for signs of imperfection.

But on that late summer morning following the theft of my skin, there was a thin but unmistakable finger's width of loose flesh around my waist.

Still I failed to recognize the implications, assuming instead that I had been lax in my exercises, or perhaps had slipped into unhealthy eating habits. This latter explanation seemed even more credible when I discovered a cluster of small dark spots on my nose, infected pores, and by the time I had thoroughly cleaned them and applied a disinfectant, my nose was as red as a drunkard's and as painful as a prizefighter's. Resolving to ruthlessly re-examine both my diet and my training routine that evening, I set off to work mildly concerned but not yet aware of the true nature of my condition.

The feeling that something was subtly wrong persisted all day. I've worked the same position on the assembly line at Eblish Manufacturing for four years now, and I've trained my body to work as a piece of the machinery. The rhythms are a part of me as I am a part of them, and every flexing muscle, every twist of elbow and wrist, each individual stretch of skin over flesh is predictable and familiar. But not that morning.

I couldn't quite put my finger on it at first. I had fallen into the routine as always, three connections on the left, three on the right, rotate the unit, check the solder joint, rotate again, fasten the clip, arms back while the unit shifted to the next station and a new one offered itself. More than a thousand times I had merged with the operation smoothly, without a moment's hesitation. But that morning, it felt wrong; the kinesthetics were different, not enough to interfere with my performance of the work required, but enough to put my nerves on edge. I've always been proud of my self discipline, the way I've trained my body to respond instantly to everything I ask of it. If we aren't captains of our own bodies, how can we expect to control the world around us?

I was troubled throughout the day and distracted on the drive home. My work clothes went into the hamper; I never wore the same set more than once without washing them. Then my usual thorough shower, starting with my hair, which had grown to be nearly an inch long. Time for a trim. Three applications of shampoo and a rinse, then a thorough scrubbing with a stiff spined brush, followed by a final shampoo. Then my face, concentrating on my nose this time. I had installed a mirror on the shower wall years before, but it rarely proved effective, the image obscured by rising steam as quickly as I could clear it away. But I used it this time, concentrating to make certain there'd been no recurrence of the invading blackheads I'd discovered that morning.

Other than that, I kept to my routine, ears, back of the neck, then throat and chin. I scrubbed myself until the flesh was warm and glowing and the sense of wrongness started to recede. Chest and armpits and navel, shoulders and back and waist. The superfluous flesh at my midriff was still there and still worrisome, but I was confident that I could work it off in a few days.

I was tempted as always to quickly pass over my genitals, the weakest and least perfect part of the male body, but as usual I forced myself to overcompensate and lather them thoroughly, scrubbing vigorously enough that my breath became sharp and ragged. I shaved myself there once a week to facilitate this process, but there were so many folds of flesh that might conceal infections or other unpleasantness, I was never completely satisfied that my efforts were complete.

Just below my left knee, I discovered a tiny, tear shaped scar. I almost passed it by. It was faint, an absence of feature rather than a blatant disfigurement. It wasn't fresh, had in fact entirely healed. But I had never seen it before, never once in the forty years I had lived in this body.

I forced myself to eat, carefully measuring the portions, even though I had little appetite. Dressed in loose fitting pants and sleeveless shirt, I cleared away the dishes and walked thoughtfully down to the exercise room in the basement, spent the next two hours following my established pattern, pushing each group of muscles to their limit, then slightly beyond. The routine helped to suppress the growing sense of uneasiness, shift it temporarily into some recess of my mind where I could pretend that everything was normal.

Of course you know I was fooling myself, but it's easy to judge things like this from the outside, a lot more difficult to accept that someone has violated the sanctity of your most precious possession, your body itself.

I would normally have showered again, just a warm rinse this time, but as soon as I stopped, those nagging doubts returned. So I chose instead to jog for a while, even though it was already dark outside. There's a heavily wooded area threaded with paths just a block from my house, not the safest place even in the daylight, but I wasn't afraid of being attacked. There were far easier victims available and I'd never had any trouble with the scruffy punks who frequented the area.

Moving at a carefully regulated pace, I ran north until I reached the housing project, then looped back on a narrower path, one so nearly overgrown that I was forced to use my bare arms to fend off stray branches. When the parkway lights were visible to the west, I changed routes again, angling southward, knowing I would eventually cross the paved footpath that led fairly directly back toward my house. I'd never run out here in the dark before and found it somewhat disorienting, but the forested area wasn't so extensive that there was any real chance I might lose my way.

Back home, I stripped and showered, was toweling myself dry when I found the rash. It wasn't much of one, just a thin streak of red spots along my right forearm, almost certainly an allergic reaction to something I had brushed away from my face. The only problem with that was, I had never suffered from any allergies in the past. My skin was tough and resilient and resistant to irritation, just like the rest of my body.

That's when I realized I was wearing someone else's skin.

You might expect that I would have become frantic when faced with the truth, but actually I grew quite calm. Now that I had an explanation for the bizarre inconsistencies that had been showing up all day, knew that they were not signs of my own weakness, the loss of tight body control, but actually the result of a hostile act, I felt a sense of relief and prepared to deal with the situation.

Naturally my first thought was to wonder who was responsible, and why. I didn't have any real enemies, at least not since Marie walked out on me, so it wasn't malice. That left envy. Perfectly understandable, of course; everyone who knew me envied my body, the men anyway. Women admired it as well, but they just wanted to use it for their own pleasure, in ways that would weaken me. Marie had been different, at least when we first married; it was only later that she began making irrational demands, insisting that there was something wrong with using our bodies only for healthy, life affirming purposes.

I was actually quite relieved when she finally left.

But once the motive was understood, the number of potential thieves became bewilderingly high. There was no one I knew whose body could even begin to approach my own hard won near perfection, and frankly I doubted that any of them would be able to substantially improve their situation just by draping themselves in my skin. But jealousy is an irrational emotion, independent of logic.

Using a yellow lined pad, I quickly made a list of every male I could think of. It had to be a man, of course. Then I put check marks next to the ones who were closest to me in size, although I made the marks darker for those who bulked a bit more than me, mindful of the misfit at my waist. There were a half dozen prime candidates and I copied those names onto a second sheet, arranged in order of probability, based on my intuition. One of these men was almost certainly responsible, although there were a few others on my original list whom I could not completely rule out. The thought that it might be a complete stranger, someone who had watched me secretly and waited for a chance to strike, was disturbing, and I decided that if that unlikely explanation was the correct one, there was little I could do about it. It was far more likely that the man responsible was known to me, though, and I proceeded on that assumption.

Although I was impatient to act, it was impractical until the next day, a Friday. Two of my top candidates worked at Eblis, though not in my department. I would need to be circumspect. It was necessary to identify the guilty party without letting on that I knew of the switch.

I was able to eliminate Ned Sanders before the shift started, disappointing since I'd placed him at the top of my list. He was having a cigarette in the cafeteria, in violation of the posted rules, and I regretted the necessity of approaching closely enough that I would have to breathe that polluted air. Sanders was almost exactly my size, but soft, unseasoned. He was shop steward and the company always managed to find a way to assign him the less strenuous jobs, spot inspection, cycle counting, things like that. He saw me coming, half turned in my direction.

"Morning, Dougherty. How're they hanging?"

I was inured to Sanders' language, which was so peppered with obscenities that he has twice been reported to the shift supervisor by women working the line. Although I really hoped that he was the one I was after, I realized the impossibility of that when he raised his arm to wave at me. Sanders had a vulture tattooed on the inside of his left forearm.

Eric Nicholson was my third choice, and he worked the day shift here at Eblis, so I went looking for him at lunch time. He's kind of young, but the right size, even keeps himself in pretty good shape although his posture is bad and I've heard that he drinks. It was hot in the cafeteria and a lot of people took their lunch outside, ate it sitting on the grassy slope that faced the cemetery.

He was there all right, lying off by himself in a patch of sunlight with his shirt off. I couldn't have asked for a better chance. With one arm across his eyes to shut out the light, he didn't even see me standing there, staring down at him.

What I could see of his skin was tanned, smooth, and firm, and I experienced a sense of familiarity. There were some minor inconsistencies, but I figured whatever process had allowed him to switch his skin for mine couldn't have been absolutely perfect. Perhaps it dried out a little while in transit. The skeleton and muscles underneath had to be at least slightly different in configuration, and that would change the distribution of tautness and wrinkles, at least until the skin had a chance to adjust to its new platform. No scars, no tattoos, and the small scrape mark on his elbow was fresh, might have been done since the transfer.

I couldn't be certain, but it seemed likely Nicholson was responsible. Now all I had to do was recover my property.

Nicholson lived alone, a small rundown house in one of the older sections of Managansett. I'd driven him to work a time or two when his car was in for repairs and although I didn't remember the exact address, when I drove through the neighborhood after work that afternoon, I identified it easily. It was set all by itself at the rear of a lot cluttered with untrimmed shrubs, mock orange, rosebushes, lilacs, and forsythia. There'd be no difficulty approaching the house unseen once darkness fell.
I drove home thoughtfully, planning my attack.

For the most part, everything went quite well. I returned after midnight, parking several blocks away, then reached Nicholson's back yard by a roundabout route, easily avoiding the widely spaced streetlights that futilely attempted to bring a sense of security to the neighborhood. His doors were locked but almost all of the ground floor windows were open to the night air. I slipped inside so quietly I wondered if I had missed my calling in not taking up burglary.

The penlight in my pocket was unnecessary. A lamp was still glowing in the front room, a short neon tube buzzed over the kitchen sink. There were two bedrooms, both with their doors open, one piled high with junk, tools, furniture, boxes filled with off season clothing, even some canned goods. Nicholson was asleep in the other, sprawling naked on his stomach diagonally across the bed.

Almost as if he knew I'd be coming and wanted to make it easier for me.

I regretted the necessity to damage my stolen skin but by using the wrench to crush the top of his skull, I figured most of the incidental damage would be concealed under my hair. I might have to let it grow longer in the future, but I'd just increase the number of times I shampooed it to compensate. When I was quite sure that he had stopped breathing, I turned on the bedroom lights.

Obviously Nicholson had used some more subtle technique, since he had managed his theft without assaulting me. He'd have been wiser to finish me off, but I imagine he was smugly convinced that I'd never notice the difference, or if I did, that I'd be unable to figure out the identity of the guilty party.

I went outside and retrieved the ice chest I'd left below the window. Nicholson's methods were clearly more efficient than mine, but I didn't have time to try to figure out how he'd done it. The longer my skin spent on his body, the less likely I was to retrieve it before serious damage had been done. It was a futile effort on his part, when you think about it. Sure, for the time being he'd reap the benefits of my years of discipline and conditioning, but unless he gave up his own lax ways and poor habits, deterioration would be inevitable and he'd be no better off than before. Then I realized that logically he would strike again, find a new skin to replace the old, had perhaps already gone through this same routine in the past. I had not felt any remorse when I killed him. I mean, considering the depraved nature of his crime against me, he deserved no better. But add to that the possibility...no, the probability that I was saving many others from a similar fate. Why, in a sense, I was serving the community as well as myself, destroying a monstrous wolf lurking unsuspected among the sheep.

His skin came off quite readily under the flensing knife. I took this as further proof of his guilt; the tissues had not completely reknitted themselves. After washing it off in the shower stall, I carefully folded my skin, wrapped it in cellophane, and buried it in the shaved ice, now rapidly melting into a chilly slush. It will probably involve some experimentation to put things right, so I have returned to my own place where I can work undisturbed.

I'm writing this all down in case anything goes wrong, so that there will be a record, a warning, something to alert the rest of you to the danger. I can't believe Nicholson was an isolated case; there must be others like him preying on the innocent. Those facelifts that actors and politicians have, the ones that are so unbelievably effective -- at least some of those are probably excuses to cover up what has really happened.

There's no doubt in my mind that I will be able to reattach my skin. I took measurements to be certain, but there wasn't really time for it to shrink or stretch unnaturally, though I suppose it might be uncomfortable at first. Marie left behind her sewing basket, so I have needles and plenty of thread to close the seams. No, I don't expect to have any great difficulty with that part.

It's cutting Nicholson's alien skin off my body beforehand that poses the challenge.